TRAVELLIN' SHOES

AN RJ FRANKLIN MYSTERY

V.M. BURNS

CAMEL
PRESS
Seattle, WA

CAMEL PRESS

For more information go to: www.Camelpress.com
www.vmburns.com

Cover design by Sabrina Sun

Travellin' Shoes
Copyright © 2018 by V.M. Burns

ISBN: 978-1-60381-689-2 (Trade Paper)
ISBN: 978-1-60381-690-8 (eBook)

Library of Congress Control Number: 2017954797

Printed in the United States of America

TRAVELLIN'
SHOES

ACKNOWLEDGMENTS

TRAVELLIN' SHOES WAS my thesis project for my Master of Fine Arts degree at Seton Hill University. So, I would be remiss if I didn't acknowledge the many people who helped to bring this project to reality. Thanks to my mentors, Barbara Miller and Patrick Picciarelli. I'd also like to thank Dr. Lee McLain for her help and support. Thank you to my critique partners, Dagmar Amrhein, Kenya Wright, and Brenda Clark. As Iron sharpens Iron, great writers inspire and motivate me to write better. One of those great writers is Victoria Thompson. Thank you so much for including Seton Hill University in your bio and helping me find my way to my Tribe. Thanks to Lana Ayers, Patricia Lillie, Jessica Barlow, and Michelle Lane for always encouraging and supporting me. I'd also like to thank the rest of my WPF June 2012 Tribe, Jeff Evans, Alex Savage, Anna LaVoie, Penny Thomas, Gina Anderson, Matt O'Dwyer, and Crystal Kapataidakis. Thanks to Michael Dell for trudging through the rough draft and providing editing and great suggestions.

Many friends and family members were instrumental in supporting me in my decision to go back to school to pursue my dream to write popular fiction. This book would not have happened were it not for my mother and father, Elvira and Benjamin Burns. Thanks to my sister Jacquelyn Rucker and my late brother in law (Chris) Rucker for poodle-sitting so I could attend school. Thanks to my niece Jillian and nephew Christopher for all the holiday meals you spent listening to me talk about this book. Thanks to B.J. Magley for the recipes, prayers, and support. Special thanks to two special friends, Sophia Muckerson and Shelitha Mckee. Sophia Muckerson has provided pep talks, hair, makeup, and fashion advice and has supported me through countless ups and downs. There aren't enough words to say thank you for traveling close to six hundred miles in the middle of winter to listen to my thesis defense and for all the help and support. Shelitha Mckee had provided encouragement, support, and the occasional kick in the pants. During one of the darkest times of my life, she set aside her fear of dogs to ride six hundred miles in the middle of the night in a car with two of them while listening to me talk about this book for hours.

Thanks to Jennifer McCord and Catherine Treadgold at Camel Press and Dawn Dowdle at Blue Ridge Literary Agency for having faith in me and taking a chance on this book.

Thanks to Adrena and Deloris for allowing me to use your mom's name in my story. Mrs. Ella Bethany was a wonderful woman who lived on an alley across from a recreation center and down from the church. Even though she's gone and the house has been torn down, I still look in that direction whenever I drive past. Thanks to Mrs. Ella Bethany, the inspiration for Mama B.

Death went out to the sinner's house,

Come and go with me

Sinner cried out, I'm not ready to go,

Ain't got no travellin' shoes.

Got no travellin' shoes, got no travellin' shoes

Sinner cried out, I'm not ready to go

I ain't got no travellin' shoes

Check out RJ's Favorite Meals at the End

BJ Magley's Pork Chops

BJ's Quick and Easy Peach Cobbler

Sweet Potato Pie

Elvira Burns' Fried Corn

CHAPTER ONE

———— ∼∼∼ ————

YOU HAVE TO be nuts to run at two a.m. That's when all the crazies came out. Every town has them, even the sleepy bucolic ones like St. Joseph, Indiana. Good thing I have a gun.

My favorite route followed the St. Joseph River, winding around a park and ending in the historic district. I used to be able to run ten miles and barely break a sweat. Now I can't run half that distance without feeling like I need an oxygen tank.

Soaked in sweat and sucking air like a four-pack-a-day smoker, I finally made it to the end of the block, my designated stopping point. Resisting the urge to flop down on the ground, I bent over and massaged my knee, hoping the pain would subside. Running was no longer advisable—not after the car accident that left me with a metal plate in my leg and a scar the size of Rhode Island—but it beat lying in bed with my nightmares.

The early morning was cool and peaceful. I heard sirens but ignored them. Living near this neighborhood, I was familiar with the sound of sirens. The locals were in a no-win battle with the hospital to ban ambulance sirens between ten p.m. and five a.m. But these sirens were getting closer and louder.

That's when I got the first whiff of smoke. After a few more steps, my eyes stung and I saw flames. The fire was close. That's when the pain I'd felt just a moment ago vanished and I started to run. I ran, not away from the fire, but toward it.

I was on administrative leave from the force, but I still had my shield. The doctors patched up my body, but some scars are deeper than flesh and bone. I needed time to recover mentally. Arriving only a few seconds after the fire trucks and police cars, I pulled my shield from the chain around my neck and flashed it at the first cop I saw, which got me inside the blockade.

"Anyone inside?" I asked.

The cop manning the barricade answered, "Single man by the name of ... Warrendale." He looked at his notebook and added, "Thomas Warrendale."

That startled me. Thomas Warrendale was the choir director at First Baptist Church. Looking at the house, I concluded that if Warrendale were inside, he wasn't going to make it out alive. It wasn't long before the fire crews shifted their focus from rescue to containment. It was also pretty clear that, when church started in a few hours, First Baptist Church would soon be looking for a new choir director.

CHAPTER TWO

———∞———

As a detective with the St. Joseph Indiana Police Department (SJPD), my job was to serve and protect and to catch bad guys. As a member of First Baptist Church—albeit a fair-weather member—I always hoped to do my job without damaging the church or its reputation. "Fair-weather Christians" were what my godmother called people who only came to church when the weather was fair. That summed me up pretty well.

Today was the first Sunday in May. The weather was agreeable, but with the choir director's death headlining the *St. Joseph Tribune's* Sunday morning paper, nothing short of a hurricane could have kept me at home. The coroner hadn't officially declared murder, but the smell of gasoline was so strong, the fire chief went on record with "suspicious" circumstances. News like the death of the church choir director traveled quickly. I suspected the gossip would be flying fast and furious at the church, which was one reason for my presence. I might not be working the case, but the cop in me couldn't pass up a chance to do some reconnaissance.

First Baptist Church—FBC—was more crowded than I

remembered. The late choir director had changed the musical format, the result being that the congregation more than doubled in size during the past nine months. Instead of the traditional spirituals and hymns I remembered as a child, the choirs sang upbeat gospel tunes. Instead of merely a piano accompanying the choir, there was almost a full band with drums, bongos, and two guitars. FBC had gone from a geriatric population of five hundred regular members to a much younger crowd of well over a thousand that included more teenagers and twenty-something single parents. The church's location, in an economically declining part of town, could only be described as the *hood*, so the congregation consisted of lower income and plain old poor folk. The wood-paneled walls and red carpet that had been trendy in the '70s was in desperate need of an update. From the fake flowers lining the pulpit to the tattered American and Christian flags flanking the communion table, the church definitely showed its age. The absence of the choir director's rather flamboyant style was noticeable, but the choir reverted to their old faithful songs, and the service progressed.

"Precious Lord, Take My Hand" reverberated through the vaulted ceiling and the pews. Chills ran through me as Sister Dorothea Green, in the white robes everyone except the Children's Choir wore on the first Sunday, belted out the song, giving it her all.

The titles Sister and Brother were common throughout African-American churches. We weren't talking about nuns or monks, just brothers and sisters in the faith.

"Sis" Green was a stocky, older woman with a strong, powerful voice. She might not be a classically trained singer, but she had something special. Some called it an anointing— that voice. Whatever it was, she had it.

Feeling, rather than seeing *the look*, I glanced over at my godmother. My mother's closest friend, Ella Bethany, had cared for me and my older sister while my mother battled cancer.

After my mother died, she was more like a grandmother than my real one. That's when we started calling her Mama B. She supported my decision to become a cop when no one else in my family did. Somehow, she knew it was something I had to do. My parents were both dead now, and my sister had married, had two kids, and moved away. It was just me and Mama B now, and she was no spring chicken. Mama B was in her mid-sixties, with gray hair and soft brown eyes. She was a lot slower than she used to be, and she'd put on more weight than was good for her, but far be it from me to mention weight to a woman.

Mama B was one of those women who never dreamed of coming to church without a hat. Today she sported a purple turban with a large white feather. Not every woman could carry it off, but she wore it well.

She leaned in close and whispered, "Robert James Franklin Junior, wake up!" She delivered a sharp nudge to the ribs. If I hadn't been awake before, I was now. I rarely got the full name unless I was in trouble.

"I'm not sleeping." I stifled a yawn. It had been a long time since I'd sat through early service. On the rare occasions when I drag myself to church, it is at eleven. Attending church at eight a.m. was a penance that no kind, loving God would require of his children.

Nevertheless, here I was. In addition to performing reconnaissance, I was attending the first service in response to a message from Pastor Hamilton requesting my presence.

The choir finished singing, but many in the congregation were still feeling the effects. Some wept. Others stood with their hands raised and faces lifted to the heavens. Emotions overflowed, and the musicians played quietly while various members of the congregation regained their composure. I settled in for the main event—the sermon. As Reverend Moses Chapman approached the pulpit, I unfolded my legs and tried to find a comfortable position.

Wooden pews are torture on a good many parts of the human anatomy. Taking pity on my six-foot-three-inch frame, the ushers generally gave me a seat on the aisle, allowing for extra leg room.

Reverend Chapman approached the pulpit, and I pondered how he came to be here. A few months ago, Reverend Chapman was just plain ol' Moe Chapman, the church financial secretary. That was before he got *the call*. As I child, I had heard Reverend Hamilton talking about *the call*. In many African-American churches, the role of minister was not a career choice but a spiritual calling. I pictured a biblical scene with angels singing, blinding light, and the booming voice of God. Maybe that's what had happened to Moe. Someday I'd ask.

Moe Chapman and I were alike in many ways, starting with our age—thirty-three. We both had skin the color of coffee, although his was a dark espresso and mine was more like a latte with plenty of cream. His eyes were light gray, where mine were dark brown. Both of us were over six feet, though I had a couple of inches on him. The biggest difference between us was our girth. At well over four hundred pounds, Moe would only balance a scale with me if my clone stood alongside. Moe didn't let his weight hold him back in any way. For a big man, he had a surprising swagger, and he dressed well. Women were attracted to him, and he never seemed to lack companionship. But for some reason, Mama B didn't like him. She claimed he had too many teeth. As far as I could tell, he had the same number of teeth as every other adult. But he did smile a lot, which is more than likely what made her distrust him. His call into the ministry came at an opportune time. Three months ago, our pastor, Reverend Hilton V. Hamilton, had a heart attack and needed to take it easy. Three sermons each week were deemed too many, and Reverend Hamilton had to slow down. The church elders asked Moe to step in and ease the load.

The mood was understandably somber today. During the

reading of the announcements, the church clerk got choked up over a statement expressing the congregation's loss at the death of Thomas Warrendale. Reverend Hamilton always shared a few inspirational words after the announcements and before the first offering, and he spoke quietly of the loss the church felt and said funeral arrangements would be announced soon. All in all, the church had taken a low-key approach. Nothing shocking or, pardon the pun, *incendiary* had been communicated, although I had been hearing rumors of Warrendale's lascivious behavior from Mama B for the past nine months. The unexpected death of the church's choir director was being handled calmly, quietly, and carefully. So, it was surprising to hear Moe Chapman declare the title of his sermon, "The Wages of Sin Are Death." From his shocked expression, Reverend Hamilton was clearly as surprised as the congregation. The shuffling, shifting, and whispering stopped, and everyone settled in for what promised to be an exciting sermon.

I looked toward the pulpit at Reverend Hamilton, a wise old man whose gray, thinning hair, worry lines, and scars showed he'd been through hard times. Despite the obvious wear and tear on his body, a kindness shone from those intent brown eyes. Only those closest to him knew how it pained him to step aside and leave his flock in someone else's hands.

Moe Chapman never actually said Thomas Warrendale's name at any point in his twenty-minute sermon. But references to Lucifer's beauty and angelic voice seemed to especially point to the handsome, golden-voiced choir director. Moe Chapman was a charismatic man who was more of a preacher than a teacher, a style that contrasted sharply with Reverend Hamilton. They also differed in their portrayal of God. Reverend Hamilton taught the congregation about the love and forgiveness of God our Father, while Moe Chapman preached on the vengeance of God. Mama B looked as though she was about to burst. This was going to be the talk of the congregation, and Mama B loved to talk. If you wanted to know what was really going on in the church, in the neighborhood, or in the town, all you had to do was spend a little time sitting on Mama B's front porch. And that was my plan after the service.

Following the sermon, Reverend Hamilton "opened the doors of the church," which is Baptist-speak for extending the invitation to accept Christ into your life. This was followed by baptism, communion, and benediction.

There was only about thirty minutes in between the completion of the early service and the start of the next one, so I hurried downstairs to have a quick word with Reverend Hamilton. When I got to the office that was carved out for him in the basement of the church, I could see through the glass door that he wasn't alone. Nevertheless, he waved for me to enter.

"RJ, it's good to see you," Reverend Hamilton said as we shook hands. "How're you feeling? How is the knee?"

"I'm fine." My tone was sharper than necessary, but it had been six months since my accident, and I was tired of fielding questions, no matter how well intended. "How are you, Moe ... uh, I mean, Reverend Chapman?" It was hard to adjust to the new title after so many years of calling him just Moe, Mama B had told me he felt it was disrespectful when people didn't use it. That was probably why she never included the title when referring to him.

"Blessed." Moe flashed his toothy grin. "I'm blessed, Brother Franklin, and highly favored of God." Ever since he'd received his call, his conversation was littered with inane phrases like this.

"RJ, I was hoping to have a word with you, but it looks like it will have to wait." Reverend Hamilton frowned. "Perhaps we can talk later."

"I look forward to it."

The basement of the church was starting to fill with people, choir members getting ready for the next service and children heading for Sunday school. I made my excuses and my exit.

Waiting for a break in the crowd, I made a dash for the door. If dodging hugs, kisses, and handshakes was an Olympic event, I could be a gold medalist. On a good day, I could be sitting at home eating a burger before the pastor finished shaking hands with all the parishioners. But today I was in no hurry. I lingered on the front porch of the church and listened to the whispered questions flying around. Several people brought their newspapers with them. Most were shocked by the death. There weren't a lot of personal details in the newspaper, so the theories whispered on the church steps included everything from arson to a meth-lab explosion. No facts. With the second service starting soon, the church-porch crowd thinned, and I made my way across the street to the parking lot.

MAMA B LIVED only two blocks from the church on what can only be described as an alley. Few houses remained standing on either side of the narrow, graveled path. Most were partially burned and boarded-up shells where the homeless sometimes took refuge during the cold winter months. The buildings that hadn't been torn down were falling down of their own accord. The absence of street lights left the alley pitch-black once night fell. Normal people didn't like the looks of that alley, but Mama B wasn't normal. She didn't even think twice about walking through there day or night. To make mail delivery easier, the post office gave the alley a name, even though Mama B's house was the only one on "Columbia Court."

Within thirty minutes of the benediction, I sat on the front porch waving as various members of the congregation drove by and Mama B changed out of her Sunday best and put on something cool and comfy. Even from the front porch, the aroma of Sunday dinner worked its magic. I could almost taste the fried corn, collard greens, and hot water cornbread with fried pork chops. It was my favorite dinner, and she knew it, God love her.

Even if I hadn't been hungry enough to eat a small cow, I would still have shoveled the food down with gusto. I knew the cook well, and I'd eaten here before. After the second service got out, half the congregation would stop by to say "hey" and talk about the goings on. I was determined to get at least one plate down before the onslaught.

The first visitor to arrive at Mama B's was Laura Leigh Jackson. Laura Leigh was a forty-something Southern maid. Mama B had taken her in like an adopted daughter. Unfortunately, I always felt Laura Leigh had a more intimate relationship planned for me, so I never felt completely comfortable around her. I could hear her biological clock ticking like a time bomb. It wasn't that Laura Leigh wasn't attractive. She was close to six feet tall and slender, with long legs and a very pleasant, soft-spoken personality. She wore her hair in a short afro, and her skin was what Mama B referred to as high yellow.

"Laura Leigh, come in and have some supper," Mama B yelled from the back of the house.

I tried to sound polite and a little distant. "How're you?"

"Good," Laura Leigh said in her West Georgia accent. "I thought I saw you at early service this mornin', but I knew that couldn't be right."

"Why the surprise?"

Laura Leigh laughed. "I didn't say I was surprised, but I think you were about twelve the last time I saw you at early service."

She was probably right.

Mama B was still yelling from the kitchen, "Sis Green really tore up that song, didn't she?"

"She sure did," Laura Leigh yelled so Mama B could hear her. She made herself at home on the sofa.

The first plate of food had taken the edge off my hunger, and I felt a lot more social when Mama B came into the living room and plopped down into her favorite chair, a large leather recliner. The chair had probably been green leather once, although it was so old and cracked now it was hard to tell the original color. There were rips and tears, and much of the bottom was held together with duct tape. Stained with sweat, the chair had molded over time to fit Mama B's backside perfectly. One year I'd tried to get her another chair for Christmas, but she made me take it back. She and that chair were bonded together for life.

"Laura Leigh, go fix yourself a plate," Mama B said.

"Oh, I will."

As Mama B had a favorite chair, so too did Laura Leigh. Her spot was the sofa on the end closest to Mama B. Of course, given the small size of the living room, everything was pretty close to that chair. I decided to go back for thirds as they settled in for what promised to be a long gossip. Normally, this would be my cue to exit stage right. However, I hoped to hear some tidbit that no one would volunteer to a cop. My job was to listen for any information that might shed light on the murder.

Mama B settled into her chair. "That was the best I've heard y'all sing in almost a year—since that fancy-pants choir director got here."

"I can't believe he's gone," Laura Leigh said. "Was it an electrical fire?"

"We don't know for sure yet what caused the fire," I said between bites. "We'll have to wait until the fire inspector completes his report."

"Well, I never did like those old houses. They have all kinds of problems. I'll bet it was the wiring. It felt strange, him not being there. He *never* missed Sunday service. We was all runnin' 'round like chickens with no heads tryin' to figure out what to do."

"Y'all should have got down on your knees and thanked God," Mama B said as she rocked. "I never could stand that little fancy boy."

To say Mama B never liked the new choir director would be like saying the Grand Canyon is a nice little hole in the ground.

"Well, you're 'bout the only one who didn't like him," Laura

Leigh said. "Half the choir was fallin' over themselves to impress him when he was alive. They was all bawling in the basement before service like they'd lost their best friend."

"I don't know why," Mama B said. "I don't go for all that showy stuff. All those fancy outfits and choreography." We laughed as she shimmied and shook, arms flailing and feet stomping, all from the comfort of her La-Z-Boy.

"Young people like all that showy stuff," Laura Leigh said. "You have to admit, it really has drawn in the people. They like those modern songs."

"Bringin' the street into the church." Mama B scowled.

Mama B wasn't alone in her opposition to the changes the new choir director had brought into the repertoire of the various choirs performing for our small congregation. Thomas Warrendale's musical taste was contemporary and lively. Every song had arm movements, flamboyant dance steps, or props. The songs he chose were controversial as well, especially for the younger choirs. The traditional gospel hymns and anthems were replaced with upbeat, hip-hop gospel, and even gospel rap. This one change had practically split the church in half. The older members of the congregation, like Mama B, considered the new repertoire blasphemous. I didn't think anyone would be upset enough to kill him because of his song selections, but I forced myself to listen anyway and hoped they'd get to the meat soon.

"Well, you can't argue with the fact that it has drawn a lot of younger people to the church," Laura Leigh said.

Mama B shook her head. "Just coming to church won't save your soul."

"I know, but we've got to at least get them in the pews. You can't deny the church has more than doubled in size since Minister Warrendale came."

"He was *not* a minister, and just having your rear end on the pew doesn't mean you've been saved. If you've truly been saved, you should see a difference. They don't even tithe. I was always taught to pay your tithes—one dime from every dollar."

Many Baptist churches considered the choir to be a ministry. Therefore, the choir director was referred to as the "minister of music." No formal calling was necessary for this position, just an ability to sing, play an instrument, or direct a choir. Again, I doubted that anyone would kill for the position. Some churches didn't even pay their minister of music. But money was always a good motive for murder.

"Nothing shows commitment like cash," I said.

Laura Leigh pouted. "It's nice to have a larger church."

First Baptist Church had grown substantially. To accommodate the crowds, Reverend Hamilton was now preaching three sermons every Sunday, at eight, eleven, and five. The pews of First Baptist Church were crammed full each and every week, or so I was told. The new members were young, loud, and extremely rhythmic. Unfortunately, they had more passion than money. This, I learned from a conversation with the pastor. To be fair, Reverend Hamilton wasn't as concerned about the money as he was about the eternal souls of his flock. Nevertheless, he was walking a tight rope trying to keep the two factions together. Similar situations had split two of our sister churches, and he was determined the same fate wouldn't befall FBC. So far he had only succeeded in keeping the two sides from tearing each other apart. Funny, you wouldn't think by looking at the congregation there was so much strife and discord hiding behind those feathered hats and silk choir robes.

"They certainly didn't need him today," Mama B said. "Sis Green sang her wig off. Speak of the devil."

Sis Green knocked on the front screen. The door was never closed when it was warm and Mama B was home. She just yelled from her chair, "Come on in."

"How do? How do? How is everybody?" Sis Green spoke with the enthusiasm and country charm of Minnie Pearl.

Mama B was a gracious and welcoming hostess even

though she rarely got up from her seat. From the recliner, she welcomed Sister Green. "Good. Come in and take a load off. How're you?"

"Oh, I'm tolerable fair." Sis Green laughed. She had a great laugh, and when asked how she was doing, she always responded in the same way. She came inside. Laurie Leigh slid down on the sofa, leaving the spot closest to Mama B open. Sis Green flopped down into the spot without missing a beat. Seating in Mama B's house indicated the hierarchy of the visitors. The older and more respected you were, the closer you sat to Mama B. I was intrigued by the unspoken and unconscious protocol. I'm sure no one in the room even realized the silent game of musical chairs they were playing, which made it even more intriguing from an observer's standpoint.

"Dorothea, you know you tore that song up today," Laura Leigh chimed in.

"Thank you. Thank you kindly."

"We missed you at the missions meeting this week, Ella," Dorothea said, kicking off her shoes and settling in.

Mama B rocked and avoided my eyes. "My sugar was up. I didn't feel like walking down there."

"Lawd, I know what you're talking about. It seems like it's one thing or another. If it ain't my sugar, it's my pressure."

I tuned out on the ensuing medical rehash. From A to Z, there was a disease or a med for everything. These women covered everything from Mother Lovelace's Alzheimer's to debates on the effectiveness of garlic for high blood pressure. If this topic held sway much longer, I'd be forced to guide the conversation back to Thomas Warrendale. I didn't want to do that. I wanted everything to flow naturally. Thankfully, I didn't have to wait much longer.

"So that fancy-pants choir director finally got himself killed," Mama B said with relish.

"It might have been an accident," Laura Leigh said.

Mama B snorted. "Pshaw. It wasn't no accident. You read

the newspaper. It said *suspicious circumstances*. That means somebody set that house on fire."

Everyone turned to me, and I shrugged and continued to eat. I wanted them to forget I was there so I could listen to the gossip and the *word on the pews*. I didn't want them on their guard. Information flowed easier when people thought I was just one of them rather than a cop who could arrest someone.

Laura Leigh crossed her legs and leaned in closer to Mama B. "You make it sound like he tried to get himself killed."

Like any seasoned performer, Mama B enjoyed having an audience, and she had excellent timing. That's when she made her statement.

"If looks could kill, Thomas Warrendale would have died at least three times last Sunday."

Mama B rocked and waited for the room to recover from the bombshell she had just dropped.

"What?"

"*No!*"

Insincere words of shock and surprise echoed while the ladies urged her to continue.

"I was watching that floozy, Mercedes Jackson, last Sunday," Mama B said, "and she was looking at Warrendale like a starving dog at a hambone."

"What?" Laura Leigh said. "I heard she been messin' around with Reverend Chapman."

Mama B continued to rock. "Yeah, she messin' around all right. She got *that man* so tied up he couldn't get free if his life depended on it. He kept staring at Warrendale like he was 'bout ready to spit bricks. And so much steam was coming out of Tonya Rutherford's ears, it 'bout took all the curls out of her hair."

"But what makes you think they were angry at Thomas Warrendale?" I asked.

" 'Cause that's who they was all looking at," Mama B said, as if talking to a halfwit.

I leaned forward in my chair and tried not to seem too obvious. "Any idea why they were so angry?"

Laura Leigh squirmed a little in her seat. "Well, I had heard Nettie Fay said she thought there was something going on between Tonya Rutherford and Warrendale. She thought she saw them kissing in the back parking lot after choir rehearsal a few weeks ago. But, well, I figured that was just Nettie Fay being spiteful."

Not to be left out, Sis Green added, "And I heard Mercedes Jackson used to be foolin' around with Warrendale for a while, but he broke it off."

Mama B shook her head and let out a harrumph. "I guess even Warrendale must have had some standards."

Before I could ask more questions, I noticed Reverend Hamilton at the front door. "Reverend Hamilton. Hello, sir."

Mama B welcomed the pastor to her home. "Come on in."

"Good afternoon, ladies and gentleman."

"How do, Reverend," Mrs. Green said as she moved down to make room for Reverend Hamilton.

"Interesting sermon today, Reverend," Mama B said. "We enjoyed it, didn't we, RJ?"

"Yes, I really did enjoy the sermon this morning."

"Did you now? I have to admit, I have missed seeing you in church. I know your job is very demanding, but it's good to see you. How is the knee? I—"

"Fine. My knee is just fine." I didn't mean to be short, but my accident and my knee were the last things I wanted to talk about, especially with this crowd.

"I will continue to keep you in my prayers," Reverend Hamilton said. "It was very good to see you. I think you must have been twelve the last time you came to church that early. Sort of took me by surprise. But I thought I noticed you nodding off once or twice."

I tried not to look as puzzled as I felt. Surprised? Why would he be surprised to see me, especially after he sent me a note specifically asking me to come to the early service today? Whatever his reasons, Reverend Hamilton didn't want to discuss it in this crowd. So I played along.

"Oh no, Reverend. I'm sure I was in deep meditation and prayer."

Reverend Hamilton got a big kick out of that one.

"I thoroughly enjoyed the sermon, although I admit it did seem a bit … *forceful*." I struggled to find the right word to express my feelings in a manner that wouldn't offend Reverend Hamilton.

"Reverend Chapman is a passionate man." The ladies laughed, and even Reverend Hamilton had to suppress a smile before adding, "Well, it certainly smells good in here."

"Reverend, would you like some supper?" Mama B asked as she pushed herself up from her chair to prepare a plate. But he motioned her back into her seat.

"Please don't trouble yourself. I can't stay. I just wanted to stop by to say hello. I have dinner waiting at home."

Mama B returned to her seat, and Reverend Hamilton stood up slowly to leave. After years as a cop, I recognized a stall. He wanted to talk, but not in front of the ladies.

"Are you sure you don't want to take a piece of pie home? It's delicious." I patted my stomach. "I'll be happy to cut you a slice."

"Well, if you don't mind. I know Miss Ella's pies are like a small piece of heaven on earth." Reverend Hamilton followed me into the kitchen.

Taking a knife from the drawer, I cut Reverend Hamilton a slice of pie and wrapped it up quickly. "They'll be suspicious unless you walk out of here with pie."

"Oh, yes. Thank you," Reverend Hamilton said rather hurriedly. "RJ, I really do need to talk to you alone. Can you stop by the parsonage tomorrow around ten?"

"Yes, sir," I said, handing over the pie. "I'll be there."

Reverend Hamilton thanked Mama B for the pie and said his

goodbyes. The rest of the afternoon's conversation consisted of gossip, none of which was helpful in finding out who killed Thomas Warrendale. After checking my watch for the third time in less than ten minutes, I decided to make my exit. As I stood up to leave, Sis Green immediately jumped up and grabbed her bag.

"Lawd, look at the time. I better go. RJ, can I trouble you for a ride?"

It wasn't dark outside and Sis Green, like Mama B, had nerves of steel. Yet, she certainly seemed nervous.

"Of course."

"Your plate's in the fridge." Mama B never sent me home empty-handed. "And bring my good Tupperware back with you when you come by tomorrow."

"Tomorrow?"

"I knew you'd forget. Tomorrow I gotta go to the beauty shop. You said you'd take me."

"I didn't forget. What time is your appointment?"

"Nine."

"Okay. I'll see you in the morning." I gave Mama B a quick kiss, then held the door for Sis Green.

On the short drive to her house, Sis Green seemed unusually quiet. She lived only two blocks from Mama B's.

"Well, here we are. Let me help you with that door." With one hand on the handle, I was just about to jump out when Sis Green reached over and grabbed my arm.

"Wait. I need to talk to you."

Settling back on the seat, I noticed the tears on her face for the first time. Mama B had trained me to always have a clean handkerchief, which I was very glad to hand over, as it gave both of us something to focus on.

"I'm sorry. But I'm so worried about my boy." Her *boy* was the fifteen-year-old grandson she'd raised since he was six months old.

"What's going on?"

Sis Green choked up. After a moment, she recovered enough to add, "Chris is a good boy. I've done my best to raise him to fear the Lord and to be respectful and to stay in school. But, those good-for-nothing hoodlums won't leave him alone."

During the next few minutes, Sis Green spilled out her concerns and fears. Most of them were the same concerns any parent has for teenagers. However, several items raised red flags for me. Though Chris had always been a good student, his grades had dropped dramatically. Once talkative and outgoing, he had become introverted and secretive. His new friends, those she'd seen, both looked and acted tough. She was scared.

"Do you want me to talk to him?"

"Would you? Chris always looked up to you. He respects you. He used to follow you around like a puppy. Said he wanted to be like you ... play ball like you used to. He even said he wanted to be a policeman, just like you. I don't know what else to do. I've talked till I'm blue in the face."

"I'll talk to him."

"Thank you. Thank you. Thank you. Jesus knows I thank you. That boy is 'bout all I've got on this earth, and I don't know what I'd do if something happened to him. I've done all I know to do. I've prayed so long and so hard, I think God is 'bout tired of listening to me."

"Well, you keep on praying, and between the three of us— you, me, and the Lord—we'll figure out something."

You could almost see the weight lift from her shoulders. I was happy to see her smile again, but I knew if her observations were true, talking might not be enough. I'd known Chris since he was a baby. He was one of the nicest, most well-mannered kids I'd met. Sure, he was your typical teenager who liked baggy jeans and rap music, but I'd been around too many of those 'hoodlums' Sis Green referred to, and Chris wasn't one of them. Not yet, anyway. Those are the ones who are hardened from the inside out. You look in their eyes and you see nothing. No soul. No fear. No feelings. No hope. But these new friends might turn out to be a bigger problem than Sis Green knew.

CHAPTER THREE

A T FIVE THIRTY on Monday morning, I watched the sun rise over the river from the window of my townhouse. I had enjoyed four hours of continuous sleep, an improvement over the past few months. Since my accident, my sleep had been sporadic. Six months ago, I was driving on the interstate when I was hit from behind by a sixteen-year-old girl texting on her cellphone. The impact forced my car into another vehicle—killing two people. One was a six-year-old kid. I spent twenty minutes praying and doing CPR. But it was too late. I see that kid's face in my sleep every night. She was wearing one shoe and clutching a Barbie doll. I fractured a ton of bones in my knee. Two surgeries later, it only hurts when I push myself too far. The surgeries were probably the last times I've slept through the night, and that night was the last time I talked to God.

After the short-term disability ended, I went on administrative leave. My shrink said the limp was in my head. If that was true, I had bigger problems. I could probably do my job with a physical limp, but I wasn't sure about a mental one. I needed time to get my head straight.

My townhouse is the end unit of a newly constructed complex, built to resemble a converted warehouse. My home is a Zen-like retreat. It was a foreclosure so I got it for about one third of its market value. Thanks to great timing and some excellent grants the city created to encourage cops and teachers to live in inner-city neighborhoods, I bought a place a lot nicer than most cops could afford. Three stories, brick walls, seventeen-foot ceilings, exposed pipes, minimalist modern furniture, and outstanding river views were the things I loved most about my space. Everything was orderly and neat. I'm sure the department psychologist would say my home reflected my need for order and control.

But the best thing about my townhouse was the oversized two-car garage underneath it. I carved out a small space for a woodshop. I love working with wood and keep a number of tools in my garage. When I need to think, working with wood helps me make sense out of chaos. There's nothing like the hum of a table saw to help sort out the mental pieces.

After a hot shower and a bagel and black coffee with my morning paper, I was ready to face anything.

After dropping Mama B at the hairdresser, I arrived at the parsonage at exactly ten. Mattie Young, Reverend Hamilton's housekeeper for the past twenty years, was there as always and welcomed me. We exchanged pleasantries as she escorted me into the study and then discreetly left, closing the door behind her.

First Baptist Church was well over a century old, and the parsonage had all the character, charm, and problems of a hundred-year-old building. The plumbing was archaic. The boiler and radiators belonged in the Smithsonian. The hardwood floors squeaked, and the draft from the molding around the leaded glass windows could blow papers from the top of a desk. But thanks to Mrs. Young's tender loving care and a generous application of Murphy's Oil Soap, the floors and wood moldings shone like the top of the Chrysler Building.

The hand-carved wood staircases, bookcases, and mantles were unique objects of beauty with stories all their own, and exquisite hand-blown glass tiles surrounded the fireplace. Reverend Hamilton fit perfectly into this environment.

When I entered the room, I got a glimpse of the reverend as he gazed out the window. I hadn't noticed the lines around his eyes and forehead yesterday, nor the look of heaviness that seemed to weigh him down. His hair was almost completely white, and he seemed shrunken.

Still, when he looked at you, it was as though he had X-ray vision. He saw the parts you tried to cover. As a kid, I was terrified of him. Here was someone who actually talked to God, and I honestly believed God told him all my deep, dark secrets. In Reverend Hamilton's eyes, I saw all the lies I'd ever told. He'd seen me steal candy from the corner store, and he'd seen the dirty magazines I'd gotten from Herschel Washington and hidden under my mattress. I believed Reverend Hamilton saw it all. And maybe he did. He always seemed to know things, but he never said a word. In the mind of a guilt-ridden kid, that just made matters worse. Here was a man with the power to destroy my world. I figured he was just waiting for the right time to do it. Maybe he was still waiting.

For a moment, the veil was lifted, and I got a glimpse of the real man behind the mask.

"RJ, I didn't hear you come in. Welcome. Sit down."

I took a seat in one of two wingback chairs in front of his desk and waited.

Reverend Hamilton paused for a moment and then, with a sigh, leaned forward. "I don't know how to begin. But I asked you to come because I'm concerned. As you know, attendance has doubled in less than a year. We've always been fortunate to have a good congregation that has been extremely generous in their giving. But lately, it seems there have been some inconsistencies with the offerings."

My radar went up. "What kind of inconsistencies?"

He paused. "The deposit amounts seem to be a lot less than what we would normally expect."

"Someone's taking the money. Is that what you're getting at?"

"Yes. That's exactly what I'm saying."

"Who do you suspect?" I couldn't help the sharp tone that entered my voice.

He waited so long to respond, I thought he wasn't going to. Eventually, he shrugged.

Reverend Hamilton was older, but he knew everything that went on in that church. There was no way he didn't at least have an idea of who was stealing money. Besides, not many people had access. "How much money are you talking about?"

"Between tithes and offerings, we are down approximately fifty thousand from what we took in last year at this time."

That was more than I expected. "So, with more members, you have substantially less money?"

Reverend Hamilton nodded.

"Have you talked to the financial secretary? Checked the books? Called the bank?"

"I've looked over the envelopes," Reverend Hamilton said quietly, "and talked to the bank."

"Have you talked to the financial secretary?"

Normally not one to shy away from problems, Reverend Hamilton returned his gaze to the window. When he finally spoke, his tone was soft and deliberate. "As you know, Thomas Warrendale was a CPA with one of the local firms. Moe Chapman was the financial secretary, but after he received the call and began preaching, the deacons felt it was too much to expect him to do both."

Years on the force taught me he was holding something back. "Is that the only reason?"

Reverend Hamilton thought for a moment and then shrugged. "We had no *reason* to change financial secretaries."

"But you suspected something wasn't right?"

With a sigh, Reverend Hamilton said, "I wasn't sure. There

was nothing I could prove. It was ... just a feeling. Thomas Warrendale agreed to take on the responsibility of financial secretary as well as minister of music."

I was getting annoyed and could feel my temper rising. "Did you talk to either one of them about your feelings?"

"Warrendale was extremely creative. I'd heard him called a financial genius. He was going to have our accounts analyzed by someone at his firm."

"Why didn't you go the deacons or the trustees? Or the police? Why did you wait so long before doing anything?"

"I have no proof. You've been a member of the congregation long enough to know what would happen if I went to the deacons or the trustees. Thomas Warrendale and Moe Chapman would've been convicted in the eyes of the congregation within a day.

"So, instead you let one of them steal from the church?"

Reverend Hamilton's eyes flashed. He quoted, " 'Dare any of you, having a matter against another, go to law before the unjust, and not before the saints?' First Corinthians six: one." Taking a breath, Reverend Hamilton regained his composure. "I can't prove any money is missing. Not everyone pays tithes. There are a lot of very low-income people with great need."

As Mama B had complained, not everyone paid tithes to the church. It was very possible the new members weren't adding to the church's coffers. Reverend Hamilton's problem was not uncommon. Many churches were apt to allow sin and sometimes outright crime to go unpunished rather than risk a scandal by involving the police in internal matters. I'd grown up with that ideology. Forgive and forget. Repent and be washed clean of all your sins. Coming to me must have been hard. I swallowed my frustration and waited. After all, if he hadn't told me about the money, chances were good we might never have found out about it. And there could be a connection to the murder.

"What about Moe Chapman?" I said. "He's certainly no financial genius."

"He's … a dedicated and passionate minister. I can't believe he would be involved in this." Reverend Hamilton took a moment to think and then shook his head. "Moe Chapman is very straightforward. This … well, this required some finesse."

"So, he isn't smart enough to have done this?"

Reverend Hamilton didn't respond immediately. Finally he said, "I don't believe this would fit Moe Chapman's character."

"Do you think there is any connection between the money and Thomas Warrendale's death?"

Reverend Hamilton stared. "I don't see how."

"You have got to be kidding," I said. "We have missing money and a dead man."

Reverend Hamilton gave me a long look. "RJ, I understand what you're saying. But, if what you're implying is true, that would mean someone from the church … someone close to the money, is a *murderer*. And *that* is something I *cannot* accept."

I might not agree with his logic, but I could understand it. Reverend Hamilton was hanging on to the belief that those closest to him wouldn't be capable of this type of treachery. I wondered briefly if the same thought had crossed Jesus' mind when he realized Judas betrayed him for thirty pieces of silver. "What do you want me to do?"

"I want you to investigate. Not officially, mind you. I don't want the scandal of a formal police investigation. You know the church well enough to know that if word of a police investigation got out, reputations would be destroyed. I want you to investigate privately—quietly. You can say it's part of the investigation into Thomas Warrendale's death."

That part was true. If I investigated the murder, I'd need to look into anything and everything that might possibly be connected to Warrendale's murder. The coroner might not have officially declared this to be murder, but in the event of a suspicious death, we were apt to treat it that way so we didn't lose time later. Something in my gut told me this was not a random house fire, even without the smell of gasoline. But, aside from the fact that I was not investigating this murder, I was still on leave.

Reverend Hamilton lifted a shopping bag from the floor and slid it across the desk. Inside, I saw an old-fashioned accountant's ledger, a CD case, and index-card boxes filled with offering envelopes.

"Reverend Hamilton, I'm not sure I can help. I'm a detective, not a financial wizard. You need a lawyer, not a cop. Plus, I'm on leave."

"That's why it would be an *unofficial* investigation. Being on leave should mean you have more time, right?" His X-ray vision penetrated my outer shell and pricked my conscience.

"I don't even know where to begin."

Looking down at his Bible, Reverend Hamilton smiled for the first time since I arrived. "I do. You start with the Word and with prayer. Let's pray."

It had been at least six months since I'd prayed, but I assumed the position—head bowed and eyes closed. With any luck, he wouldn't notice I was faking. Reverend Hamilton prayed for guidance and direction and finished with praise and thanks in advance for the solution.

I stumbled outside in a daze, lugging the bag Reverend Hamilton had given me with the church's receipts and bank statements. I swear it got heavier with every step. Tossing the bag in the trunk of my car, I felt a brief moment of relief. Out of sight, out of mind. Sooner or later, I'd have to tackle this problem, but not right now. I couldn't prove a connection between the money and Warrendale's death, but I felt they were somehow tied together. If there was a link, I would find it.

I NEEDED TO pick Mama B up from the beauty shop, which was actually only a few blocks away from the parsonage. When I arrived, she seemed a bit out of sorts. It was just about lunchtime, so we headed to get a bite to eat. Despite the excellent lunch at her favorite restaurant, a little dive called St.

Joe Café, she was still not quite her normal, jovial self. After fifteen minutes of probing questions, I ascertained she wasn't happy her hairdresser was out of town, even though she'd arranged for someone else to do her hair—which by the way looked quite nice. However, during dessert, the true source of her frustration came out.

Mama B took a bite of pie. "You know you ain't foolin' nobody. I can see right through you. And they should have put a bit of lard in the dough."

"I think the pie tastes great." I ignored the personal commentary, even though I knew it wouldn't matter. When Mama B got hold of something, she was worse than a dog with a new bone.

"You ain't sleeping. I can see the dark circles under your eyes."

I focused on my pie and kept eating.

"Boy, you're too young to be working this hard and not sleeping and probably not eating right."

"I'm eating very well," I said, taking another bite of pie.

"You know what I mean. You're running yourself into the ground, and you need a wife."

I laughed, despite the serious look on her face. "How is having a wife going to help me sleep better?"

"A wife would make sure you were looked after."

"Well, I don't need a wife to look after me. I'm perfectly able to take care of myself."

Mama B rolled her eyes and snorted. "Pshaw."

"Look, I know you're concerned, but I'm fine. I slept longer last night than I have in a long time."

"Men! You don't even know what you need. If you had a wife, she'd be able to tell you."

I laughed so hard, people at a nearby table actually started to laugh too. Mama B was totally serious, but she eventually let it drop. I knew she was biding her time. She wouldn't give up until she had me safely married off to a young woman of her choosing.

After lunch, I dropped Mama B at home then swung by the courthouse. Judge E.L. Browning's retirement party was today, and I wanted to stop in and wish him well. After forty-five years on the bench, Judge Browning was finally calling it quits. Over the years, we'd gotten to be something just short of friends.

Judge Browning was the first African-American named to the bench in St. Joe, Indiana. After a short but distinguished career as a public defender, E.L. ran for and won his seat on the bench after Judge Richard Thomas was caught in a scandal involving drugs and an under-aged prostitute. E.L. was heavily involved in civil rights and education. In fact, for the last fifteen years, he'd served as a part-time professor at the local law school. Word around the precinct was he wasn't leaving the bench for a life of leisure but would soon be named as the new dean at the law school. Oftentimes, cops and lawyers seem to be on opposite sides of the table. But, down to the last man and woman on the force, every member of the SJPD would attest to the fact that, while we may not have agreed with every decision E.L. handed down, we respected him. He treated everyone— cops, lawyers, victims, and criminals—with respect.

Streamers, music, cake, and balloons filled the courthouse cafeteria. I grabbed a piece of cake and a fork and looked for his familiar face. I spotted E.L. in the middle of well-wishers and elbowed my way close enough to say, "Congratulations, Judge."

"Thank you, RJ. I was hoping you'd show up. Have you had a chance to consider my proposition?"

"I'm still thinking about it."

Grabbing me by the arm, he guided me toward a less crowded corner of the room.

"I know you don't like the idea of talking in public. I still remember the first time you testified in my courtroom." His lips twitched with the effort to keep from laughing. "I thought you were going to puke right there in the witness box."

"So did I. Which is why I don't know why you want me to

humiliate myself. I'm not a lawyer. I'm just a cop, nothing else—nothing special."

"That's exactly why they need to hear you. They need to hear you because you're a cop—an honest cop. Because you have something to say that these young kids need to hear. They're going to hear enough about the law from a lot of men and women who haven't practiced in over twenty years, if at all. I want them to hear about the law from someone who upholds it every day. There's more to the law than written rules and regulations. Whether they're prosecutors or public defenders, we should all be on the same side. The side of law, the side of order, the side of justice."

"No pressure, right?" I barely hid a smile. "I agree with everything you're saying, but I just don't know that I'm the right person to do it. Talking to a bunch of twenty-two-year-old wannabe Clarence Darrows isn't my idea of fun. Being a cop takes up a lot of time. I've never taught anyone before. I don't know the first thing about teaching."

"You'll learn, and I'll help you. Just give it a try—one semester. If you hate it, then I'll get someone else. I promise. It's only part-time, and there are perks that come with being on the faculty—like discounted football tickets."

He was pulling out all the stops now. "I'm not qualified to teach at a law school. I have a bachelor's degree. Don't you need a PhD to teach at that level?"

"Normally, yes—"

I started to interrupt, but Judge Browning didn't get where he was by being unprepared.

"You're right. Normally you would need a terminal degree like a PhD or JD to teach at this level. But we have a program where we allow experts in their field to teach as long as they have a college degree, more than five years of experience, approval of their manager, and if they work with a tenured professor."

"Wow. That seems a lot."

"That's the problem with our law schools. We have a lot of tenured professors who have studied law for years, but they've never practiced a day in their lives. Besides, I want these students to learn the other side of the law. The relationship with the police needs to be established early. We're a team."

"But why me?"

"You've been working with at-risk kids at the rec center already. This will give you an opportunity to help future prosecutors and defense attorneys as well."

"You're not going to leave me alone about this, are you?"

"I didn't get where I am by giving up. You should know that. It's just one class—one semester. It's part-time, and I'll be there to help you."

"All right, one semester. That's it. After you get all the letters from parents asking for their money back, you'll see I was right."

What had I gotten myself into? Suddenly, the cake I was eating tasted like sawdust. I needed air.

THE BASEMENT OF the courthouse was linked to the jail through a tunnel, and that's where I was headed. The tunnel made it easy to transport prisoners back and forth. Somehow, just leaving the courthouse seemed to alleviate a great deal of tension. I was finally able to breathe again. Back on familiar turf, I felt confident. Maybe that's what I needed to do, teach the class from the basement of the county jail.

The tunnel between the courthouse and the jail was actually very large and had a café and tables where police, lawyers, and judges could grab a cup of coffee and a bite to eat. I ran into several people I knew in the basement, including my temporary partner, Officer J. Harley Wickfield IV.

St. Joe's police department had about 261 sworn officers and over a hundred civilian employees. In the Investigative Division, there were sixty-five sworn and civilian personnel. We were assigned to a wide variety of duties, but our main responsibility was to investigate major crimes. This included robbery, homicide, suspicious deaths, domestic violence (repeat offenders), and aggravated assault. Crime had been up over the past few months, and investigators were stretched thin, which was one more reason for me to feel guilty for the administrative leave.

Harley had been assigned to work with me so he could learn the ropes in preparation for his investigator's exam. The fact that Harley and I were friends was amazing; on the outside, we're complete opposites. Harley was a twenty-six-year-old white male from a rich, Southern family. His vibrant blue eyes made him very popular with women, which could be quite useful during an interrogation.

His ancestors owned a large plantation outside of Nashville, Tennessee. The dilapidated slave quarters were still there as a "testament to the family's prestige and social standing." At least that's what J. Harley Wickfield III told me. Having met Harley's parents, I was further amazed he and I were friends. Number Three (as I liked to refer to Harley's dad) still bemoaned the financial loss that weakened the family's fortunes after the Civil War, or the "unconstitutional acts of Northern Aggression"—another quote from the illustrious Number Three.

But for some reason I couldn't explain, Harley and I were friends. In fact, he was almost like a brother to me. Personally, I considered it one of those freakish anomalies of life. But Harley had a different philosophy. Despite all facts to the contrary, Harley believed we were related. His theory was one of his slave-owning ancestors must have fathered one of my ancestors, making us blood relations. None of my relatives could be traced to Tennessee, but he didn't let facts interfere with his beliefs.

I went to the table where Harley was having a cup of coffee.

"What're you doing here?" Harley said with his Southern drawl, which despite five years in Indiana, he hadn't dropped—although, it did become more pronounced when he needed to turn on the charm.

"Just getting some air," I said. "Stopped by Judge Browning's party. But I was hoping I'd run into you. I have a question."

"I've got one for you too. You first."

"What do you know about the Skulls?"

Tilting his head to the side and raising an eyebrow, Harley asked a question without saying a word.

He was astute—another reason I liked him. "I know you recently spent a few weeks working on the mayor's Gang Prevention Taskforce. It's been a while since I was involved in anything gang related."

Harley was perceptive enough to know I wasn't being completely honest, but also smart enough not to push. He was a good officer and would make an excellent investigator one day. "I know they're one of the toughest gangs in the Midwest. Scary bunch. They have a really complex structure with different levels, modeled after the Italian mafia. Mostly they're into drugs, everything from harvesting to distribution. No one really knows how many members there are—could be in the thousands. I read only a week ago that they're trying to corrupt people from all areas of society. Lawyers, judges, bankers. They focus on the area between Cleveland and Chicago."

"What about St. Joe? Have you heard of the Skulls getting a foothold around here?"

"Nothing concrete. Only rumors. Why? What do you know?"

"Not much, just have some suspicions." I didn't think Chris Green was actually a member of the Skulls. He'd have to kill to become a full member, and I didn't believe he'd sunk to that level. But Sis Green's descriptions of a few of the kids Chris was hanging with sounded like some thugs we were watching closely for ties to the Skulls. We didn't have any proof the Skulls had made their way to St. Joe, but a couple of known gang members had been spotted in town, and we knew they had relatives here.

I hoped to change the subject before Harley got too suspicious. "So, what did you want to ask me?"

"I was going to—"

Before Harley could finish, Division Chief Mike Barinski walked up and interrupted our conversation.

"Just the men I'm looking for," Chief Mike said. He grasped my arm and steered me to a corner, allowing a guard escorting a prisoner to pass. "You saved me from having to track you down. I need everything you have on Thomas Warrendale and quick. The mayor wants a briefing first thing tomorrow morning."

Death went out to the gambler's house

Come and go with me

The gambler cried out, I'm not ready to go,

Ain't got no travellin' shoes

Got no travellin' shoes, got no travellin' shoes

Sinner cried out, I'm not ready to go

I ain't got no travellin' shoes

CHAPTER FOUR

———

"Look, RJ, I'm not supposed to be talking to you and we're not even having this conversation." Chief Mike looked over his shoulder.

"What conversation?"

It took him half a second and then he slapped me on the back. "Exactly." He glanced over his shoulder again. "I'm between a rock and a hard place, and I need your help with this Warrendale murder. I'm understaffed and Harley is a good cop, but he's never investigated a homicide before. Plus this guy Warrendale lived too close to the mayor's neighborhood for comfort, so he's asking questions. I need my best man on this."

I opened my mouth, but he held up a hand. "I know. I know. You're on administrative leave, but I talked to the mayor who talked to Human Resources. If you're agreeable, there's two ways we can do this." He held up a finger. "Your shrink's willing to sign off that you're fit to return to work." He stared into my eyes.

I stared back without blinking. "What's the second option."

He took a deep breath. "If you were to take early retirement from the force, I could hire you back as a consultant. You'd be a contractor. You work with Harley and teach him the ropes."

I had been seriously considering leaving the force, but had grown too accustomed to having a roof over my head. My pension might keep me from starving until I figured out what else I wanted to do with my life, but consulting would provide an income. I would definitely think it over.

Chief Mike, as he liked to be called, was large, both vertically and horizontally, and looked as though he slept in his clothes. A linebacker with a heart of gold. He had the knack of inspiring the cops who worked for him to go the extra mile. Tough but fair, he'd have taken a bullet for any one of us, even the shots fired by the media. He often did.

"Come on, RJ, I really need you. I'm desperate."

I reached in my jacket and pulled out the note from my shrink that I'd been carrying around since my last visit.

Chief Mike hesitantly took the paper and read it. Then he released a sigh and used a handkerchief to wipe his forehead. Relief oozed out of every pore. He froze when I added, "I'm back, but I want to think about that consulting thing. For now, I will continue to be a detective for the police force."

He reluctantly nodded.

The briefing didn't take long. The smell of gasoline was so strong, the fire had definitely been set deliberately. But the coroner's preliminary report stated the fire wasn't the cause of death. From what was left of Warrendale's lungs, the coroner determined he'd died before the fire. There was also a hole in Warrendale's skull just the right size for a small-caliber bullet. We were holding that part back from the media.

Afterward, Harley and I spent the next few hours reviewing the case file, including pictures and video from the crime scene. But there were still some foggy areas. Pictures and videos were great tools in police work, but nothing really takes the place of seeing things with your own eyes. We needed to talk to the coroner.

If there was one thing I hated about being a cop, it was visiting the county morgue. Don't get me wrong; the coroner was a nice guy, but the morgue held too many bad memories. It was sterile, cold, and impersonal. Maybe that was a good thing. If your loved one ended up at the morgue, you probably needed something hard and solid to ground you. Perhaps the sleek, steely-gray counters combined with the white walls and white-coated personnel could help you keep your sanity at a time like that. It didn't help me with the images of that six-year-old girl with one shoe. But then maybe cops are different.

The official report wasn't ready yet, but the overworked, underpaid, and eternally jolly coroner promised the report would be in my hands first thing in the morning. He wasn't ready to stake his reputation on it, but he felt strongly that Thomas Warrendale died from a gunshot wound to the head. The fire—probably an attempt to cover the murderer's trail—was the work of a rank amateur.

I had a little time left before I was scheduled to meet Harley at the crime scene, so I made a small detour and swung by my old high school. St. Joe High School was a tall, stately building on the Northwest side of town. Walking through the halls, I was inundated with the sights and the smells of my youth—cold-gray lockers, sweat-soaked athletes horsing around in the halls, and the thump of rap music that blared through headphones. My senses were almost overwhelmed as I relived moments from my youth. Most of those memories were good, but I wouldn't trade places with these kids for any amount of money. At sixteen, I'd been sure I knew more than anyone else on the planet, just like these kids. Amazing how the older you get, the more you realize how little you really know. Maybe that's the key to maturity, realizing you don't know anything. I didn't have to wander long. It was just a few minutes before I saw Chris.

Was it my imagination, or did he look scared? "Hey, Chris. Got a minute?"

"Yo, man. What brings you here?"

We did a knuckle punch and a manly half hug.

Chris was about five-eight with a slight build. He wore his hair cut short, and he had one visible earring, a diamond stud. I didn't notice any tattoos or other markings that indicated gang connections.

"Just checkin' on some things. How's it going?"

"Good. Good. Things are good."

Maybe I would have believed him if he wasn't looking around like a cornered rat. Gang colors weren't allowed in school, but I looked for other signs of gang affiliation on Chris, caps turned a certain way or jewelry. After a quick assessment, I concluded he looked much the same as all the other kids.

"Really? I saw your grandmother the other day. She's worried about you."

"Oh well, you know ... she's always worried about something," Chris shrugged.

"Does she have any reason to be worried about you?"

He held my stare for a moment and then blinked and backed away with a laugh.

"No. No, man, of course not."

I got closer, my face only inches from his, and stared him in the eyes. Chris squirmed a little before he dropped his gaze. "Come on, RJ, you know me."

"I do, and you know me."

The warning bell sounded, but I stood my ground for another few seconds before stepping back. "Go on. I wouldn't want you to be late for class."

Chris ran down the hall. He looked back only once and then opened a door and scurried into his classroom. It was a brief conversation, but I'd learned quite a bit. No noticeable tattoos, clear eyes, and no smell of alcohol or weed. Chris was still just an impressionable kid. As I walked out of the school, I chuckled at the way he'd rushed to get away from me. I don't think I've ever seen a kid happier to get to class.

* * *

MY HOUSE WAS very close to the historic district of St. Joe.

On the other side of the river, large Victorian, Georgian and Craftsman homes sat on tree-lined cobblestone streets. The cherry trees, with their big white blossoms, filled the air with a soft, floral scent that reminded me of spring. Many of the large homes in this area had been converted into duplexes, triplexes, and quads. Several of the largest homes had definitely seen better days. But the area was undergoing a rebirth, as young families started to move back. Sitting high on a hill, the grandest of these homes had a view that couldn't be rivaled, at least not in St. Joe. The St. Joe River, Martin Luther King Memorial Park, and a view of the St. Joe skyline, such as it was, were the sights these lucky people saw each and every day. The mayor lived in the grandest of the grand homes.

Thomas Warrendale had lived on the edge of the historic district. No river views, no view of the park, and a lot less square footage. These homes retained few of their historic details. They were far enough away from the historic district that the neighborhood association didn't harass the owners about paint colors, but they were apparently too close for a criminal to commit arson without incurring the wrath of city hall.

All that remained of the house was a charred shell. Through the home's skeletal remains, I could see Harley in full gear, sifting through the rubble.

"It's official." Harley's greeting wouldn't make sense to an outsider, but I understood the fire chief had formally announced arson. That *suspicion* led to the fire chief notifying the state fire marshal. The fire marshal would be sending an inspector to investigate.

In Indiana, the Office of the State Fire Marshal had eleven investigators. Each investigator was responsible for between nine and thirteen counties. Their caseloads were huge.

"Do we have an ETA?" I said.

"Not yet. Maybe by noon."

"That's fast."

"The mayor's office strikes again."

Sifting through the remains of a fire was a dirty and tedious job. Technically, the Uniform Crime Scene Technicians (UCST) collected evidence, photographed and diagrammed the crime scene, and documented the evidence, which was then passed on to the investigators, who in this case were me and Harley.

In the trunk of my car, I kept a bag with boots, coveralls, and gloves. There's no way you can walk through the ashes of a burned house without coming out covered in dirt and soot and smelling like smoke. In addition to the dirt, until the fire marshal determined what chemicals were used to ignite the flames, there was also a risk of inhaling potentially dangerous chemicals. The Crime Scene Unit had already done their jobs, but I wanted another look, and it would do Harley good to see things up close and personal. All geared up in a jumpsuit, gloves, boots, and cap, I grabbed a few more essentials from my trunk—flashlight, camera, evidence bags, and a small shovel. Harley already had a video camera. We were determined to leave no stone unturned.

"We better get to work," I said.

Three hours, a hot shower, and a change of clothes later, we weren't any closer to the truth. At the precinct, I reviewed the pictures from the crime scene, along with the crime scene technicians' reports and the evidence they'd collected, as well as the report from the fire marshal. Apparently, the mayor had lit a fire of his own that had spread throughout the station. Our lab was overworked and underpaid, but I'd never seen such a quick turnaround.

Harley came around the corner with his nose in a file folder. He looked up briefly. "Find anything?"

"Where'd you come from?"

"Lab." Harley sat at his desk and flipped through the folder. "Anything useful?"

"Not yet. What's the word going around the church? What's the Oracle got to say?"

From the moment Harley met Mama B, he referred to her as "The Oracle." He said that every time he watched *The Matrix,* he was reminded of her. It might have something to do with the fact that Mama B had just baked cookies, and there we all were, cops and hoodlums, sitting on Mama B's porch eating cookies and drinking sweet tea.

"Couldn't keep his pants on," I said. "Apparently, he had a rep for being a *playah.*"

Harley snorted.

"You kiddin'? She said that?"

"She did. She thinks he got those girls all worked up, and one of them killed him."

"Any truth in it?"

"Beats me. We've got to start with the basics. Motive 101. Who wanted him dead and who benefits?"

I should have known by the smile plastered on Harley's face he was holding something back.

"Maybe his wife." Harley grinned.

"Wife? Thomas Warrendale was married? I'm pretty sure he never mentioned a wife. It would have been all over the church."

"Maybe the problem is his real name wasn't Thomas Warrendale."

Harley dropped the file on my desk. "They managed to get enough DNA to run it through the database." He leaned over my shoulder while I scanned the file.

Our friendly neighborhood choir director had a rap sheet. Mostly petty teenage stuff, shoplifting, and vandalism, and nothing recent. Thomas Warrendale was Tyrone Warren, a CPA from Cleveland. Wife. No kids.

"Anyone contacted the wife?"

"Not yet. Called the Ohio State Police. They'll notify her and call us back."

"Now, why would a respected CPA move to another state, change his name, and pretend he was single?"

"Lots of people dream of running away from their ordinary lives and doing something different."

"True, but few actually do it. We need to find out what Tyrone Warren was running away from, and whether or not his past caught up with him. Or whether someone in St. Joe ended his life."

"Is that it?" Harley asked.

"No, but it's a start."

THE WEATHER WAS unseasonably warm for May as I drove by Mama B's. The days were getting longer, so it was still light outside. Seeing her sitting on the porch, I honked and then pulled in beside the house. She was enjoying the basketball game across the street.

The front of the house looked out on the back of the Southeast-Side Recreation Center, an old rec center where men, young and old, hung out. Concrete and two poles with rims passed for a basketball court. The nets disappeared long before I could remember. This was not a place for the weak. These die-hard basketball fanatics were serious about their game. If you came to the Center talking trash, you'd better be able to back it up. While people of every race were welcome to watch, only serious *ballers* were invited to play. Today's game was pretty intense, considering it was only Monday. Weekend games were the best, but I recognized some high school hotshots along with the regulars and knew this game would be worth watching. This was not a place for the faint of heart or those who lacked skills. Some of the toughest kids in the city passed Mama B's house to play ball at the Center. Most stopped to speak. Some asked for a glass of water or a bite to eat. All of them cleaned up their language, even when passing, because if the weather was nice, Mama B was almost always sitting on the front porch.

"Go on in the house and get yourself something to eat and some lemonade. It's hotter than East Hell out here."

"Hotter than East Hell" was one of Mama B's colorful colloquialisms. Apparently, East Hell was somewhat hotter than West Hell. How a good, Bible-quoting church matron like Mama B knew the temperature of Hell was another question I pondered as I went to the kitchen.

No small talk where food was concerned. Mama B cut straight to the chase. Since I was single, she was sure I couldn't possibly be eating enough. And there was no way I was eating a balanced meal. Resistance was futile. Plus, the scents drifting out to the porch were enough for me. Pot roast, leftover collard greens, and cornbread.

After eating till I was stuffed like a turkey, I went out on the porch, but Mama B wasn't alone.

"Hello, Moe … ah, I mean, Reverend Chapman." I extended my hand.

Mama B snorted and continued rocking. Moe and I pretended we hadn't noticed.

Moe Chapman occupied one of the sturdier chairs Mama B kept outside for her heftier guests. Made of metal, it was technically considered a chair and a half. Moe flashed his largest, toothiest smile. "Praise the Lord. Good afternoon, RJ. I was just on my way home from the weekly Sunday school teachers' class at the church and saw Miss Ella out here rocking. Thought I'd come set for a spell."

Moe was a big man, and his flesh oozed out of the sides of the chair. Each time he moved, the chair creaked, and I could see a vein begin to twitch on Mama B's neck.

I decided to make the best of the situation and see what I could learn. "I'm glad you stopped by. You saved me from making a trip out to your house. With Thomas Warrendale's murder, I need to ask a few questions."

Moe stopped rocking and turned toward me. For a moment, I thought I saw a flash of panic in his eyes, but it only lasted a moment. Police tend to have that effect on a lot of people.

Moe leaned forward and spoke quietly, as if I were coming to him for spiritual advice. "How can I help you?"

"How well did you know Thomas Warrendale?"

Moe gave the question some thought. "Not very well, I'm afraid. We didn't exactly run in the same circles."

"Really? That seems odd. I mean, St. Joe isn't that big, and First Baptist Church is even smaller."

He smiled big. "Of course we knew each other from church, but we didn't hang out otherwise."

"You used to be the financial secretary—"

"I helped out with the books. But I wasn't no 'financial genius' or nothin'. I heard Warrendale was a financial genius." Moe laughed heartily. "But that was before I got the call into the ministry and started preaching the Word of God. Praise the Lord."

"And once you started preaching?"

"Once I started preaching, I didn't have the time to do the books. That's when Warrendale took over."

"Did you like Warrendale?"

He squirmed a bit in his chair, but maybe that was because he was wedged in so tight, his flesh had started to go numb.

"Well, I can't say I exactly liked him. I heard some rumors." Moe halted and looked down a bit sheepishly. "I don't like spreading no rumors, but I suppose this is important." He looked at me expectantly.

"Very important. We're trying to solve a murder."

Moe hesitated just a second. "I guess you're right. Besides, I don't suppose anything I say will do any harm now."

I took my notebook out, and Mama B rocked in silence.

Moe Chapman had his audience. "I was at choir rehearsal on Friday night, and I heard a big argument."

"Who was arguing?" I asked.

"Thomas Warrendale and Sister Williams." Moe leaned forward in his seat.

Mama B let out a noise that sounded like "Pshaw."

"Who's Sister Williams? I don't think I know her."

"Sister Paris Williams. She sings in the choir. She was furious." Moe shook his head at the recollection. "She really let Minister Warrendale have it."

"What were they arguing about?"

"It sounded like Sister Williams was accusing Warrendale of stealing. She was madder than a wet hen, and claimed she'd make sure he paid for what he'd done."

I looked up from my notebook. "Why didn't you come forward with this sooner?"

Moe tried to look sheepish, but his lopsided grin came across as sneaky instead. "I wasn't sure it was important. Besides, I don't like getting involved."

"Did she say anything else?"

"I sort of came in on the tail end of the conversation, so I don't know what Minister Warrendale said, but she was so hot you could have fried an egg on her arm." Moe shook his head again and chuckled. "After that, she stormed out."

"Did anyone else see or hear this?"

"I wasn't paying a lot of attention. I just noticed the time and had to go pick up Mercedes ... ah ... I mean, Sister Jackson."

"And where did you go after you left the church?"

"Like I said, I had a sort of date with Sister Jackson, so I went and picked her up, and then we went to dinner and spent some time together." Again Moe flashed his big toothy grin.

I asked a few other questions, but Moe didn't have anything further to add. After a few more minutes, he pried himself out of the chair and left. When he was gone, I sat in the chair Moe vacated.

"So, what do you think of that?" I asked Mama B.

Mama B rocked in silence for a few seconds. "I thought I was going to have to call 911 to get that fat tub of lard out of my chair."

"I meant, what did you think of what he had to say?"

"Moe Chapman's a liar. He was a liar as a child. Once a liar, always a liar."

"He's popular with the ladies."

Mama B scrunched up her nose as though she'd smelled sour milk. "You would be too if you paid them."

I spat out my lemonade. "How do you know that?"

"That Mercedes Jackson was bragging to Nettie Fay how Moe sends flowers to her job every week and pays for her to get her nails and hair done. He buys her clothes, pays her rent, and springs for expensive vacations and jewelry. They went on a cruise to the Bahamas over Christmas. Can you imagine all that fat lying on the beach? Lucky they didn't mistake him for a beached whale and try to harpoon him. If that ain't paying for a woman, then I don't know what is."

Whew. That wasn't exactly what I was expecting when she said he "paid" for women, but it didn't restore my faith in this supposed *man of God.* Where had all that money come from? I spent a few minutes trying to get her reaction to his comments about Sister Williams, but she remained uncharacteristically quiet on the subject. No matter how much I asked or what I said, she couldn't or wouldn't say more. Eventually, I decided to change the subject and had her fill me in on the dirt she'd gotten since yesterday. There wasn't anything new, so I filled her in on my latest bombshell.

She snorted. "I don't believe that boy was married."

I knew *that boy* referred to Thomas Warrendale. Mama B's likes and dislikes ran deep. Once she made her mind up about someone, there was no turning back.

"I assure you he was."

"He certainly didn't act like it. Just because you have a marriage certificate doesn't mean anything." Mama B rocked slowly. "A lot of people have diplomas, but that don't mean they know the front end of a mule from the back."

"Any truth to the rumors you all were talkin' about yesterday?"

Mama B pursed her lips. "I don't lie."

"I know you don't lie. I mean are you sure? Was Thomas Warrendale fooling around?"

"Mm-hmm … that's what I heard. Where there's smoke, there's fire."

"Was there anyone in particular?"

Mama B rocked on. "I don't know how par-tic-u-lar he was." Mama B enunciated each syllable to make her point. "But I heard Francis Montgomery was one of the people."

Francis Montgomery seemed like a nice, straight-laced kid. She dressed older than her nineteen years, but if that were a crime, our jails would be packed. She'd grown up in the church. Her father was on the Deacon Board, and her mother was a member of the Nurses' Aid.

"Anyone else?"

"I heard Mercedes Jackson's name mentioned, but I didn't believe it. Even a little fancy pants like Warrendale wouldn't be that desperate."

"I thought Mercedes had hooked up with Moe Chapman? They looked pretty cozy on Sunday."

"Any port will do in a storm." Mama B rocked. "I heard Tonya Rutherford got herself … in the family way. Some say it was Warrendale's."

"Is it true?"

"She's expecting. I can tell by her face. They say she wears a tight girdle to hide her belly."

Mama B was a font of information.

"Anything else?"

Mama B rocked on for a long moment before adding, "You need to talk to my hairdresser, Paris Williams. He used to do her books. I think he was up to no good."

"Is this the same Paris Williams Moe Chapman was talking about?"

"I couldn't tell you what he was going on about. But Paris Williams is a good woman. And I think you should talk to her."

Mama B wouldn't elaborate on anything other than to suggest I talk to Paris myself.

"I've got a cobbler in the fridge."

I'm going to have to go to the gym tomorrow.

BACK AT THE historic district, not far from Thomas Warrendale's house or what was left of it was the home of Paris Williams. It was almost nine at night but it was still light outside, so I decided to stop, in spite of the time. It had been a long day, but when you're working a murder investigation, time is important.

Paris Williams' house was a large, three-storied Georgian with a brick exterior and leaded-glass windows. Prominent and stately, it sat back from the curb like a well-preserved grand dame. Large, flowering white dogwoods and orange blossoms filled the air with a sweet, fruity aroma and dropped white petals onto the manicured lawn. From the cobblestone driveway to the wrought-iron fence, this house exuded grandeur and had river, park, and skyline views. It was not on the outskirts of the historic district like Warrendale's home. No, this house *was* the historic district.

Up close and personal, the house had seen better days. While not perfect, it had class. It looked like the one-hundred-fifty-year-old home that it was, and it wore its years well. Pausing to admire the view, I felt like I'd stepped back in time. But this trip back was a short one. At the time when this house was built, I would not have been welcome, at least not at the front door. Memory Lane was not always a street I wanted to linger on. I rang the bell.

"The salon business must be *really* good," I mumbled to myself as I waited.

It didn't take long before the door opened. I started to speak, and my mind went totally blank.

"Yes?"

"I'm Detective Franklin."

"Yes, I know."

"You do?"

"Do you want to come in?"

The home's interior had high ceilings, incredible crown molding, and marble floors. The walls were taped and patched and ready for paint. Paris led me into a room that was once a parlor. Drop cloths protected the hardwood floors, and a large door she was in the process of stripping was spread across two workhorses.

Focusing on the house gave me time to catch my breath. I wouldn't describe Paris as beautiful. Tall, medium build, with dark skin and gray eyes, she wasn't a runway model. If you were into super-thin women, you wouldn't have looked at her twice. But if you did look twice, you'd see that her skin was smooth like chocolate milk and her eyes were light gray with little golden flecks in them that sparkled when she smiled. She had great curves. But mostly there was an inner beauty, peace, intelligence, and a twitch at the corner of her mouth that hinted at a sense of humor. That's what left me speechless. But I had to say something.

"And the answer is 'yes,' " she said.

"Excuse me. The answer to what is 'yes'?"

"The salon business is good."

"You heard that?"

"Yeah, I heard that." Paris tried to hide a smile. "The doorbell is also an intercom. I've heard a lot of interesting comments on that thing. But this house was a wreck when I bought it. It was slated for demolition. I only paid ten thousand for it. Of course, it's costing a small fortune to renovate, but that's where the fun lies."

Paris had put on a pair of rubber gloves while she talked, and she returned to stripping the pair of doors in the living room.

"You're not doing that right," I said.

"What?"

"You're not stripping that properly. You need to go with the grain of the wood."

"Really? Who're you, Bob Villa?"

"Let's just say I've stripped wood before. Let me show you."

Putting on the spare pair of heavy-duty rubber gloves lying on the mantle, I took the scraper. Normally, I don't go looking for extra work, but there's nothing like the smell and the feel of wood. Maybe when this case was over and I fulfilled my consulting obligation, I could spend time woodworking.

"I'm not complaining, mind you, but I can't believe you've come here to strip the paint off my doors." She picked up another scraper and started scraping, this time with the grain of the wood. "I know the police are here to serve and to protect, but isn't this taking service a bit far?"

"We aim to please. Actually, I came to ask you some questions about Thomas Warrendale. I understand he worked for you."

"That's a little misleading. I wouldn't say he exactly *worked* for me. He did the books for my salon. He *used to* do the books. That doesn't mean he was an employee."

"Did you know him well?"

"Depends on what you mean by 'well.' He started doing my books about six months ago."

"And …?"

"And what?

"Mama B said you had suspicions."

"Mama B?" She stopped and stared at me.

"Mrs. Ella Bethany. You do her hair. She's my godmother."

"Oh, of course. I knew that. I just hadn't heard her called Mama B. Well, I have, ah, had suspicions."

"Would you like to elaborate?"

"Not really. But I suppose I'll have to, just not here." She removed her gloves. "I've got to get out of this room. The fumes are getting to me. Would you like some tea?"

Taking my agreement for granted, she headed off to what I could only assume was the kitchen. I followed the sounds toward the back of the house.

Along the way, I noticed the interior. Some rooms were totally renovated, while others were still works in progress.

The kitchen, however, was completely done. Paris' kitchen was a totally new space, tastefully designed to look old—from the farmhouse sink, bay windows, built-in window seat and brick fireplace to the reproduction vintage stove, which must have cost a small fortune. Hardwood floors, marble counters, and a butcher-block island were all functional as well as beautiful. I took a seat at the large farmhouse table and watched as she prepared the tea.

There was a comforting smell of cinnamon and music piped in from somewhere, which made for an extremely peaceful and inviting atmosphere.

"Is that Diana Krall?"

"No. Actually, it's an artist I've just discovered named Kitt Lough. Isn't she great? I love her voice. She reminds me of … I don't know. It's like a different time."

"You like jazz? I've never heard of her, but I like her voice. I love jazz. It's so pure, so unique. I know when I get to heaven, the angel blowing the horn of welcome will sound something like Duke Ellington or maybe Najee." I felt awkward sharing so much with a perfect stranger, but she smiled, and the awkwardness disappeared.

The tea kettle whistled, and she finished the preparations.

"Is there some place I can wash my hands?"

"The powder room is just around that corner."

The powder room was renovated to include a pedestal sink, hexagonal black and white floor tiles, a small toilet, and not much else. The décor was tasteful and subtle but not overdone. I hate it when people buy an old house and spend a fortune turning it into a modern one. I liked how this one-hundred-fifty-year-old house felt like a home. From the imperfect plaster walls to the scuffed-up molding and radiators layered in paint, this was a *home*. People lived and loved here.

"Give my compliments to your decorator," I said as I returned to the table.

"My sister will be happy to know you approve."

"Your sister's an interior decorator?"

"Actually, she's got a master's degree in electrical engineering, but she's working on completing her associate's degree in interior design. She's always been good with decorating and sewing. She says that when she's ready to retire, she's going to move someplace warm and sunny and open an interior-decorating business. She's great with finding period pieces in second-hand stores. Plus, she fits my budget."

Teas, cookies, cinnamon rolls, and other goodies filled the table.

"That's some spread."

"One of the things I loved when I traveled to England was high tea. It's a tradition that's going out of style there, but I think it's great. My sister and I just about lived on scones and clotted cream when we went to London a few months ago. I try to continue the tradition as often as I can. But I'm sure you don't want to hear about me. You were asking about Thomas Warrendale."

"You said you had suspicions."

She poured tea and passed the tray. I felt remarkably relaxed. This kitchen was definitely a comfortable retreat.

"I own two salons, and he approached me about doing the books."

"How did he know you?"

"Church."

"You go to First Baptist? I don't remember you."

"It's a big church."

"Not that big. I would have remembered you."

She smiled, and I think I blushed. Not an easy task for a police officer, and even harder for an African-American.

"I just mean I'm a highly trained professional," I said with a smile and a wink. "Plus, I've gone to First Baptist Church my entire life."

"I've only been going for about eight months, and I usually go to the early service. Unless you attend the early service,

we would miss each other. I sing in the choir and that's how
we met. Anyway, when he heard I had a couple of salons, he
offered to do my books. I was doing the books myself until
I opened the second salon. Between the new salon, house
renovations and ... well, life in general, I was overworked. At
first I was double-checking everything he did, but I got busy
and didn't check for a while. About a month ago, I got a call
from the president of my bank."

"Wow, the bank president. Business must be good."

"Not that good. They wanted to change my account. My
account was overdrawn, and my overdraft protection was low."

"So, business wasn't going well?"

"My first salon was doing very well, but I'd sunk almost all
my profits into opening the second one. I don't make a fortune,
but I try to live within my means. No way should my account
have been overdrawn. That call got my attention. So, for the
last three weeks, I've been going over my books with a fine-
toothed comb. I may not be a CPA, but I have an MBA. And
when it comes to my business, I watch over each penny very
carefully."

"You have less money than you should? How much less?"

"I don't even know yet. Warrendale was supposed to be some
kind of a financial genius. He set up accounts and transferred
funds and did things I haven't even figured out yet. My guess is
I lost close to twenty thousand—maybe a little more."

"That's a lot of money. What happened after you realized it
was gone? Did you confront Warrendale?"

"You better believe I confronted him. I told him in no
uncertain terms exactly what I thought of him."

"And what did he say?"

"He denied everything, of course."

"When did this all take place?" I sipped my tea. This was
beginning to sound like a motive, and I didn't want to arouse
suspicion I was interested in anything other than finding out
about Warrendale's embezzlement.

"Friday night, just after choir rehearsal."

"That would be one day before he died?"

After a pause, a light came on in her eyes. "Hey, I didn't kill him, if that's what you're thinking."

"I'm not accusing you of killing him. I'm just listening. But if it makes you feel better, you do have the right to remain silent. Anything you say can be used in a court of law. You also have a right to talk to an attorney." I said it as casually as possible, trying not to raise alarm.

"Why do I need an attorney?" Her pitch rose. "I didn't kill him."

"Wait a minute, hold on," I said jokingly and held up both hands in surrender. "I didn't say you needed an attorney. I'm just letting you know you have the right to an attorney."

After taking a moment to consider, she relaxed, and I knew my reassurance had worked. She was going to keep talking because she felt she had nothing to hide. And I'd managed to read her rights without raising any red flags.

Paris took a drink of tea. "I didn't kill him. So, I might as well tell you."

"You confronted him on Friday, right?" I took out my notebook. "You don't mind if I take a few notes, do you?"

She shook her head.

"It must have been around seven o'clock."

"Why did you wait until after choir rehearsal was over before you confronted him?"

"I didn't wait. I worked late. I was actually on my way to a hair show in Indy that night. I was heading out of town when I drove by the church and saw choir rehearsal was just letting out. I decided to stop."

"So, you went in the church and saw Warrendale, and then what?"

"He denied everything. He said my bank must be mistaken, but I told him I wanted all my money back or else I'd …."

I waited. She stalled and took a sip of her tea before the silence became too much for her.

"All right, I might have threatened to make his life a living hell." She paused before adding hurriedly, "And I might have suggested a few changes to his anatomy. I might even have mentioned the police, the FBI, and possibly the media, but that was about it. Just words, nothing more."

I couldn't help myself. I laughed. After a moment, she joined in.

"So, after these threats, then what happened?"

"Nothing. I stomped out and left for Indy. I'd already opened a new bank account he couldn't access, and my employees were told not to turn any money or checks over to him, so I thought I was safe."

"Was anyone there in the church when this transpired?"

"I don't remember seeing anyone. But honestly, I was too mad to notice. I think everyone had left."

"And this hair show you attended, where was it?"

She got up, rummaged through a purse on the counter, and pulled out a brochure, which she handed to me.

"When did you get back to St. Joe?"

"Not until late Monday night. I was supposed to get back Sunday, but I was so tired I stayed over an extra night."

That's when the light dawned. "Were you supposed to do Mama B's hair yesterday?"

"Yeah, I'm really sorry about that. I know she doesn't like to switch stylists, but I was sure Nichole would do an excellent job."

Now I understood why Mama B had been so upset yesterday when I picked her up from the beauty shop. She'd planned to introduce me to Paris, and her matchmaking plans were foiled. Despite my best intentions, I laughed again.

"What's so funny?"

Maybe I'd let her in on the joke someday. "Oh, nothing." I held up the brochure. "Mind if I take this?"

She shook her head, and I pocketed the brochure. It looked like Paris Williams had a really good motive and the possible opportunity to kill Warrendale. Indianapolis was only three hours from St. Joe. I would have Harley verify her alibi, but Ms. Williams was looking like a good suspect. That should have made me more excited. Instead, I felt a bit depressed.

I had a lot to think about on my drive home, and not all of it was related to the murder. One side of my brain wondered what Thomas Warrendale was up to. The other side was focused on Paris Williams, and it had absolutely nothing to do with this case. I had a lot of questions, and I had a feeling I knew where I might be able to get some answers—Mama B.

THE MAYOR WANTED to be briefed on our progress. Bright and early the next day, I made my way to the top of city hall, which in St. Joe meant the twelfth floor of the County-City Building. Chief Mike was already there. Harley arrived the same time I did. I've only been in the mayor's office a handful of times, but each one left an impression. The combination of plush carpeting, large mahogany furniture, and two full walls of floor-to-ceiling windows overlooking the city was impressive, even for a cynic like me. The room was large enough for a conference table and ten chairs.

Not surprisingly, the mayor was on a tight schedule. Mayor Charles Longbow was an elegant lawyer turned politician. He was a sharp dresser and smart as a whip. He wore handmade French shirts, custom-tailored suits, and expensive Italian shoes. Mama B said he was as slick as a greased pig. Despite this not-so-flattering description, she liked him. She'd voted for him. He was Native-American, and a classic example of a man who'd pulled himself up by his bootstraps. He'd worked his way through college and law school by cutting grass, shoveling snow, waiting on tables, and doing any odd job he could. He'd started his political career on the School Board, then progressed to the City Council, the Indiana General Assembly as part of the Indiana Senate, and finally the Mayor's Office. He'd moved up the ladder "faster than a scalded dog," another of Mama B's phrases. And a ton of people were discussing the possibility of a run for U.S. Senate or even governor. Mayor Longbow was first and foremost a politician, but he seemed to be the rarest of politicians—an honest one.

Chief Mike had briefed him on the details we'd discovered to date, which wasn't much.

"I want this case solved quickly," Mayor Longbow said. "It doesn't look good to have murder and arson in my neighborhood, especially in an election year. Do you have any suspects?"

"Not yet, sir," Harley said. When Harley was nervous, his Southern accent was more pronounced than ever. Despite his family's connections, Harley was awed by the mayor. He was always afraid of talking too much—afraid he'd make a fool of himself. He rarely said more than a couple of words whenever he was around Mayor Longbow.

Mayor Longbow leaned back in his chair. "Tell me what's not in the report."

Harley squirmed. Chief Mike was normally unshakeable, but for some reason, even he looked a little rattled. All eyes turned to me. Not sleeping afforded me a lot of time to think, and last night I'd had several hours to mull things over. I'd developed a speck of an idea, but it wasn't ready to be spoken out loud. Another reason I was reluctant to verbalize it: I hadn't had a chance to talk things over with Harley or Chief Mike first. But someone had to say something.

"I think Thomas Warrendale's murder may be tied to his past," I said. "It's the only thing that makes sense. But we need to dig more."

"What about his past?" Mayor Longbow asked.

"For nine months, Tye Warren, aka Thomas Warrendale, lived in St. Joe pretending to be someone else. He stole money from the members of the congregation, and there is a possibility he was stealing from the church too. Why was he hiding? Who was he hiding from? He left his wife, his job, and all his connections for a job as a choir director at a church? I think we need to find out what he was hiding from."

I expected the mayor to badger me. Based on the shocked expressions on Chief Mike's and Harley's faces, they were expecting the same. I hadn't intended to keep my partner and boss in the dark, but my nightmares made sleep a fleeting visitor. I didn't think either of them would have appreciated a call in the wee hours of the morning. The silence that followed lasted about thirty seconds but felt like an hour. Mayor Longbow gave me a long look, sizing me up, and stood. Just as he was about to speak, his phone buzzed and his secretary's voice rang out over the intercom.

"The governor's on line two."

Mayor Longbow sat back down and picked up the phone.

"Keep me posted on what you find out."

And just like that, the meeting was over and we were dismissed.

CHAPTER FIVE

———

CITY HALL WAS two blocks away from the police station, if you didn't use the tunnel. Harley and Chief Mike pumped me for details the moment we got outside.

"What was that?" Chief Mike said. "Do you really have something or were you just faking?" He was incensed, and rightly so. I should have briefed him before going into that meeting. No excuses.

"I think Thomas Warrendale—or Tyrone Warren—may have been involved in some illegal activities in Cleveland."

It took the entire walk back to the precinct and ten additional minutes sitting in Chief Mike's office to fill him and Harley in on what had puzzled me in the early hours of the morning.

"So Warrendale was swindling the church and this salon owner?" Chief Mike said aloud as he pondered the information.

"I wonder who else he was stealing from," Harley said.

"Exactly." Chief Mike was warming up to this idea. "Maybe someone caught him with his hand in the cookie jar, and they didn't like it."

"I can't think of any other reason why he would leave

Cleveland and hide out in St. Joe under an assumed name," I said, "unless he was hiding from someone."

"There might be something in those rumors about a scorned lover too," Harley said.

Chief Mike paced his small office. "Love and money are two powerful motives for murder. You two need to investigate both angles."

"A leopard doesn't change his spots," Harley said with a little more confidence. "If he was stealing from the church and at least one other person we know of, how many other people was he stealing from?"

"I want you two to talk to Mrs. Warren and to some of those women from the church. Find out if there was anything there. It could still turn out to be a jilted lover or jealous spouse. And keep investigating the money angle. See if you can find out if there were any other people Warrendale was stealing money from." Chief Mike picked up the phone to notify the Cleveland police that Harley and I would be coming and to arrange for cooperation.

By the time I was back at my desk, Detective Mari Lawrence was waiting for me.

"You're working that arson/murder that took place in the mayor's backyard," she said. It was a statement, not a question.

At five-foot nothing and one hundred pounds dripping wet, Detective Mari Lawrence looked like a lightweight, but looks can be deceiving. With black belts in judo, karate, and a couple of other martial arts, she was someone you wouldn't want to surprise in a dark alley.

"That's right. Why? What's up?"

"Got a call on a break-in at Starling and Schuck. Accounting firm downtown."

"That's the CPA firm Thomas Warrendale worked for."

"Yep. Thought you might be interested."

"Definitely. Anything taken?"

"That's the suspicious thing. They've had several break-ins downtown, probably kids doing a snatch and grab. Brick through the window and grab a laptop off the desk. This time there was no brick. And no laptops were stolen. Just ransacked the office and left."

"Any idea if anything was taken?"

"Like what?"

I shrugged "Did they pay particular attention to Warrendale's office?"

"Sure did. And Warrendale apparently worked from home most of the time. He was more of a subcontractor than an employee and rarely came into the office. He mostly helped out during tax season. He didn't keep much there, but since his was the only office ransacked, I thought there might be a connection."

"Wonder what they were looking for?"

"Don't know, but here's a copy of my report." Detective Lawrence handed me the case folder. "Maybe it'll help."

"Thanks." I added the file to the others on my desk.

Harley and I would need to interview someone at Starling and Schuck sooner or later. Might as well be sooner.

STARLING AND SCHUCK was a mid-sized CPA firm started in St. Joe almost fifty years ago by Fred Starling and Robert Schuck. Over time, this two-man business grew to the almost a thousand employees who operated out of five Midwestern branches. Never aiming to compete with the big international firms, Starling and Schuck built a solid reputation and a large client base by providing quality services at reasonable prices. It was a local fixture. I learned this by watching the video that played on a continuous loop in the lobby while we waited for Abigayle Bennett, chief operating officer. She narrated part of the video, so we recognized her immediately.

The lobby was elegant and modern, with large windows and vaulted ceilings. The furniture was high-end and extremely uncomfortable. Fortunately, we didn't have to wait long.

"Detectives, I'm pleased to meet you. I'm Abigayle Bennett. How may I help you?"

She handed out business cards and instructed us to call her Abbi.

After escorting us to a small meeting room located right next to the reception desk, she started right in. "I've been expecting someone from the police ever since I read about Thomas Warrendale's death."

"How long did Warrendale work here?"

"Mr. Warrendale hadn't been with us long. He was a contractor, not an employee, so I'm afraid I don't have a lot of information."

"Perhaps you can tell us what you know of Thomas Warrendale's background?"

"Well, that's just it. We relied on the contract agency that recommended him to ensure he met our criteria." Mrs. Bennett slid the two folders she'd brought with her to the conference room across the table to us. Harley and I opened them and flipped through the paperwork inside.

"Mr. Warrendale was temporary. December through April fifteenth is our busy tax season, and we hire a lot of people to help us process tax returns during that time."

Harley glanced over the skimpy files. "Did he have any friends or perhaps co-workers who might know more about him?"

"Mr. Warrendale worked out of his home. Most of the work we do is electronic, anyway. With a laptop, high-speed internet, and a fax machine, there's no reason to come to the office. In fact, I don't believe he actually showed up at the office more than once or twice. We keep a desk for our contract employees in case they want to come in for whatever reason, but few of them take advantage of it. I doubt very seriously if most people here would even recognize him if they saw him."

"So why did he have his own office?" I said, thinking about the police report I'd seen earlier.

"He had a lot of experience and was working at a senior

level. I believe he requested an office, and we had the room and were happy to accommodate."

"Isn't that unusual?" I tried to think of a reason Warrendale would ask for an office and never use it, but I couldn't come up with anything.

Mrs. Bennett smiled. "Not really. This is a profession where walls and doors signify status, even if you aren't using them."

The file showed Warrendale used his real name with the contract company and on his CPA license. However, he also included a written request to go by Thomas Warrendale, as he was *officially* changing his legal name. Apparently, neither the contract company nor Starling and Schuck thought that strange. We tried coming at Mrs. Bennett from several different angles, but there was nothing useful she could tell us. There were no discrepancies in previous returns from one year to another. No complaints from clients, nothing unusual in any way whatsoever. She was polite, but she wasn't able to shed light on why anyone would want him dead. It didn't take long before we were on our way. I wouldn't say it was a totally wasted trip. I had no doubt Warrendale's work was now being checked and any discrepancies with his accounts would be identified, but nothing had come to the surface yet. So, any threat from Warrendale's illegal activities might not be connected to his accounts with Starling and Shuck.

ST. JOE, INDIANA, was a mid-sized town. St. Joe lacked the skyscrapers, the crowds, and the energy of big cities. One thing it had in abundance was banks. Warrendale was making deposits into Paris Williams' bank, St. Joseph Bank and Trust, and the church's bank, First State Bank. I don't know if there was a link, but it was a starting point. First State Bank's corporate headquarters were close to the precinct, so I started there, while Harley went back to the precinct to try and put a dent into some of the paperwork and forms that were piling up.

The main branch of First State Bank was located in the largest building in St. Joe; at twelve stories, that wasn't saying much. Most of the building was now a hotel. The executive offices were on the second floor, and that was where I waited for the bank president, Henrietta Thomas.

Mrs. Thomas was not only the president of First State Bank but the first female bank president in St. Joe's history.

"I need your help."

She looked hesitant. "Well, I'll certainly try." She directed me to take the seat facing her large mahogany desk. "Without a warrant, I may be limited on what type of information I can provide, but I'll do my best to help if I can."

It was clear that Henrietta Thomas was sharp as a tack. In her mid-forties, she was only slightly shorter than me at about six-one and probably over two hundred pounds. Although she looked solid as a rock and had the physique of an athlete, she had glossy dark hair that might have softened her appearance if she hadn't worn it pulled back into an unflattering bun.

I gave her a rough sketch of the situation before asking, "Have you noticed anything unusual?"

"I suppose that depends on what you mean by 'unusual.' I certainly haven't noticed anything that would be of importance to a police detective. You'll have to give me a bit more to go on."

"I'm wondering if you noticed anything unusual relating to withdrawals—money transfers, deposits, money laundering."

She leaned closer. I now had her full and undivided attention. Clearly, this was not what she'd been expecting to hear.

"I thought you said you were investigating a murder."

"I am. But I've run across some inconsistencies that led me to believe there might be illegal transactions."

"That's very serious, Detective Franklin. May I ask what led you to this conclusion?"

It only took a few minutes to explain what I knew about Warrendale. Mrs. Thomas asked some pertinent questions but allowed me to relay the facts, such as they were.

"Detective Franklin, I don't know if I can help you. I can certainly look into the accounts he had access to. It sounds like Mr. Warrendale—or Warren, or whatever his name is—may have been involved in something unusual. Embezzlement is more common than you'd think, but money laundering isn't something we see a lot of in St. Joe."

We talked for a few additional minutes and ended with Mrs. Thomas promising to launch an investigation.

"Typically, we would have our CPA firm take care of this, but under the circumstances, I think we'd better use our own internal audit team."

"Why? Who's your outside CPA firm?"

Mrs. Thomas smiled. "Starling and Schuck."

She was indeed a sharp cookie. She had picked up on the fact that Thomas Warrendale worked for Starling and Schuck, and if there were illegal activities happening, it was possible Warrendale had run them through the auditing firm.

"I'm not implying Starling and Schuck are in any way involved in illegal activities," I said.

"I know, Detective, and I certainly am not accusing them of anything either. Since one of their employees or contractors is possibly implicated in criminal behavior, they are required by law to abstain from involvement."

"I understand. We'll do what we can and let you know if we find anything."

I rose to leave and Mrs. Thomas offered her hand.

As I left the bank, I felt inexplicably heavier—more weighed down than before my meeting. Finding a murderer was my number one priority. However, Reverend Hamilton and FBC were like family to me. Something inside me didn't want to find a link between the murder of Thomas Warrendale and the church's missing money. If my hunch was right, these two things were linked together, and that meant someone I knew was a cold-blooded murderer.

* * *

THE TALK WITH the president at St. Joseph Bank and Trust, Paris' bank, went roughly the same way. Both bank presidents were concerned and agreed to initiate internal investigations. Since 9/11, rules around money and deposits were much stricter and more regulated. I didn't believe the former choir director was a terrorist, but I wasn't ruling anything out. Where was the money? Unless Warrendale left a paper trail, I doubted we'd be able to find anything. Between the forensic accountant, our anti-fraud and money laundering experts, and the resources of both banks, I hoped we'd find out something soon.

Harley was finishing up a special assignment with another detective, so I was on my own for the day. Leaving no stone unturned, I decided to interview the women Mama B mentioned as possible paramours for Warrendale.

I wanted to get the worst over with first. Mercedes Jackson worked at the Department of Motor Vehicles, so that's where I went. Mama B described Mercedes Jackson as *ghetto fabulous*. Her clothes were cheap, trendy, and two sizes too small. Leopard-print leggings and three-inch heels were a common look, with an excess of big, gaudy jewelry and long, elaborately decorated nails. Despite the youthful attire, Mercedes seemed older than her twenty-five years. Something in her eyes made her look hard and worn out. Maybe it was the cigarettes. She was a chain-smoker, and her teeth and skin bore the signs.

"Hey, RJ. I ain't seen you in forever. You looking fine." She looked me up and down like a piece of meat she was about to devour, and I wondered how she fit in with the other choir members.

I forced a smile. "I need to ask you a few questions, if you don't mind."

"You can ask me anything you want." Mercedes snuggled up closer, overwhelming me with the odor of cigarette smoke and cheap perfume. I hoped my clothes wouldn't reek of it after I left.

"I heard a rumor you were involved with Thomas Warrendale."

"That just goes to show you shouldn't listen to every rumor you hear, doesn't it?" Mercedes laughed and took a fingernail file out of her pocket that looked like a straight razor. But given the length of her nails—which were so long they curled down and included diamonds and what appeared to be tiny hundred-dollar bills—she'd need something long to tackle those claws.

"So, you never had a relationship with Thomas Warrendale?"

"Nope. He wasn't my type, if you know what I mean." Mercedes smacked her gum and leaned in. "I prefer the tall, dark, and handsome type. You know, someone about your height and color. Minister Warrendale was too short and too yellow."

"I also heard you and Moe Chapman were an item." I didn't need to mention that Moe Chapman's four-hundred-pound frame didn't fit that description either.

"Yeah, me and Moe been hanging out lately. He's a big man, but he knows how to treat a woman." She flashed a sly smile and patted the expensive purse flung over her shoulder. "He got me this purse just the other day."

"Have you ever heard Thomas Warrendale mentioning money to you?"

"Nope."

"Did you hear anyone threaten Thomas Warrendale?"

She shook her head.

"Where were you on Friday night?"

"Umm, well, Moe took me out to dinner. Then we went to the movie, and then … he took me home. You wanna hear what we did when we got home?" She asked the question with a wicked grin, which told me everything I needed to know.

"No, I think that will be all."

She laughed. She didn't have any ideas on what might have happened to Warrendale or who wanted to harm him, but before I left, she asked for a card with my telephone number just in case any ideas came to her later when she was home alone and had time to think about it. I gave it to her reluctantly. Thankfully, it only included my work number, where my associates monitored the answering machine, but she definitely knew enough people at the church that she could track me down if she needed to.

Next on the list from Mama B was Francis Montgomery. I caught up with her at the mall, where she worked at a local department store. Business was slow, so she was able to talk to me while she folded towels.

"I'd like to ask you some questions about Thomas Warrendale. You don't have to answer them if you don't want to. And you can have an attorney present if you'd prefer." I waited. Francis was scared, but that was normal. Most people are nervous when talking to the police.

Francis Montgomery was a sweet young girl of about nineteen. She was rather plain and dressed a tad frumpy compared to other girls her age. But her parents were older and known to be rather strict. "I thought he loved me," she whispered so softly I barely heard.

"What happened?"

She continued to fold in silence, and then I noticed the tears trickling down her face and handed her a handkerchief.

"He told me he loved me. He told me he wanted to marry me. But then I heard he was messing around with Mercedes and Tonya, and I knew he was just playing me." Excusing herself, she went to the break room, returning after a few minutes. She'd reapplied her makeup but still looked tired and worn.

"I said I wasn't going to waste any more tears on him." After a final sniffle and a shrug of her shoulders, she was back in control.

"How did it end?"

"I confronted him about the rumors. At first, he tried to deny them, but there was too much evidence. He admitted it finally. And I told him we were done."

"When was this?"

"Two weeks ago."

"Did you have any further contact?"

"Only at church. I dropped out of the choir. I couldn't stand seeing that hypocrite pretending to be so dedicated to the Lord. Singing and dancing and praising the Lord in church when I knew what a lowdown skunk he was. I knew something like this would happen."

My antenna went up. "What do you mean? You knew he'd be killed?" I liked Francis; I really hoped she hadn't done something stupid.

"I know you can't play in the Lord's house. The Bible says, 'God is not mocked, whatsoever a man sows, that also shall he reap.' I don't know where it is in the Bible, but I know it's in there. He was mocking God, and God wouldn't put up with that."

Like Moe Chapman, Francis Montgomery saw God as an avenger. I took a moment and thought how busy God would be if he murdered every man or woman who cheated or lied.

"So, you think God killed Thomas Warrendale?"

"I know God works through people, and someone killed him. God may not have actually struck him down, but He *allowed* him to die. So, yeah, God killed him."

"What did your parents think about you dating Thomas Warrendale?"

"They didn't know. They still don't know. He said it would be best if we didn't tell anyone at the church. I thought he was protecting my reputation. Now, I see it was his own reputation he cared about, not mine."

We talked for a few more minutes, but she had been out of town at her family reunion last Saturday. In fact, her entire family was about six hundred miles away. I would get someone to verify her alibi, but it looked like Francis and her immediate family were off the list. That meant Mercedes Jackson was back on top. I'd have to look into Francis' claims that Mercedes and

Warrendale were involved. This was the second time I'd heard that allegation. I was not looking forward to that. Maybe I could send Harley. The thought brought a smile to my face that I had a hard time removing.

Tonya Rutherford was harder to track down. According to her mother, she was visiting a sick aunt in Detroit. She was expected back in a couple of days. Her interview would have to wait.

Chief Mike arranged for a quick flight to Cleveland for Harley and me. But I had one stop to make first.

The sun was going down and had taken most of the heat with it. Mama B wasn't sitting on the porch, but the front door was open. I found her in her favorite chair just inside the house.

"I fixed a snack for you to take with you to Ohio."

"They have food in Ohio, you know. Besides, I'll only be there for one or two days."

"You don't want the food, just leave it in the kitchen. One of the boys will eat it."

The "boys" Mama B referred to were the *ballers* who played at the recreation center across the street. Most people took one look at those rough-talking kids and clutched their purses, locked their doors, and called the police. But Mama B fed them sweet tea and banana pudding. Thirty years she's lived on that alley, and no one has laid a hand on her or her property. I'd like to think that somehow they knew she was connected to the police and that knowledge kept her safe. But the truth was Mama B had connections of her own.

Mama B befriended a kid most people ran from. Taz was a thug with a rap sheet about a mile long. Breaking and entering, disorderly conduct, and a few other charges had kept Taz—I can't even remember his real name—in and out of juvenile detention most of his life. Maybe Mama B reminded him of his mother or grandmother. Maybe she was the only person who took an interest in him. Whatever the reason, Taz put the word on the street Mama B was protected, off limits. I found out about it when I ran into a group of kids drinking lemonade on the porch one afternoon. I waited until Mama B went into the house and then threatened to come down on them like stink on a skunk—one of Harley's favorite sayings—if they so much as looked at Mama B crooked.

I expected anger, indignation, anything but what I got, which was laughter. When they finally got control enough to talk, one of them told me about Taz's threat. Apparently, in their world, his threat was more frightening than mine. I was even more surprised when Tiny, a three-hundred-pound delinquent who sounded like he had a mouth full of marbles, told me Mama B and her house were declared Switzerland. In St. Joe, declaring someone or something Switzerland meant neutral ground. Mama B was off limits. Anyone touching her would be hit hard from all sides.

Tiny mumbled, "Man, between the T-Devils, the RZs, and all the minor leaguers, plus the cops, Mama B is safer than the president of the United States."

I wanted to believe I could keep my loved ones safe, but I knew the streets. If these hoods wanted to take her out, they could do it before anyone could dial 911. Looking in their eyes, I saw they cared about Mama B too in their own way. She was the glue that linked us together.

"You still feed all the thugs in St. Joe?" I asked. "For a church-going woman, you hang out with some of the lowest scum in the city."

"Dem boys ain't a bit more dangerous than I am. Two of them came over yesterday and fixed my washing machine."

"Did you check your silverware after they left?"

"Pshaw. They ain't never stole nothing—not from me, anyway. B'sides, I ain't got nothin' worth stealing. They got more gold, silver, and diamonds in their mouths than I ever seen in my life. That cross-eyed boy they call 'Doc' came by here one day, and I had my teeth out. He pulled out his plate.

That thing had so much gold, it, 'bout blinded me. I think he called it a stove."

I sputtered. "I believe they call it a 'grill.'"

Mama B continued to rock. "Well, I knew it was something you cooked on."

She was tickled by kids buying what she considered false teeth. I sat amazed thinking how this sixty-year-old woman hung out with more hoodlums than some of my fellow police officers.

"So you just eat your Cleveland food," she said. "What you got to do in Cleveland anyway?"

"I'm going to talk to Thomas Warrendale's wife."

"I still don't believe that little fancy pants boy was married. What kind of woman would marry someone like that?"

"There's someone for everyone, I'm told."

Mama B smiled and rocked on. After a while she added, "Two weeks ago there was this strange woman that came to church. We've had so many new people, I wouldn't have really noticed, 'cept I saw Fancy Boy look out, and I'd swear he turned white as a sheet."

"Did you notice anything special about her?"

"She didn't belong here. Her clothes were too nice, too expensive. She looked too sophisticated. She had on more makeup than a prostitute."

"How would you know how much makeup prostitutes wear?"

Mama B could not have looked more serious as she said, "Baby, I do have cable."

It took me a few seconds to get myself together after that one. But eventually, I was able to follow up. "Did you see them talkin'? Warrendale and … the woman?"

"No. But now you mention it, I did think it was strange because he left during the sermon. The choir was supposed to sing one more song during the invitational, but he wasn't there, so they just sang a congregational hymn instead."

"Are you sure?"

"I may be old, but I'm still in my right mind, thank you very much." The gleam in her eye told me she wasn't really offended. The smirk on her face told me she was pleased to have passed on information I didn't already know.

"I know you're sane. But I still have to verify all the facts."

"So that little namby-pamby mama's boy was married," Mama B mused. "Did his wife kill him?"

"Don't know yet. Maybe. I'll know more after I talk to her. Speaking of talking … I talked to your hairdresser, Paris Williams. How long have you known her?"

"About three months. Don't tell me you believed those lies Moe Chapman was spreading. You're too smart to suspect Paris of killing that little weasel."

"Harley checked out her alibi. She was in Indianapolis all day Saturday and Sunday. It's possible she made the three-hour drive back but not likely. The times don't line up. She's not off the list yet, but she's not near the top. I was just wondering how well you know her. I mean, for example is she … uh, well, is she married?"

I was making a real mess of this. During normal circumstances, Mama B could read me like a book. With me stuttering and sweating like a pig, she was reading my mind loud and clear.

"She ain't married. Shame before God, but she's single, 'bout your age too." Mama B had the slightest smile on her face. "Paris is a nice woman, best hairdresser I've ever had. Smart too. She's got two salons."

"Did she tell you her suspicions about the embezzlement?"

"Not in so many words, but she heard Mrs. Green talking about you being a policeman and asked if I'd see if you could drop by sometime. She didn't want any rumors until she was sure. She made me swear on my life I wouldn't mention anything to anyone but you. You think that has something to do with his death?"

"I don't know yet."

"Is Paris in any danger?"

Mama B was very good at getting to the heart of the situation. She'd made the leap I'd been avoiding ever since I heard about the break-in at Starling and Schuck. Whatever Thomas Warrendale was involved in most likely got him killed. That might mean not only Paris but also Reverend Hamilton might be in danger. I wanted to lie, but I knew she'd see right through me.

"Probably not, but I'll check up on her anyway." Did I sound casual enough? From Mama B's smirk, I'd say that was a no. But she just smiled and kept on rocking.

CHAPTER SIX

S T. JOE'S AIRPORT was the size of a large shopping mall but serviced the Greater St. Joseph Metropolitan Area. The biggest usage was from the University. St. Joe was the home of the prestigious Saint Mary Catholic University, or SMACU, as the locals called it. So, unless it was the beginning or the end of term, parking and check-in were not even close to the harried, stressful experiences one had in large urban areas.

Harley had just stepped up to the counter when I arrived. To the dismay of those standing in line, I joined him. We showed our shields to the ticket agent, who cut his spiel short and moved us right on through to screening. Our shields got us around rather than through the metal detectors. Two armed men setting off the metal detector would frighten the passengers. However, after September eleventh, airlines (and passengers too) have appreciated armed police on airplanes.

The trip from St. Joe to Cleveland took less than an hour. Detective Carl Hastings met us at Hopkins airport. Bald, and maybe five feet tall, Detective Hastings was just about as wide. His girth took up a substantial portion of the front seat, while paper, receipts, pop cans, and miscellaneous debris covered most of the backseat of a bright orange 1970s Volkswagen Beetle. With Hastings' girth and Harley's and my height, it was a tight ride. When we pulled up in front of the Warren house, I found it difficult not to think of circus clowns piling out of a trick car.

"I was one of the detectives who told Mrs. Warren about her husband's death," Detective Hastings told us as we walked up the drive to the front door. "She's one cold fish. No tears. No hysterics. Just wanted to know when his belongings would be shipped back. If she didn't have an iron-clad alibi, I'd think she had something to do with the murder."

Harley beat me to the punch. "You checked?"

"She was lying on an operating table having her appendix removed."

"That is a good alibi," Harley said.

"They let her go the next day—"

"That's pretty quick, isn't it?" I asked.

"Doc said they normally keep people twenty-four to forty-eight hours, but she insisted on going home. Irregardless, he assured me there was no way she would have been in any shape to make the trip to St. Joe, kill her husband, and get back in less than twenty-four hours."

I stopped listening after he said *irregardless*. It's one of my pet peeves. The word is *regardless*. Like fingernails on a chalkboard, it made me grind my teeth. When I spoke, I was a little shorter with Hastings than he deserved. "True, but the lack of an alibi is only part of what we need. Motive and means are a lot more important than opportunity." I shook my head to shake off the mood.

Mrs. Warren lived in one of the new subdivisions that had cropped up all over suburbia. I've seen neighborhoods like this throughout St. Joe. The houses were all large, with a builder's standard landscaping. A brick front and three sides of vinyl were now the norm. I'm sure it saved a lot of money not to brick all sides on a house, but it looked as if they'd run out of money.

We rang the bell and were admitted without really seeing who was behind the door.

Inside, the house looked like it had been taken from the pages of a magazine. White carpet, white furniture, and glass and mirrors made the room feel cold and uninviting.

"Mrs. Warren, I'm—"

"Would you mind taking off your shoes?"

We all promptly took off our shoes. Detective Hastings struggled to hide a small hole in a pair of dingy socks, and for the first time in my life, I was thankful for a mother who stressed the importance of clean socks and underwear. I always thought her rationale that I'd need them in case I got hurt and ended up in the hospital was ridiculous. The one time I had been in the hospital after my accident, my socks and underwear were the last things on my mind. But standing in Mrs. Warren's fancy foyer in clean socks certainly added a lot more strength to my mother's argument.

Settled into the austere living room, Mrs. Warren seemed more of an actress than a grieving widow. She was in her early forties and had a light complexion that seemed overly made up, as if she were about to enter a beauty contest. Suddenly, I understood Mama B's remark about more makeup than a prostitute. Like a queen on a throne, Mrs. Warren condescended to receive us.

"Mrs. Warren, I'm sorry for your loss. Do you know anyone who wanted Thomas dead?"

"Who's Thomas?" Mrs. Warren tilted her head and brought her hand up to her throat.

"I meant Tyrone. Mrs. Warren, why was your husband using another name?"

"I have no idea." Mrs. Warren looked at the wall, the floor, and down at her hands in her lap as though the answer must be written somewhere.

She was lying. It wasn't just the little telling signs that gave her away, like her failure to make eye contact or the way she touched her throat. There was something in her eyes that gave her away before she opened her mouth.

I tried again. "Why was he in St. Joe?"

"I have no idea." Leaning forward, Mrs. Warren adjusted a vase on the coffee table so that it was now directly in between us rather than slightly to the side.

Another lie. Liars often try to place objects in between themselves and the people they are lying to.

Third time's a charm, so I asked, "Mrs. Warren, your husband had been living in St. Joe, Indiana, for the past nine months. Yet you never filed a missing person's report. Why?"

"Why should I? You only file a report if you want the missing person found. I didn't."

That wasn't what I expected. "So, you and Thomas—I mean, Tyrone—weren't happily married?"

"That's not a crime, is it?" she said softly, with a little less defiance in her voice.

"No, but someone murdered your husband, which is a crime. So ... back to my original question. Do you know anyone who was so *unhappy* with your husband they wanted him dead?"

That did it. The ice queen finally started to thaw. She knew that if she didn't give us someone else who wanted her husband dead, we would be looking at her. I expected her to be nervous. Her husband was murdered, and she was a suspect. I expected her to squirm. What I wasn't expecting was the look of outright terror that flashed across her face.

"Tye was murdered? I thought he," she motioned to Detective Hastings, "said he was killed in a fire?"

"We have reason to believe the fire was set deliberately in an attempt to hide the murder," Harley said.

"But that's ... that's not possible. I mean, it was an accident. It had to be an accident."

"Why does it have to be accident?"

Mrs. Warren winced when she got up. Holding a pillow to her abdomen, she paced. She walked with a hesitation that showed she was still recovering from her surgery. Hastings was right. There was no way she murdered her husband, unless she paid someone else to do it. And based on the look of surprise at realizing her husband had been murdered, I was willing to risk my reputation she hadn't planned his death. So, why was she lying?

"Mrs. Warren, I'm sorry to have to tell you your husband was murdered. I thought you already knew."

Hastings shifted uneasily in his seat. "We told her about his death right after we received the call, but we hadn't gotten the information about it being murder until this morning."

I waved him off. Under normal circumstances we like to share the information with the family of the deceased as soon as possible. However, I was glad I was here to see Mrs. Warren's reaction in person. She hadn't known he was murdered. I was certain of that. But she was terrified of something.

"I don't feel very well."

I was sure this was a desperate attempt to buy time, but to be honest, she wasn't looking very good either. I haven't seen very many African-Americans turn pale, but Mrs. Warren did. She looked like she was going to pass out, and if Harley hadn't jumped to assist her, she just might have.

"Would you like us to call an ambulance?" I motioned for Hastings to go to the phone, but he was already dialing.

"I just need to lie down. Can you help me?"

Mrs. Warren pointed toward the back, and Harley helped her to the family room, which was off the kitchen. It was decorated in a safari theme with faux animal skins, African masks, and a plethora of giraffe and elephant statues. There was a large plasma television and a leather recliner, which was apparently where Mrs. Warren wanted to be led.

"Since the surgery, I've been sleeping in the recliner. It's a lot easier on my stomach and back muscles. If you can just help me into the chair, I'll be fine."

I felt her wrist. "Mrs. Warren, I really think you should let us call an ambulance. You've had a big shock."

"No. I'll be fine. I just need to … to rest."

We tried a little longer to convince her to let us call a doctor but eventually gave up and decided to leave and come back a little later. You couldn't force her to accept medical treatment. She looked pale and her pulse was racing. Either she was a first-class actress or she was really ill. But there was something else. Mrs. Warren's eyes darted around like a frightened rabbit's. The signs were there. Mrs. Warren was terrified of something or someone.

AT A TABLE in a nearby restaurant, we regrouped. Harley and I had coffee while Detective Hastings munched on a mid-morning snack of pancakes, scrambled eggs, bacon, fried potatoes, and oatmeal.

"Are you two sure you don't want to try this?" Hastings said with a mouthful of food. "It's really good."

I could feel my arteries harden just looking at it.

"No thanks," Harley and I said simultaneously. With Detective Hastings engrossed in his food, we continued our discussion.

"Where do we go from here?" Harley asked.

"We've got to figure out why she's so scared. The answer might help us find out what led Warrendale to St. Joe."

"Running away. Hiding." Harley tapped his fingers on the table.

I turned to Detective Hastings. "What else do you have on Tye Warren?"

He gulped down the potatoes he'd just shoveled into his mouth. "You saw the report. He had some petty stuff in his jacket from years back but nothing recent. For the last ten years, he's been clean as a whistle. Although …."

Hastings squirmed and looked uncomfortable. I doubted his discomfort was related to the large quantity of food he had managed to consume. He was definitely an experienced eater. There had to be more to this.

We waited.

"I don't know if there's any connection to your homicide, but the CPA firm Warren worked for was under investigation a while back." Hastings reached down under the table, which was a bit of a tight maneuver with his stomach wedged under the table, but he pulled a folder out of a backpack he had lugged around with him. "Two years ago, the accounting firm Warren worked for came up in an investigation into gambling and drugs. Evidence disappeared. We had an internal investigation."

"What kind of investigation?" It was hard to believe an investigation from two years ago could be linked to this murder, but I wasn't ruling anything out.

"There was suspicion of money laundering, but each one of the companies Warren worked on came out squeaky clean. The forensic accountants thought there was something unusual about the way he transferred funds, but they couldn't find anything concrete."

Harley and I mulled over this new information and tried to figure out if this could have any bearing on our case. It seemed like a long shot.

Harley asked, "So what happened?"

"Nothing. The firm, including Warren, were off the hook. Like the three Hebrew boys in the Bible, they came out of the fire and their clothes didn't even smell like smoke."

Detective Hastings belched and then excused himself from the table. He squeezed his rotund frame out of the booth, sliding the folder closer to my hand as he vacated the seat. He walked to the men's room without glancing back. Harley and I reviewed the case file. Nothing in the folder seemed related to our murder investigation, but I looked for anything that might in any way help us find our killer.

Detective Hastings returned. "Well, gentleman. Where would you like to go next?"

"I think we better get a hotel room, since it looks like we're going to be here a little longer than we expected."

"I know just the place."

The hotel was less than a mile from the station. After we checked into our rooms, I made a call to Chief Mike. He listened and promised to call some friends he had on the force, unofficially, and get what information he could. After the call, it was time to strategize.

Harley had advanced from fidgeting to pacing. "What now?"

"We keep going. Nothing's changed. Not really. We investigate this like we do any other case." I hoped I sounded a lot more confident than I felt, but my uneasiness was more a result of unanswered questions than a fear of doing anything that would lead to career suicide. I could always retire and come back as a consultant. But Harley couldn't. He was young and had a lot to learn. I needed to make sure he had the chance.

I walked to the window. "A man packs up and leaves his wife, his job, and his friends. He changes his name and settles into a new community where he is seemingly unknown. He starts a new life, but then he gets murdered. Why?"

"And why is his wife terrified?" Harley asked.

Now I was pacing. "She's afraid of something, and it isn't the police."

"You think she knows who killed him?"

"She knows something." I was confident of that much.

"Can we trust Hastings?"

"He withheld information, but if he hadn't come clean and told us about it, we might never have known."

"So, what do we do now?" Harley asked.

"Let's start by getting a car."

Getting a rental car gave us something to do and was more of an ego boost than a reflection on Detective Hastings' trustworthiness or the state of his vehicle. A car represented action and freedom.

By the time we picked up our new Toyota Camry, I was feeling more in control. We needed to go back and talk to Mrs. Warren, without Detective Hastings present, and find out what she knew.

It took quite a while for Mrs. Warren to get to the door this second time. The look on her face showed she expected us. She didn't say a word but stepped aside to permit our entry. Harley and I removed our shoes without being asked and followed Mrs. Warren back to the family room where we'd left her on our last visit.

Settled into her recliner, she waved her arms to indicate we should sit. All this and still no words had passed between us. The silence had gone on long enough.

"As a matter of routine, I need to tell you anything you say can and will be used in a court of law. You do have a right to an attorney or to have an attorney present. Now, you know why we're back. We need to know what happened to your husband."

Mrs. Warren seemed to age twenty years in twenty seconds. Her face crumbled, and for the first time since we'd met, I saw honest emotion.

"He left me. He packed a bag and he left. Now he's dead."

I looked her directly in the eyes. "Why?"

"I don't know. Things change. They always change. We weren't swinging from the chandelier in ecstasy, but we were ... comfortable."

Harley took notes and stopped to hand Mrs. Warren a handkerchief. I'd trained him to always keep a couple in case he ran into a crier. He gave her a moment before asking, "Was there another woman?"

Warrendale certainly had plenty of them in St. Joe. He might have left a string of broken hearts in Cleveland too.

"I don't know. He said he was tired, said he needed to get

away. He wanted to start over. I didn't know what that meant. I still don't. How do you start over? Why would you want to? I didn't. He couldn't explain it."

"So, you knew he was leaving?"

"No. He said he *wanted* to. He asked me to go. Just pick up and leave. Drop everything. Leave our home, our friends. Everything. He didn't want to tell anyone. He didn't even know where he wanted to go. Just get in the car and drive. Wherever we ran out of gas would be our new home. Start over."

She was on autopilot now. The words tumbled out as though it was a relief to say them out loud.

"I couldn't do it. No … that's not right. I *wouldn't* do it." She shrugged. One day I came home, and he was gone. No note. No card. Just gone."

"Why didn't you call the police?"

"So they could tell everyone my husband left me? I would have been the laughingstock of the neighborhood. No. I had some pride left. I knew he wasn't dead. He took the car."

"Didn't anyone ask about him?" Harley said, looking as puzzled as he sounded. "I mean, his job? The church? Surely, someone questioned where he'd gone?"

"They did at first." She leaned back in her chair. "I just told them he had a nervous breakdown and was recovering in a hospital. After the big investigation at the firm and all that media attention and stress, no one even questioned it."

"Do you think his disappearance had anything to do with that?" I said.

She took so long considering the question, I thought she wasn't going to answer at all.

"I don't know. It was hard. The police and the IRS were going through our house. They went through his files at the office. It was horrible. We were so relieved when they dropped the whole thing. I thought we were finally going to get our lives back. Then he wanted to up and run away, as if …."

"As if he really had done something wrong?" Harley asked.

She nodded.

"Had he?" I asked.

"I don't know."

For the first time during our return visit, she was lying. She knew. From the set of her chin to the glint in her eyes, Mrs. Warren was not going to admit to anything that would jeopardize her reputation.

I tried another tactic. "Mrs. Warren, who wanted your husband dead? Who did you tell where he was hiding?"

Surprise. Panic. Fear. All three emotions flashed across her face.

Before she could deny it, I added, "You found out where he was, and you went to see him at the church. You were recognized." *Okay*, maybe *recognized* was stretching the truth a little, but based on the description Mama B gave me, it was clear Mrs. Warren was the woman she'd seen at church.

"I guess he forgot and used one of his credit cards," Mrs. Warren said. "I saw it on the statement. I found out where he was, and I went to visit him. But I didn't kill him, and I don't know who did." She leaned back in her recliner, closed her eyes, and turned her head away. "I'm very tired. I don't have anything else to say, and I'd appreciate it if you would leave and allow me to rest. I'm still recovering from surgery. Please show yourselves out."

With that, we were dismissed.

WE STOPPED AT a restaurant before heading back to the hotel. "I think she did it," Harley said.

"How? You heard what Hastings said. There's no way she could have gotten to St. Joe and killed him. Besides, you saw her. I don't think she could have physically done it."

"She may not have pulled the trigger or started the fire. But I think she arranged it. For months, he was fine. But right after she shows up in St. Joe, he ends up dead. Too much of a coincidence."

"You better watch it, Harley," I said with a smile. "You're beginning to sound like a detective."

He was right. The facts were against Mrs. Warren, but it didn't feel right.

We went to our rooms. For some reason, I didn't believe Mrs. Warren had her husband killed. Facts were facts, but my gut was saying something else. In my current state, I was feeling very sentimental about love and marriage. Visions of a certain hair stylist kept entering my head. I wanted to call her but couldn't think of a good excuse, so instead I tortured myself with thoughts of Paris rejecting me for a doctor or a lawyer or some other wealthy, highly educated man with a safe job and regular hours. Fortunately, my cell rang, interrupting this masochistic moment. I didn't recognize the number.

"Hello?"

It was Paris. I couldn't erase the smile from my face, but I tried to sound casual and nonchalant anyway. As I listened, the smile left of its own volition.

"I'm sorry to bother you with this," she said. "I know you're out of town, and it's certainly not important. But Mrs. Bethany insisted. It's nothing to worry about, I'm sure—"

"Paris, what happened? Are you okay? Did something happen to Mama B?"

"No. She's fine. We're both fine. It's just that someone broke into my shop. I'm sure it's just teenagers or something, and I doubt it it has anything to do with ... well, any of this ... but well ...."

"Are you okay? Was anyone hurt?"

"No. The shop was closed and nothing was taken. It was only a few minutes before the security system alerted the police. They rifled through papers and files, but it appears nothing was taken."

"Where are you now? Are the police there?"

"I'm at the shop, and yes, the police are here."

"Paris, I'm going to have one of the officers take you home."

I could feel the objections rising in her voice and immediately elevated my own. "I want you to pack a bag and go to Mama B's."

"That's crazy. I think you're overreacting. It's probably just some kids trying to find some money."

It was time for a reality check. "Do you keep anything valuable in the shop?"

"No, just the equipment and a little petty cash in the safe."

"So, why break in? There's nothing of value, and the few valuable items were not touched."

"You think it's related to the murder, don't you?" She seemed surprised and a little frightened.

"I don't know, but I'd rather be sure. Now, let me talk to the officer in charge."

She handed the phone to the officer on duty, who quickly and concisely relayed the facts. I informed him the break-in could be related to an open homicide investigation and asked him to escort Paris home, secure the premises, and stay with her while she packed. Then I gave him Mama B's address.

Mama B liked to listen to the police radio at night. She might even have heard the call about the break-in. What was going on? First, someone had broken in to Starling and Schuck, and now there was a break-in at Paris' hair salon. The common denominator was Warrendale. I needed to figure out what was going on before someone I cared about got hurt.

CHAPTER SEVEN

———∿∿∿———

THE NEXT DAY, I updated Harley on the call I'd received from Paris. It was probably nothing to worry about, but better safe than sorry.

We drove to the precinct where Hastings was stationed. There I called Chief Mike and filled him in on the break-in and what we'd discovered about Mrs. Warren. Chief Mike listened and then said he would call an old friend from the Cleveland District Attorney's office. If there was anything that might help with our murder investigation, he'd let us know. With that, we got back to work.

We made a trip to Benson, McCormick, and Chandler, LLC, the accounting firm where Tyrone Warren had worked.

The lobby was a large, glass, plant-filled space with brick-paved hallways and an interior atrium that included a fountain. It was opulent and stuffy, and I had a difficult time imagining Thomas Warrendale in this maze of blue suits and starched white shirts. Perhaps Tye Warren had been at home here, but the energetic, singing, dancing, flamboyant Thomas Warrendale from First Baptist Church wouldn't have fit in at all.

At the front desk was a small, well-coiffed woman in her early sixties. She seemed petite and fragile, but you could tell her spine was made of steel. Something in her eyes showed she would gladly toss us out if we upset the delicate balance of her world.

"Welcome to Benson, McCormick, and Chandler. How may I help you?"

Harley and I flashed our shields, and she held out her hands. Most people don't bother to look closely when you flash your shield, but not her. She took them and wrote down our names and badge numbers before handing them back.

"Thank you, Detectives Franklin and Wickfield. How may I help you?"

I'm sure she was trained to use customer names, but we weren't customers. I guess some habits die hard. "We'd like to speak to whoever is in charge."

"Well, that will depend. This is a large company. In charge of what?"

Harley must have been annoyed by her tone. Normally, he turned on the Southern charm, and women, especially elderly women, melted. But he was all business now. "We need the person in charge of handling murdered employees. We're investigating the murder of Tyrone Warren."

For a brief moment, she looked as though she would like to rip our faces off. I didn't think it possible, but she sat up straighter than she had before. She picked up a phone and dialed. "There are two police officers here. They want to talk to someone about the death of Mr. Warren. Is Mr. Chandler available?"

She waited politely for a few seconds before responding, "Thank you."

"Gentlemen, if you would take a seat, someone will be down shortly to show you the way." She pointed to a seating area with overstuffed furniture and plush carpets.

With that, we were left to wait. We weren't kept waiting long.

I guess two police officers carrying guns were probably not good for business. It wasn't long before a twenty-something woman with long hair, longer legs, and a really short skirt asked us to follow her.

From the outside, the building looked tall, but both of us were surprised how large it actually was. We followed her through a maze of hallways and cubicles to the back of the building, where we took an elevator to the sixteenth floor. She led us to a door that belonged to Bryce Chandler, CEO—at least that's what the brass door plate said. Our guide knocked twice and then opened the door, and Harley and I entered before she backed out and closed the door behind her.

I've seen some nice offices in my time, but Bryce Chandler's office was definitely one of the most luxurious. Two walls were made entirely of windows. One wall looked out over the Cuyahoga River, while the other looked out at the Cleveland skyline. Harley whistled softly under his breath as we approached the massive desk behind which Bryce Chandler sat.

Mr. Chandler stood to shake hands with us. He wasn't a tall man, probably five feet six, but he had a presence that made him seem taller. His dark suit was custom-made, and from across the room I could tell none of his clothes were purchased off the rack.

"And I thought Mayor Longbow's clothes were expensive," Harley whispered so only I could hear.

Mr. Chandler's clothes, his office, and his bearing were intended to impress and probably to intimidate. We were on his turf and he knew it. However, I wasn't about to be intimidated.

"Mr. Chandler, I'm Detective Franklin and this is Detective Harley Wickfield." My voice was five degrees colder than normal.

Harley sat down and pulled out his notebook.

"I was stunned to hear of Mr. Warren's death. We knew he had been under a great deal of pressure. Poor Marla must be frantic."

It took me a moment to realize Marla must be Mrs. Warren. "I'm sure she is. But we're hoping you can shed some light on the case."

"I'm not sure I understand." Chandler's innocent look was as fake as his perfect teeth and phony smile.

"Perhaps you can tell us why Tyrone Warren left here suddenly and disappeared without telling anyone where he was going?" I knew I had made a tactical error when relief flashed across his face.

"Well, Tye was always a little high-strung. He was a good worker, don't get me wrong, but he was ... the nervous type. We assumed the pressure of the job had gotten to him. He had a brilliant analytical mind, but they do say genius is a close kin to insanity."

"So, you believed Mr. Warren was insane?" Harley asked innocently, barely looking up from his notebook.

"No. No. Not really *insane*. Not insane in a dangerous way. No. I merely meant that geniuses are often ... well, eccentric. Yes. That's a better word. He was eccentric." Mr. Chandler smiled, pleased with himself for coming up with just the right word.

"How do you mean? Can you give us an example of some of his ... eccentricities?" I was willing to indulge in this little game while I waited for just the right moment to wipe the smug look from his face.

"Well, I don't know that I can lay a finger on any one thing he did or said. It was more a combination of a lot of little things. Certainly, picking up and moving to St. Joseph, Indiana, without one word to his wife or his friends is a perfect example of eccentric behavior, wouldn't you say? If he'd wanted a transfer, we certainly could have arranged it. We have a small satellite office near St. Joseph."

"How did you know Mr. Warren had moved to St. Joe?" Harley looked innocent as a lamb as he quietly waited for Mr. Warren to respond.

Chandler's smile vanished briefly as he realized what he'd let slip. Smiling again, he stood up and walked to a bar by the window, which allowed him to look away from us and collect himself.

"Would you gentlemen care for a beverage?" Opening the refrigerator behind the bar, Chandler took out a couple of bottles of water, offering them to us. "I also have Coke, or would you care for something a little stronger?"

We both shook our heads, and he smiled knowingly. "Oh yes, you probably can't drink while on duty." This little diversion bought him about two extra minutes to think, and Chandler was taking advantage of each second. I could almost see his wheels turning. "Now, where were we?"

Harley glanced in his notebook as if he needed a reminder. "You were about to tell us how you knew Mr. Warren had moved to St. Joe, Indiana."

"I'm sure I must have read about it somewhere." Chandler took a drink. "Wasn't it in the paper?"

"No, it hasn't appeared in the Cleveland newspapers yet. We haven't released that information to the press. The paper only mentioned he was dead."

"Oh, then it must have been Marla. She called, of course, to tell us of his death. She was, as you would imagine, very distraught. Poor woman."

"You know Mrs. Warren well?" I asked.

"No, not well. She was married to one of my employees. That's all."

It was time to turn up the heat. "Since you seem to be on a first-name basis with her, I have to wonder *how* well you knew her." Based on how quickly the color rose up Chandler's neck and face, I'd say he was starting to simmer nicely.

"What are you implying? I knew her, yes. But, that's it. We belonged to the same country club. Her husband worked here. We went to functions, *company* functions, fundraisers together. That's all."

Chandler's cheeks were on fire. He took another drink of water.

"Mr. Chandler, do you know anyone who would want to see Mr. Warren dead?"

"No, I don't, but I wasn't very close to him. I don't know what he did in his personal life. Perhaps someone from his past … I couldn't say."

"I thought you said you belonged to the same country club?" Harley asked.

"What are you implying?"

"I'm not implying anything, sir. You just said you didn't know what he did in his personal life. But you belonged to the same country club."

Chandler just stared.

"What about one of his clients?" I said. "What accounts was he working on before he left?" I could tell by the frightened look on Chandler's face I'd made a hit. *Bingo*.

As quickly as the blood had rushed to his face, it drained away. "I doubt very seriously if any of our clients would sink to that level. I mean, really, we are a highly respected CPA firm that has been in business for more than sixty-five years. We service some of the largest, most well-respected companies in the world. Our clients are not murderers."

Chandler took another drink, and I noticed his hand was shaking.

Whether by prearrangement or as a result of a well-placed panic button located on the underside of Chandler's desk, there was a knock at the door.

"Come in," Chandler yelled. The door opened, and our stunning escort entered.

"Mr. Chandler, I'm sorry to bother you, but your three thirty appointment is waiting."

Chandler came around the desk and held out his hand. Obviously, we were being dismissed. Harley and I stood. Taking Chandler's hand, I held it in my grip, looked him in the eye, and said, "Rest assured, we're going to find out what happened to Mr. Warren. We'll be back to finish our discussion."

I released Chandler's hand and left him standing there with his fake smile. I hoped one day I'd get a chance to wipe it off his face.

LATER, OVER DINNER, Harley and I discussed the case and tried to make the pieces fall into place. Bryce Chandler was hiding something. I just wasn't sure what he was hiding was murder. I didn't have anything to base that on other than a gut feeling.

"Where do we go next?" Harley asked.

Before I could answer, my cellphone rang. It was Chief Mike.

The call didn't take more than five minutes; Chief Mike was a man of few words. When it was over, I filled Harley in.

"Several of the companies Warren worked with had a large supply of cash. More than could be explained by receipts. They suspected money laundering but couldn't prove anything." I felt my blood pressure rise at the thought that Reverend Hamilton and Paris might be involved in this scheme, but I knew the danger of jumping to conclusions without getting all the facts straight.

"They thought there was a link between drug traffickers and a casino owner, but were never able to prove anything."

"So, what happened?" Harley asked.

"Nothing. They worked on it for months, but in the end, they just didn't have enough for arrests."

Harley shook his head. "This whole thing sounds big. It's a lot bigger than a small-town choir director getting himself killed. What did Chief Mike want us to do?"

"He said to remember why we're here. We're not here to bring down an international drug cartel. We aren't here to investigate money laundering. We're here to find the murderer of Tye Warren, aka Thomas Warrendale."

"But how do we do that without looking into the other stuff?"

I shrugged before adding, "He's right. We can't get sidetracked. We do our jobs. We interview suspects and follow leads. I think the two cases are tied, but if we follow the clues to the murder, maybe the rest will fall into place. Tomorrow, let's get a copy of his client list, start running some names."

We scoped out a plan of attack for the next day and went back to the hotel.

FIRST THING THE next morning, we stopped by Chandler's CPA firm and got the list of clients that Tyrone Warren had been working on before he left. I thought we would have a hard time getting the information. Almost every company you deal with tries to claim the same confidentiality privileges as doctors and lawyers. But Chandler must have preferred to comply quickly and avoid another face-to-face meeting. By the time we arrived at the reception desk, an envelope with our names on it was waiting for us.

"I can't believe Chandler just gave us the information without a subpoena," Harley said as we returned to the car. "Either Chandler isn't concerned about the names on the client list, or the list he gave us isn't complete."

"Almost all Tyrone Warren's clients were publicly traded companies, those required by law to make some information available to the public."

"We'd have gotten the information one way or another. He just saved us a little time," Harley said after he scanned the names.

I nodded. "Looks like Benson and friends are good, law-abiding citizens who are eager to help the authorities." I started the engine, which hadn't even had a chance to cool off.

Harley and I went back to the station and got to work. We logged on to the computers they'd set up for us and pulled up records. We cross-referenced names; we compared company staff with known criminals. It was a slow, tedious, time-consuming, and exhausting job. By late afternoon we had no hits. Not surprising really, since most companies require extensive background checks before hiring a janitor, let alone someone who handles money.

"Take a look." I shoved a printout at Harley.

After hours of looking over records, Harley seemed happy to get away from the computer.

"One of Tyrone Warren's clients, Cuyahoga Citizens Bank, had a subsidiary company that owned a hotel and resort casino."

"So what?" Harley asked.

"Chief Mike mentioned the casino connection over the phone last night."

"We must be getting closer. At least it's something. I haven't found anything." Harley sounded discouraged.

"Another holding of the bank is a coffee plantation in Columbia." I pointed to it on my screen. "Columbia could mean drugs." It wasn't much but it was better than nothing.

We were both excited to find some possibility, no matter how remote.

AT DINNER THAT night, we discussed the case.

"I think we should visit the Casino Warren was working on," Harley said.

"And do what? Ask if we can review their books? Or maybe we should ask if any of their staff killed Tye Warren a few days ago?"

"Well, we've got to do *something*."

"Let's review what we have."

"We have a dead choir director."

"We have a successful accountant who ran away from his job, his wife, and his friends and hid in St. Joe, Indiana."

"That's not much."

"We also know he changed his name and took on a new identity. Why?"

Harley thought for a moment. "He didn't want to be found."

"But why? We know someone has broken into two places where he had a connection. Why?"

Harley shrugged, but I could tell by the look in his eyes his wheels were starting to turn. "We know he was having an affair with at least one girl from the church but probably more."

"Those are the facts. Now we make some assumptions. I think Warren was running from someone."

"Makes sense," Harley said.

"And I think he was hiding something. That's why the break-ins. I think they're looking for whatever Warren had."

"Any idea what?"

I hadn't fully worked out a theory yet. "I don't know for sure."

"Hey, if you have even the germ of a theory, throw it out there. It's got to be better than anything I've got, which is nothing. At least it will give us a starting point. We've been here three days, and I don't know if we've gotten anywhere."

"I think Warren may have been laundering money. That's what the police thought—that's why the investigation. And, I think he stole some of it."

"How do you figure?" Harley looked puzzled.

"A leopard doesn't suddenly change his spots. We think he's been stealing from his clients in St. Joe, so maybe he was stealing before he got there. I think someone found out and he ran. But old habits are hard to break. So he gets to St. Joe and starts in again. He steals from the church and he steals from Paris."

"So you think he was killed because he stole laundered money? And someone came looking for it?"

"Yeah, maybe." I hesitated because something didn't seem right, but I couldn't put my finger on exactly what was bothering me. A piece was definitely missing. "I think it's the way he died that bothers me."

"The way he died?" Harley looked puzzled.

"The type of people involved in drug cartels would have done a better job of killing him. First off, they wouldn't have killed him until they found out where the money was. They might have tortured him, but they wouldn't have killed him until they had what they were looking for."

Harley nodded. "Makes sense."

"This murder is too messy. They would have hired a professional hit. It would have been a lot cleaner than this obviously botched arson. Do you remember what the coroner's report said?"

Harley thought for a moment and then held up his fingers and ticked off the information, "Blunt trauma to the back of the skull. Death caused by bullet to the side of the head. Body soaked in gasoline and set on fire." Harley nodded. "Seems like overkill."

"It screams amateur. Whatever is going on, murdering Thomas Warrendale didn't solve the problem. Why break into Starling and Schuck and Paris' salon?"

"Someone was looking for something. But what?"

I shrugged. "I don't know, but if I had to guess, I'd say he must have had written records." I tried to reason through the logic of the case.

"Records? Accounting records?" Harley was starting to see the picture that had been floating around in my mind.

"Yeah. I think he had records or documents someone wants pretty badly."

"Bad enough to kill."

"And if they've killed once …."

"They'll kill again."

CHAPTER EIGHT

———

B ACK IN THE hotel, I was pacing and trying to figure out exactly how to word my call to Paris when my cellphone rang.

"Hello." To my surprise, it was Paris. Again, I grinned, then the policeman in me kicked in. "Is anything wrong? Are you okay?"

"I'm fine. Listen. I'm sorry to bother you, but Mrs. Bethany was adamant."

"What's up?"

"I'm sure it's nothing to be concerned about, but I've noticed a strange car parked near the salon."

Okay. Now my radar was up and my heart was pounding so hard I had to strain to hear.

"What does it look like? Did you get a license plate number?"

"It's just a car. I'm not really into cars. It's white. I can't see the license number. Whenever I try to get close, it takes off."

"How many times have you seen it?"

"Well, this is the third time. I noticed it yesterday twice and now it's back today. When I went outside, it took off, so I thought maybe I was just imagining things. Now it's back."

"Did you call the police?"

"No. I don't think it's important. I wouldn't be calling you if Mrs. Bethany hadn't insisted. It could be some poor guy waiting for someone on the street. It may have absolutely nothing to do with this whole mess."

"Paris, I don't want you to look at the car or go near it. Promise me?"

I could almost hear her hesitating. "I promise."

"This is important. I really need you to do this."

"I promise. I won't go near the car. What do you want me to do?"

"Are you still staying with Mama B?"

"Yes. But I want to go home. I don't want to inconvenience her. She's been wonderful, but …."

"I know. She's pushy and opinionated. But that's the safest place for you right now." That was definitely not my best choice of words.

"Safe? What's wrong? What aren't you telling me? Am I in some kind of danger?"

I probably should have lied and told her she was safe and there was absolutely nothing to worry about. But that just stops people from panicking; it doesn't keep them safe. If they are on guard, they're better able to protect themselves and tend not to walk into situations unprepared.

"I do know you are safer if someone is with you. If someone is following you, then I don't want you to be alone. I want you to stay with Mama B. *Okay*?" I waited for an answer, then added, "Paris, I need you to trust me."

A heavy sigh, a long pause, and finally, "Okay. How long before this is over? When are you coming home?"

For some reason that question put the silly grin back on my face. "I should be home in a day or two."

A few more minutes of small talk and she was off the phone.

THE NEXT DAY was the memorial service for Tyrone Warren.

On TV shows, the detectives show up at the funeral and wait for the murderer to give themselves away by dropping a clue of some kind. This has some truth to it. Most murderers don't have to make much effort to go to the funeral, because most murderers are related to their victims and are already there. Most murderers kill the ones they love.

Smart murderers don't return to the scene of the crime, unless they're looking for something. Pros rarely use the same spot or method more than once. Patterns are too easy for the police to recognize. Thomas Warrendale's home was set on fire, but I doubted seriously if it was the act of an arsonist. The fire that destroyed Warrendale's home was set by an amateur. A professional would have used a different accelerant, something harder to detect than gasoline. Thomas Warrendale was killed first and the fire was set to try and hide the murder. Or, they may have been trying to destroy evidence. I didn't believe there was an arsonist loose in the city of St. Joe just waiting for an opportunity to set another blaze.

"Remind me again why we're going to a funeral?" Harley asked.

"We're going to observe. FBI reports state that more than half—fifty-four percent—of all murder victims were acquainted with their assailant."

"You think the murderer will show up?"

I shrugged. "Odds are in our favor that Warrendale's murderer knew him." Chances were he or she knew him well enough to attend the memorial service. Whether the murderer would give us a clue that would lead to their capture was unlikely. Still, it was worth a shot. "Maybe it'll give us another path to follow. Regardless, we're going."

He nodded. "Okay, then show me what a highly trained investigator can learn by attending a funeral."

He was joking, but there's a lot that can be learned by observing. "Sometimes who doesn't show up at a funeral can be as important as who does show up. How people interact with each other can tell us a lot too. I once got a line on a murderer because he seemed too distraught at the funeral service of his wife's best friend. His reaction was enough to get me to cross-check the numbers on her cellphone. Once we knew what direction to look, it didn't take long to figure out they were having an affair. She tried to end it and he killed her. Sometimes all you need is a spark."

We drove to the funeral home where the memorial service was to be held. It was a massive place built to resemble a Southern plantation house. Four huge, white marble columns lined the porch while a circular drive led to the brick paved stairs and heavy mahogany doors.

"This place makes the white house look like a nice little summer cottage," Harley whispered as we walked up the stairs and stood in line in the marble-tiled entry. There was a short line of people waiting to sign the guest book. It didn't hurt to have a quick glance up and down the page to see if any of the names were familiar. Seeing nothing that leapt off the page, we followed the crowd to the parlor where Tyrone Warren was to be memorialized.

The parlor was large and open, with furniture set up to resemble a real home rather than a funeral parlor. Paris would have appreciated the heavy rugs, which muffled the noise. I don't know a lot about antiques, but the heavy furniture that dressed the room certainly looked old and expensive. Strolling by a side table, I noted the intricate detail some craftsman had probably spent months, if not longer, hand-carving.

There weren't a lot of people at the service. The women were conservatively and fashionably dressed. They were deeply tanned and well-preserved with jewels that sparkled as only the real ones can. The men wore dark suits and white shirts, looking as if they had just left an important board meeting. Who knows? Maybe they had.

In the front of the parlor was a table with massive floral sprays and plants lined up on each side. Directly in front of the table, a large picture of Tyrone Warren rested on an easel. The Tyrone Warren in the picture looked conservative and reserved, unlike the Thomas Warrendale who sang, danced, and directed the choir with total joy and abandon. It was hard for me to reconcile that man with the Tyrone Warren in the picture.

In the front of the parlor sat Mrs. Warren, appropriately dressed in black.

The service itself was short, sweet, and to the point. There were no public displays of emotion. No hysterics. A recital of Psalm 23, a few scriptures, and a brief word from a funeral director who obviously didn't know the deceased, and we were released. Tyrone Warren's remains were to be cremated when released by the coroner and placed in a crypt. So there was no internment at the gravesite. All in all, the entire proceedings didn't take more than thirty minutes.

People grieve and cope with death in different ways. But there was something chilling about the lack of tears at the death of one so young. Perhaps in a much older man who had lived a long and productive life, or one who had suffered through an agonizing illness, death might have come as a relief. But the sudden death of a young man, barely in his mid-thirties, should have generated more emotions. Anger, sadness, shock … something, anything would have been better than this polite acceptance.

Only once during the service did Mrs. Warren appear to lose her cool. As she was leaving the parlor, she stumbled. Maybe it was a moment of emotion, or maybe her cane got hung up on the oriental carpet. Whatever the reason for the slip, Mrs. Warren would have fallen if it weren't for Bryce Chandler.

"Ever the gentleman is Mr. Chandler, isn't he?" Harley whispered as we watched him assist Mrs. Warren out of the parlor. Following at a discreet distance, we watched as he helped Mrs. Warren into the waiting limousine before sliding into the car himself. The limousine pulled off almost at once.

Standing by, somewhat surprised at being left behind, was a woman I assumed was Mrs. Chandler. Puzzled and slightly embarrassed, she searched through her purse for her keys and then headed for one of the many BMWs gracing the parking lot. Hers was an impressive, black 760Li.

Harley whistled as we watched her pull out.

"Nice ride."

"That, my friend, is the BMW 760Li. Starting MSRP is one hundred twenty thousand dollars; however, I'm guessing Mrs. Chandler's tushy is resting on comfortable Nasca leather seats. Walnut dashboard, and if my eyes don't deceive, those are eighteen-inch tires with custom rims. All that luxury probably set Mr. Chandler back one hundred fifty thou."

I do love cars. While I am not a big fan of German cars, the BMW is a totally different story. That isn't a car. It's a finely tuned vehicle designed to hug the road. The suspension and turning radius are things of beauty. It's also not bad to look at.

"That car cost more than my house and it definitely cost more than either one of us will ever make serving and protecting the public." Harley's family was wealthy, but he didn't flaunt it. He lived, to the complete and utter dismay of his parents, totally off his policeman's salary.

We got into our rental car, which seemed smaller now than before we entered the funeral home, and drove to Mrs. Tyrone Warren's house.

There were few cars at the house, but we did note Mrs. Chandler's BMW was not in the driveway as we walked up to the front door. I wondered if Bryce Chandler would have the limo take him home or if he planned to stay over.

Entering the house, we noticed new rugs provided a pathway across the great expanse of white carpeting that led into the living room. Apparently, Mrs. Warren had found time for a little redecorating before her husband's funeral. We'd only been in town for two days, so she must have been in a hurry.

In the living room, Mrs. Warren sat as if on a throne, while the guests came up and paid their respects. Waiters and waitresses dressed in black pants and white shirts circulated amongst the guests, offering hors d'oeuvres and white wine. Mrs. Warren had gone all out for this affair, but something about the entire thing made me sad.

Funerals and memorial services at First Baptist Church almost always include a sermon and a choir. They are emotional occasions for a lot of reasons. I think there's something comforting about tears and grief on such an occasion. The choir sings what Mama B called, "gone to be with Jesus" songs. Songs like "Swing Low, Sweet Chariot" and "Goin' Up Yonder" or "I Stood on the Banks of Jordan," which were sure to bring a tear or two.

After the service, the processional followed the hearse to the graveside for a prayer and a few final words. Then everyone went back to the church for a meal. The Mother's Board, Missionary Society, and all the other women who can truly cook brought food so the family ate and fellowshipped. You can actually get some of the best food you've ever tasted at an old-fashioned funeral. There's sure to be chicken, dressings, green beans, corn, sweet potato pie, caramel cake, and fruit punch to wash it all down with.

Something about this catered plate of appetizers and white wine seemed sacrilegious. I smiled to think what Mama B would say if she saw it.

Harley and I made our way to Mrs. Warren. She seemed angry, or was that fear? I extended my hand. "Mrs. Warren, I am very sorry for your loss. I only knew your husband for a few months, but I can honestly say he made a big impression on our small town and on our church, where he will most assuredly be missed."

She shook my hand, and I saw the first glimmer of true emotion. For a moment, her eyes watered and her voice shook.

"Thank you. I didn't realize you knew him personally."

"Yes, ma'am, I did."

Bryce Chandler had moved from his position beside Mrs. Warren when we arrived, but now he watched us from across the room.

"Mrs. Warren, we are truly sorry." Harley had turned up the Southern accent and the charm a notch as he handed Mrs. Warren a business card. "However, if you think of anything that will help us in our investigation, please give us a call."

Mrs. Warren fingered the card before placing it on a nearby table.

"Yes. I will, but I don't …. I will. Certainly."

She glanced at Bryce Chandler, who was having a whispered conversation with a man we'd seen earlier at the memorial service.

"Is there something you remembered?" For a split second, I thought she was going to say something. Perhaps she would have if Bryce Chandler hadn't chosen that moment to turn and make eye contact. You didn't have to be a psychic to know something was going on between these two.

"I was just wondering when my husband's personal belongings would be released."

"Unfortunately, there isn't a lot left. Practically everything burned in the fire. We're still investigating. Any evidence collected will be returned after our investigation is complete." I thought Mrs. Warren seemed a little anxious. Maybe it was just the stress from the funeral.

"I see. Well, thank you."

We were holding up the lines of mourners waiting to extend their condolences to Mrs. Warren, so we moved on.

Other than some stolen glances between Bryce Chandler and the widow Warren, there didn't appear to be much going on.

So we ditched the finger food and left. Outside, a Rolls Royce was parked at the curb. It hadn't been there when we went in. Trust me, I would have noticed a Rolls.

Harley whistled and said, "Nice ride."

"That model is about two hundred fifty thousand. Only a small percentage of Rolls Royces are even imported into this country each year." I do *so* love cars.

"Tye Warren must have some rich friends."

"You got that right."

"I wonder who?" But Harley didn't have to wonder for long. Just as he finished speaking, the door opened and the Incredible Hulk got out of the front seat. Wearing jeans so tight I wondered how he could breathe, he zipped up a black-leather jacket to hide a shoulder holster. Harley and I both made sure our hands were close to our weapons as the Hulk opened the door to the backseat.

Compared to the Hulk, the elderly woman who stepped out of the car looked like a child. She was extremely petite and wore a full-length fur coat despite the warm May weather. Perhaps she wasn't *dripping* in diamonds, but there sure seemed to be a lot of them adorning her small frame. We nodded as she approached and were both surprised when she stopped in front of us, holding on to Hulk's arm for support.

"Good afternoon, gentlemen. I was hoping for an opportunity to speak to you."

We mumbled good afternoon and shook the small, frail, wrinkled hand she extended.

"Let me introduce myself. I'm Mrs. Elizabeth Hartford-Graham."

"Hartford-Graham? Are you the Hartford-Graham who owns the Easy Street Casino?" Harley had done his homework after all.

Smiling, she said, "Well, yes. My husband owned it, but after he passed away, I found I enjoyed owning my own casino."

"I'm Detective—"

"I know who you both are," she said.

"What can we do for you?"

"Would you gentlemen mind if we sat down and talked? I'm not a young woman and I tire easily. I'm sure we can find someplace quiet to sit and have a private conversation inside. You weren't leaving so soon, were you?"

It was obvious we were leaving but we denied it and turned to accompany Mrs. Hartford-Graham back into the house.

Turning to the Hulk, she said, "Gerald, you can leave me now. I'm sure these nice young men will help me." And with that, Gerald was dismissed as Mrs. Hartford-Graham shifted away from him, hooking one arm through each of ours. We slowly helped our frail charge into the house.

Back inside the house, the atmosphere was electrified as Mrs. Hartford-Graham entered and was immediately recognized.

Mrs. Warren rushed—as much as anyone with a cane can rush—to welcome her new visitor. "Mrs. Hartford-Graham, I'm so honored you would come to my home." To say that Mrs. Warren gushed might be stretching it, but not by much. Obviously, Mrs. Hartford-Graham was well known and extremely well respected, at least in this circle. If Mrs. Warren were physically capable of a curtsy, I think she would have done so. Instead, she bobbed her head.

Mrs. Warren became the charming hostess. "Please have a seat over by the window. That chair is the most comfortable, and it has a good view of the outside. I'm sure Mrs. Johnson won't mind switching." Mrs. Warren didn't care whether Mrs. Johnson minded or not. Mrs. Johnson vacated the comfortable chair at once, as if not minding the snub. Apparently, the ritual of seniority seating that played out in Mama B's small living room was no different than that of the rich and famous, I thought, as I watched Mrs. Johnson shift down to a less comfortable chair more suited to her rank in this hierarchy.

Sitting delicately in the chair of honor, Mrs. Hartford-Graham said, "I am so sorry for your loss. I wanted to come personally and give you my condolences."

"Thank you." Mrs. Warren bowed her head in acknowledgment, and I swear to God, bobbed again.

Harley and I were both pretty curious at this point and

wondered just how important Mrs. Hartford-Graham was.

"Mrs. Warren, I think my age and rheumatism are catching up with me. Do you have a quiet place I could rest for just a minute?"

"Of course. You can go to the master bedroom. It's just down the hall. Let me help you." Mrs. Warren moved in to assist Mrs. Hartford-Graham but was stopped with a look.

"I believe these two gentlemen can assist me, if you will just point us in the right direction." It was said with kindness, but a firmness underlined the words and prevented any rebuttal from Mrs. Warren.

"Why, of course. It's just down the hall there. Please let me know if you need anything," were Mrs. Warren's final words as we led Mrs. Hartford-Graham down the hall.

The bedroom was as impersonal and cold as the rest of the house, with white carpet and a large four-poster bed that looked like it belonged in a decorating magazine but not a home. A desk and a seating area were set up in front of a bay window that overlooked the yard.

"I think that chair at the desk will be just fine if you gentlemen wouldn't mind helping me."

After ensuring Mrs. Hartford-Graham was comfortably seated, Harley and I sat in the two Eames-inspired chairs that faced her and waited.

"Tyrone Warren was a brilliant auditor, as I'm sure you know. He did the books for my casino and several other businesses I own. Needless to say, I was shocked at his disappearance and later to hear word of his death."

Sitting behind the desk in the Warrens' bedroom, we got a glimpse not of the frail woman whose body was failing her, but of the shrewd, rock-hard businesswoman who had built a multimillion-dollar enterprise.

"Have you discovered who killed him?"

Now here was someone I would not enjoy playing poker with. She neither shrank from us nor did she provide any of the usual small signs of discomfort or anxiety. Bold and flatfooted, she stared at Harley and me as if she had every right in the world to ask this question and expected to be answered. In her eyes, I glimpsed the steel that must have propelled her to her current position, and for a split second I intended to answer her.

Instead, I replied, "Mrs. Hartford-Graham, I'm sure you understand we're working on an active murder investigation and are not at liberty to disclose any information."

She looked disappointed. As with the hulk-like bodyguard, the Rolls Royce, the fur coat, and the jewelry, it was all an act. This lady was a master manipulator, and like any good theatrical director, she had set the scene, gotten her actors, and was playing her part. I don't mean she wasn't old or that she wasn't in need of assistance. I believe that part was real. But she was not a helpless invalid. Mrs. Hartford-Graham was a dangerous woman who should not be underestimated.

One quick glance toward Harley, and the first act was finished. She smiled and nodded before adding, "I'm a pretty good judge of character, and I can see you are smart men. Quite perceptive too, I think. You'd make dangerous adversaries."

I surprised myself by saying, "So would you, I think."

Mrs. Hartford-Graham smiled. "You're right, Detective. Do I still call you 'Detective'?"

Interesting. Only a handful of people knew I was considering retirement. She wanted me to know her sources were powerful and her network extended not only to St. Joe, Indiana, but to its inner circle. "I'm still a detective."

She smiled. "I've always been vain."

Harley wasn't quite quick enough to hide his surprise, which caused another smile before she continued, "No, Detective Wickfield, I don't mean vain about looks. I was never what anyone would call a raging beauty. No, not beauty, but I have always been smart. I am vain about my intelligence. You have undoubtedly done your research and probably know more about me than I'd care to acknowledge. But did you know I graduated first in my class at Smith?"

She gazed out the window and her eyes had a faraway look as if she were remembering herself as a student at the prestigious women's college. "But I was born in the wrong time. Women were not titans of industry in my day. I had thought in my youth I could change that. I was conceited and bold enough to believe I could succeed where countless other women had failed before me." Looking directly at me, she said, "I think you understand. Society is far too concerned with the physical, outward appearance. Black or white, man or woman, young or old—it shouldn't matter. It's the brain that matters. The intellect."

Shifting her gaze toward the window, she looked out again for a full minute before continuing, "I learned there were other ways to have influence and power." She sighed and then added in a matter-of-fact tone, "But enough reflection. We cannot change the past. So, you can't or won't share what you've discovered so far about Mr. Warren's death. I shall have to be satisfied with that."

Mrs. Hartford-Graham started to rise but halted when I asked, "Is there anything you can tell us about Mr. Warren's death?"

"I have no information about Mr. Warren at all." She shook her head. "I haven't seen or heard from him in many months."

"Do you know any reason why someone would want to see Mr. Warren dead?" I kept hoping her words or behavior would provide some clue about the murder.

Again, she shook her head, "No. I didn't know him very well at all." Mrs. Hartford-Graham looked at me with wide-eyed innocence.

"But you knew him well enough to come to the funeral," Harley said quietly.

"Well, Detective, at my age I attend a great many funerals," Mrs. Hartford-Graham said with a smile.

"Have you noticed any money missing, perhaps?" I asked.

For a split second, I saw a look of anger cross Mrs. Hartford-Graham's face before it resumed its mask of innocence.

"Not that anyone has told me. Why do you ask, Detective?"

I felt sure she was lying. Mrs. Hartford-Graham was missing money and she knew I knew. I also knew she wouldn't say anything that would help us find out who killed Tye Warren, but I had to at least try. "If you know anything at all that can assist us in our investigation, I encourage you to please tell us."

She looked at me and sighed. "Detective Franklin, I wish I knew something that would help you. Unfortunately, I don't." With that, she pushed herself up from the desk and Harley and I went to assist her.

"It is terrible to get old, Detective Wickfield."

Trying to lighten the mood, Harley added, "I hear it beats the alternative."

"I don't know that it does. Perhaps if your brain grew old along with your body … but to have your brain just as sharp, or very nearly so, as at thirty or forty in an eighty-year-old body that is falling apart is not a pleasant thing."

We walked Mrs. Hartford-Graham back to the living room area where the crowd looked virtually unmoved, as if frozen in time.

Mrs. Warren hobbled over to attend to Mrs. Hartford-Graham. The older woman, however, merely inclined her head, halting Mrs. Warren in her tracks. She then allowed us to lead her out to her waiting car. Outside, Hulk leaped from the car and opened the door and helped Mrs. Hartford-Graham into the seat.

"Gentlemen, thank you both so much for all your assistance. I don't know if we shall see each other again, but I do hope that if we do, it will be under more festive circumstances."

We watched as Hulk closed the door and then got into the car. Once the car pulled away from the curb, I felt the trance Mrs. Hartford-Graham had cast over me lift.

"What was that about?" Harley asked.

"I have no idea. I think we were just sized up, but I don't know what for."

"You don't think that old bird had anything to do with murdering Warren, do you?"

"Not directly, but maybe indirectly. She's certainly rich and powerful enough to have paid someone to do it. She's smart, and if she had him killed, I think she'd make it hard to prove."

We stopped by the station one last time. We checked our messages, cleared up some files, returned our security badges and were just about to leave when Detective Hastings stopped by.

"You weren't planning to sneak out without saying goodbye?"

"You weren't here." Harley smiled and offered his hand.

"Let me take you to the airport. What time does your flight leave?"

"Four o'clock." I grabbed my bag.

"Great. That gives us plenty of time. We can return your rental car and then I can take you by a little place I know." Detective Hastings seemed anxious and nervous.

"I don't know if we have time. How far is it?" I wasn't feeling sociable and my mind was fully occupied with the strange events at the funeral. But Hastings wouldn't take no for an answer, so we stopped resisting.

After dropping off our rental car, Harley and I piled into Detective Hastings' "clutter-mobile," as Harley affectionately referred to it, and went to a small bar not far from the airport. Basically a dive, the Dew Drop Inn was cramped, dark, and dirty. The cigarette smoke was so thick it hung in the air like a heavy blanket, just waiting to suffocate any who lingered too long. My eyes stung and my throat contracted. Harley started coughing and I thought he was going to choke. I was just about to turn around and walk out when Hastings pulled us through the bar toward a door at the back. We followed in hopes that it led outside but were disappointed. It led down a flight of stairs to the basement. If leaving didn't mean returning through the haze we'd just left, we would have done it. But with the door closed and a cool breeze blowing from the basement, we decided to keep going. I did notice Harley slipped one hand inside his jacket where I knew he kept his weapon. I found myself fingering my holster too. I turned and glanced at Harley. I could see the question in his eyes. Were we wrong to have trusted Detective Hastings? We were about to find out.

At the bottom of the stairs was a basement of painted concrete blocks, stained concrete floors, and 1970s furniture in the form of a poker table, several chairs, a pool table, and a large, industrial-strength ceiling fan. Despite the outdated décor, the basement was homey and somewhat inviting. Or maybe it just seemed more inviting than the claustrophobic gas chamber upstairs. There was only one person in the lower level, and he was sitting alone at one of the tables, nursing a bottle of beer and playing solitaire.

Detective Hastings went behind the bar and grabbed three bottles of beer then sat down and motioned for Harley and me to join them.

Once seated, Hastings did the introductions. "This is my dad. Carl Hastings Senior."

We shook hands. Regardless of the age, the attire, or the situation, criminals and cops were always able to identify other criminals and cops. I knew Hastings' dad was a cop from the moment I saw him. I don't know if it was his posture, his haircut, his clothes, or the world-weariness in his eyes. Whatever it was, he had the look. In one glance, he had assessed Harley and me and found us trustworthy, because he nodded, raised his beer, and started to tell us a story.

"I was on the force for thirty-two years before I retired a year ago. I've never done anything illegal in all that time. Never even took a pencil that didn't belong to me." His eyes were moist and his voice was gruffer than it had been a moment before. He took a swig of beer to regain his composure before continuing.

For thirty minutes, the elder Hastings told us everything he knew about Benson, McCormick, and Chandler, Tyrone Warren, and Mrs. Hartford-Graham. We didn't interrupt. Talking seemed cathartic for Hastings and we let him tell his story.

After he'd finished, I asked, "How much can you prove and how much is speculation?"

He waited so long to answer, I almost repeated myself. But staring me in the eye, Carl Senior nodded to his son, who stood up and went behind the bar. When he came back, he was carrying an envelope. Back at the table, he sat down and slid the envelope across to me.

With Harley looking over my shoulder, I opened the envelope and took out a file folder with one photo. The photo was of a book opened to a page full of numbers.

"What's this?" I asked.

"I'm sure Junior told you that when we were investigating those accountants, some of the evidence disappeared."

Harley held up the photo. "Is this part of the missing evidence?"

Hastings Senior nodded. "Before you ask, I didn't take it."

"So how did you come by this?" I asked, still unsure what I was looking at.

Senior paused for a moment and took a deep breath. "I worked with a detective on the investigation. I've known the guy for years. I think he was paid to … lose the evidence."

"How? And why didn't you take this information to Internal Affairs?" I asked.

"I didn't know about it. He died about six months ago. His wife was going through his things, and she found some stuff she didn't know what to do with. She called me."

"I still don't know why you didn't turn this over to Internal

Affairs," I said, looking down at the photo, still wondering what this had to do with our murder investigation.

"I remembered seeing a page with numbers like that when we were investigating those accountants. That's a photo. I turned in the original."

"What is it? Harley asked.

Hastings shrugged. "I don't know. I wasn't involved in the case as much as Bronson. I just remember associating that page with the accountants."

"Was there anything else?" I asked.

Hastings Senior shook his head. "Not really. Most of the other stuff had nothing to do with any investigations. Bowling trophies ... personal stuff. I think he must have destroyed the evidence but somehow missed this one page. I would have missed it too, but it just struck me as weird. That's why I took a picture of it."

"Look, I don't know what we can do in Indiana. We're here trying to find a murderer, that's all. This probably doesn't have anything to do with our murder, but thanks."

CHAPTER NINE

THE FLIGHT BACK from Cleveland was short—too short. I needed time to process everything, from the funeral, to the meeting with Mrs. Hartford-Graham, to the bizarre events afterwards with Detective Hastings. It just wasn't fitting in neat little buckets, and I had the feeling I was missing something— something other than the identity of our killer. One elusive puzzle piece was hanging just out of reach, so I sat back and let the pieces weave in and out of my mind in hopes that I'd find the missing one.

I barely had time to sift through the information Detective Hastings had told us before it was time to deplane. The photo was of a page containing a combination of numbers—a code of some kind. According to Hastings' notes, they had been trying to crack that code for months. Eventually, the lawyers demanded that everything be returned, including copies. He had risked a lot keeping this. As a cop, he would have been forced to turn it in. As a private citizen, he might be protected under whistleblower laws. I had no idea. But I intended to turn it in. I had a murderer to find, and after three days in Cleveland, we weren't much closer to naming the killer of

Thomas Warrendale than we had been back in St. Joe. We had a lot of information, but none of it really fit.

After leaving the airport, I drove straight to Mama B's. She was in her chair watching reruns of *The Andy Griffith Show*.

"Welcome back."

I gave her a kiss and sat down on the sofa. "Thanks. Where's Paris?"

"She's upstairs. I hollered up to her when I saw you pull up, so I'm sure she'll be down in a minute."

"Why do you watch this stuff? You have to have seen this a thousand times."

"I have, and it's funny every time. There's so much trash on television these days, I can't hardly watch it anymore. I mostly watch the news, old reruns of television shows from the fifties and sixties, and my stories."

"Your stories probably have more sex and violence than any other shows on television." This was an old argument between me and Mama B. She loved watching those old soap operas.

"Maybe, but a woman has got to have some excitement in her life."

We both laughed at that one. Mama B's housedress had definitely seen better days; a knot she had tied at the middle of her leg was the only thing holding up her stockings. Slippers on her feet and a scarf tied around her head completed the ensemble. Mama B was at home and comfortable. She rarely got dressed up unless she was going to church, but once her hair was wrapped up, she was in for the night.

I heard Paris coming down the stairs and had to check myself to make sure I wasn't grinning. She was wearing a dark skirt, white blouse, and boots, and I felt compelled to stand. Of course, standing there, I felt rather stupid and tried to play it off by sliding down on the sofa so she could have the seat of honor closest to Mama B.

"Hi." I am a much more engaging conversationalist than

I've demonstrated from my few encounters with Paris, but for some reason I found it a little hard to get started.

"Hi. When did you get back?"

"About an hour ago. Have you eaten?" The suddenness of my invitation took her by surprise. I hadn't planned to blurt out the invitation quite like that. I'd intended a lead up.

"No. We haven't. I think Mrs. Bethany cooked though."

We both looked to Mama B for confirmation. She just rocked and smiled before adding, "It'll keep." She rocked on for another few seconds and then added, "You'd better take a sweater. It's supposed to be cool tonight."

"Aren't you going to join us?" Paris did the polite thing, including Mama B in the invite.

"Of course. You should definitely come." I tried hard to sound sincere. I think I tried too hard. She just kept rocking and smiling.

"Baby, I ain't going no place. I'm in for the night. Me and Andy Griffith have a date." Mama B rocked and smiled.

Paris went up to grab her sweater and Mama B tried to make eye contact while I aimed to avoid it. A few minutes later, Paris returned and we headed out.

"Have fun," Mama B called after us as we left the house.

I helped Paris into the car and we drove off.

"Do you have a taste for anything in particular?"

"I like just about everything, but there's a new restaurant that just opened up on the riverfront called Cesselly's."

"I heard about it too. It's a new jazz dinner club. It's supposed to be great."

I turned the car around and headed toward the river.

Cesselly's was actually located within walking distance of my home. It was part of an old warehouse that had been converted to retail shops and now a restaurant.

We talked about Warrendale. Paris couldn't remember anything helpful, but she went over the specific things she noticed when she was reviewing her books. Her attorney hadn't found anything useful, and the bank was still investigating. So far, she hadn't gotten any closer to locating the missing money. When she finished giving me her summary, she did the most amazing thing—she fell silent. Most people can't stand silence and talk just to fill the dead space, but Paris was one of those rare individuals who could enjoy the silence in between conversations.

Finally, she asked, "What do you think they're after?"

I knew she was referring to whoever had broken into her shop. "I don't know yet."

"I can't go on indefinitely staying with Mama ... ah, Mrs. Bethany." We both laughed at the momentary slip as she fell into my childhood name for Mrs. Bethany.

"She won't mind your calling her Mama B."

"Why do you call her that? Are you related?"

"I've called her Mama B since I was a small child. She was like a mother to me, and after my mother passed, she filled an empty spot."

I rarely talked about my mother. It had been almost fifteen years since her death. I'd made my peace with it. She was a strong Christian and her faith helped me and my sister through the long days of chemo and treatment. However, there was something very personal about discussing her. So I rarely did.

After dinner, we walked around by the riverfront. It had been a warm spring day, but the night was cool. There was a walking path that ran along the river. During the day, the path was usually crowded with joggers, power walkers, kids, bicyclists, and lovers who ambled hand-in-hand along the winding, fragrant trail. Tonight, it was pleasantly deserted, but well lit. We paused in the middle of the bridge that led across to the other side of the river. We were watching the waterfall when my stamina failed and I yawned.

"You must be dead tired. You flew home and haven't had any rest all day. We should go back."

"I'm used to getting just a few hours of sleep." I hadn't

intended to tell Paris about my accident or the nightmares that kept me up at night, but I did. She listened. After my second yawn, she insisted we head back. I tried to protest, but I didn't want to embarrass myself by falling asleep. Besides, we were skating on dangerous ground. I was attracted to her, but she was involved in the case. I was still on the force and I had to be careful. So, we walked back to the car. My attraction to her gave me further motivation to figure out who killed Tye Warren.

It was a relatively short drive to Mama B's. I dropped Paris off and was just about to get out when she said, "You don't have to walk me to the door. It looks like Mama B's in bed, so I'll just say good night and thank you for a lovely evening."

I waited to make sure she got into the house safely before heading home. After I got home, I went straight to bed. I was more tired than I'd been in a long time. Before long, I did something I haven't done in months. I fell into a sound sleep.

THE NEXT DAY was Friday, and I experienced déjà vu as Harley, Chief Mike, and I once again enjoyed the mayor's hospitality. I leveled with the mayor and told him everything we'd found, which really wasn't much. I shared the details of the investigation the cops in Cleveland had done two years ago and even told him about the photograph of the page with the coded numbers.

Mayor Longbow, still elegantly attired and impeccably well groomed, shocked all of us by picking up his phone, cancelling his next meeting, and asking the city's attorney to join us. We moved over to the conference table. The mayor took off his jacket and rolled up his sleeves. We talked about everything. Two hours and an untold number of cups of coffee later, Harley, the city's attorney, Chief Mike, and I left the mayor's office.

The mayor reminded us we were investigating a murder, not money laundering. The other information was outside of our purview. If the cases overlapped, and they sure seemed intertwined, then we could follow the threads. Solving a murder was time-consuming enough. Add money laundering, racketeering, and whatever else these people were doing into the mix, and it might take an entire army to get to the bottom of it.

ONE LOOSE END on this murder investigation was the other person who Mama B named as a possible love-tie to Thomas Warrendale—Tonya Rutherford. I took a few minutes and drove to the home of Tonya, the woman who, if Mama B was to be believed, was supposedly carrying Thomas Warrendale's unborn child. Harley was due in court on another matter, so I went alone.

Tonya was a young woman, not more than seventeen or eighteen. She was extremely smart, a straight-A student. Last year she'd taken the SATs and got a perfect score of 1600. It was all over the newspapers and the church had a nice write-up about her in the newsletter. That rare feat had won her a full ride to the college of her choice. I heard she was considering an Ivy League school, although her mom was hoping she'd stay closer to home. If she was indeed pregnant, that might put a crimp in her plans.

Viola Rutherford, Tonya's mother, was a single parent. She was disabled and rarely left the house. She lived in a small, rundown apartment on the edge of the 'hood. The neighborhood had once been respectable but now was littered with cars sitting on cement blocks, empty beer cans, and homes with plywood instead of glass in the windows. Men of varying ages sat on the porches drinking, laughing, and gambling 24/7. Tonya was a shining example of how, no matter what your situation, you could overcome any limitations with hard work and determination. I secretly hoped Mama B was wrong, but she rarely is about things like this.

The only thing that distinguished the Rutherfords' unit from any other was the empty beer bottles, broken glass, and tires that were piled neatly on the side of the apartment. The car sitting in the front yard was old and rusty but wasn't on cement blocks, and the empty gas can on the backseat indicated that someone held out hope that this giant yard planter would one day move again.

I knocked loudly on the door that was barely hanging on its hinges and waited while Viola Rutherford shuffled to the door.

Viola Rutherford was probably in her mid-forties, but her illness and a life of chain-smoking made her look a lot older. The fact that Viola Rutherford smoked had made her a target for a lot of the older church members when I was a kid. Some religions take a stand against smoking—First Baptist Church did not. Some of the older members felt smoking was a sin, but Reverend Hamilton never condemned smokers. However, he did ask members to smoke on the side of the church rather than on the church steps.

"RJ, what brings you down here?" Viola Rutherford moved aside to let me enter.

Despite the dilapidated exterior, the interior of the home was sporting brand-new leather furniture much too large for the room. The sixty-inch plasma television occupied a place of prominence on the wall in front of the sofa. Viola Rutherford shuffled back to a recliner and motioned for me to sit on the sofa.

"This is very nice," I gushed, hoping pride would make her tell me how she could afford all this furniture without my having to come out and ask. It didn't.

"Thank you," was all she said as she took her lighter from her pocket and lit another cigarette. Although she did pick up the remote from the arm of her chair and lower the volume on the television a smidge.

Viola Rutherford had once worked at St. Joe's one automobile manufacturing plant, Tucker. Tucker cars were hand-made in St. Joe for over one hundred years. The plant only made about thirty cars per year and shut down in the eighties. Viola Rutherford used to flash a solid-gold lighter that she received when she retired. "Just showing off" was how Mama B referred to her. Today she used a cheap Bic lighter.

"Did you hit the lottery? This is some really nice furniture in here, Miss Viola." I continued to lay on the compliments, hoping she'd loosen up a bit.

"Nice furniture isn't a crime, is it?" Miss Viola wasn't as terse as her words implied, but there certainly wasn't a lot of warmth there either.

"No, ma'am. Nice furniture certainly isn't a crime. I guess that just depends on how it's acquired." I tried to keep my voice light but my meaning was clear. She chose to ignore it.

"What brings you down our way, RJ? Slumming?" Miss Viola sneered.

"I was hoping to talk to Tonya."

"What you want with her? She ain't done nothin' wrong."

"No, ma'am. She hasn't done anything wrong. I was just hoping I could talk to her. That's all."

"She ain't here. She's still in Detroit, like I said the other day when you called."

"Any idea when you expect her back?"

"No idea."

"Well, isn't she in school?"

"Got enough credits to finish early. She's done with high school. Goin' to college in the fall."

"I know. I heard how she got all those scholarship offers. You must be very proud of her."

For the first time since I'd arrived, Miss Viola relaxed. "I am proud of her. She's a good girl."

"Yes, ma'am. Do you think I could call Tonya? If you give me the telephone number in Detroit, I won't have to keep bothering you."

Miss Viola looked like she was going to ignore me. But eventually, she rattled off a number with a Detroit area code. I thanked her and hurried out. She didn't rise or bother to see me out.

Back in the car, I hurried to dial the number I'd been given but was too late. There was no answer. Miss Viola must have started dialing the moment my back was turned. I knew I wouldn't get an answer. But I'd find her one way or another.

CHAPTER TEN

I'D BARELY SAT down at my desk when my cellphone rang. I hadn't even managed to get my greeting out before a hysterical Mrs. Green confronted me. Chris had been picked up by the police and she was beside herself. I promised I would find out what was going on.

It didn't take long to locate him. I wish I could attribute my quick results to excellent and diligent police work. But this was totally a matter of luck. As I was heading down the hall to the other wing of the building, I saw him sitting there. One quick word to Detective Cassidy and I learned Chris had been picked up as a potential witness. A stupid fistfight between two boys from the school had gone too far. One of the kids was in the hospital, badly injured, and could possibly lose the sight in one of his eyes. The parents wanted vengeance and Chris was brought in to tell what he knew. One look in his eyes and I could tell he was scared to the bone. *Good.* I asked Detective Cassidy to let him sit and stew for another thirty minutes while I picked up the phone to call his grandmother and relieve her mind. Before I could finish dialing, however, I spotted Reverend Hamilton. Mrs. Green must have been really scared. She'd called in the big guns.

"Good afternoon, Rev—"

"What's wrong with you, locking up a fine boy like Chris Green? That boy is no more of a criminal than you were at his age—probably less."

Reverend Hamilton was angrier than I'd ever seen him. He took his shepherding role seriously, and I pitied anyone who went after one of his sheep.

"Chris is only here as a witness. He hasn't been locked up. He will be going home just as soon as we've got his statement. I was just about to call Sister Green to let her know."

He breathed a sigh of relief. "Good. Well, you may not find her at home. You'd better call the church. She and the other members of the Mother's Board, Missionary Society, Senior Choir and the deaconesses are all at the church praying."

I saw a glimmer in Reverend Hamilton's eye, and after a second he couldn't contain himself and started chuckling. He looked me in the eye. "Are you being straight with me?"

"Yes, sir. Chris will be home in time for dinner. I promise."

"Praise be to God. Well, don't worry about calling. I better head back to the church and share the good news before they really get worked up. It was all I could do to keep them from marching to the jail. Can you believe they wanted me to call the NAACP, the Urban League, Reverend Jesse Jackson, Al Sharpton, and Bishop T.D. Jakes?" Reverend Hamilton laughed.

"I didn't know you knew Jesse Jackson, let alone any of the rest of them."

"I don't."

"What did they think Bishop Jakes could do? He's in Dallas. We aren't even affiliated with his church."

"I have no idea. That was Sister Bethany's suggestion. She said she saw him on television, and she thought he seemed like he could get some action because he's been to the White House."

We laughed for a few minutes. Reverend Hamilton patted me on the back. "I better get back. God alone knows what those women are capable of doing. Heaven help the poor soul who tries to harm one of those prayer warriors' loved ones. They would beat him to a pulp and pray for his healing just so they could beat him again."

I knew Reverend Hamilton was only half joking. Those were some serious women, and one of their babies was in danger. Reason was the last thing they were indulging in. Despite the humor, it was comforting to know that in times of distress, there were still people in this world who believed in the power of prayer.

I pulled myself together and put on my game face. I needed to talk to Chris, who was now in a small interrogation room just outside of one of the holding cells. The room was close enough to hear the screams of inmates as they yelled to each other. One unhappy individual was even banging on the walls cussing and screaming. Between expletives against the judicial system and his unfair incarceration, he shouted his telephone number and asked for someone to call his mother.

Chris sat with a look of sheer terror in his eyes. My intent was to let him see what running with the wrong crowd could lead to, but the look in his eyes showed me he wasn't in need of rough treatment.

"RJ, thank God. Please help me." The sincerity was genuine. I wanted to teach him a lesson, but saw no need to carry things too far.

"Come on."

"Seriously? I can go? That other cop, I mean, that other *police officer* told me to wait here."

"You gave your statement?"

He nodded.

"Do you want to stay?"

"Heck, no. No. Absolutely no. I want to go home."

I held the door, and he grabbed his jacket and ran from the room.

I had to turn my back so he couldn't see me smiling. I waved at Detective Cassidy as we headed out to my car, but I needn't have worried. Chris didn't look to the left or the right. He put his head down and marched. Once in the safety of my car, he exhaled. It took another three blocks before he took his hands from his face, and I could hear him muttering under his breath, "Thank you, God. Thank you, Jesus."

I guess the scripture is true: "Train up a child in the way he should go: and when he is old, he will not depart from it." (Proverbs 22:6.)

I DROVE TO a coffee shop I knew downtown. Sitting at the table, I tried not to notice how much Chris' hands shook as he drank his coffee.

He sat with his head bowed and just kept shaking it. "RJ, thank you for getting me out of that place, man. I couldn't take much more."

"It's not someplace you want to end up. That's real life in there."

"I never want to go back. Not even for a visit." Chris spoke with such feeling, I needed another drink to hide the smile I felt forming. He was a good kid, and I knew that if ever anyone was scared straight, he certainly was.

"You weren't even near the serious offenders. We keep them down in the basement."

Chris looked up to see if I was joking. "For real?"

"I don't even like going down there. You look in their eyes and you see nothing. There's no feeling. No compassion. Nothing. They don't care about anyone or anything. Those are the worst. Life has absolutely no meaning. Not theirs, not yours, no one's."

Chris was still shaking, but the coffee was helping. "Man, I didn't do anything."

"I know."

"You do?"

"If we thought you were guilty of something, you'd still be locked up. And trust me, if you were guilty, I would put you in that cell myself."

After a moment's pause, a slow smile came on his face for the first time. But it didn't last long. "Man, I was just standing there. Honestly, RJ, I swear to you, I didn't touch anybody and didn't have anything to do with that fight. Rico and T-Bone were just—"

"Who?"

"Rico and T-Bone. Just some guys I know."

"Chris, I know you don't think adults have a clue what you're going through at sixteen. But trust me, we do. You have to watch who you hang around with. Ricardo Miller darn near killed that kid. He's not out of the woods yet. He's still in intensive care and may never regain sight in one of his eyes. What were they fighting about?"

Chris hung his head and muttered, "I don't know."

I banged the table out of frustration, startling not only Chris but several others who were sitting nearby. I leaned closer. "Don't even think about lying to me."

After a long pause, he 'fessed up. "Rico's cousin is part of the Skulls." At the look on my face, he got defensive. "I'm not a Skull. I swear to God, RJ, I'm not. I just wanted to fit in, I guess. Because I was hanging out with someone who was connected to them, people thought I was cool. They treated me different. Nobody messed with me. Nobody made fun of me. I don't know … I just wanted respect."

I listened as Chris tried to work through his thoughts and feelings. I thought back to what it was like at sixteen, to feel like you didn't belong. At that age, all I could think about was how much I wanted to fit in.

"Chris, those boys are dangerous and can seriously ruin your life. Just being seen with them can get you killed."

"I know. I'm done. I swear. I never prayed so hard in my whole life. Sitting down at that jail, I just kept praying that if I got out of there, I wouldn't have anything else to do with any of them. And I mean it. I *never* want to go back to that place."

"I'm glad to hear it."

"Do you think T-Bone is going to make it? It was horrible. Ricco just kept hitting him and hitting him. Blood was flying everywhere." Chris unzipped his hooded sweatshirt and showed the blood splatter. "I kept screaming at him to stop. I couldn't take it. I was glad when I heard the sirens. Everybody else ran. It was like … I was frozen. I couldn't move. I just stood there." A tear ran down Chris' face. "I didn't know what to do. I was so scared."

"It's over now. You're okay. But you need to stay as far away from them as possible. Chris, there is a big difference between respect and fear. Do you really want people to be scared of you?"

"I'm done. I promise."

"Glad to hear it." Glancing at my watch, I decided I'd better take Chris home and relieve Reverend Hamilton of the ladies at the church.

As we were leaving, Chris noticed the time. "My grandmother is going to kill me."

"She might try. You know she loves you, and there's nothing she wouldn't do for you. In fact, let me tell you what your grandmother's been up to."

Chris had a good laugh at his grandmother's antics. "Man, I didn't even think my granny knew who Al Sharpton was."

I knew the image of seeing someone almost killed had left a mark on Chris. He might never get that image out of his head. That was definitely something I could relate to, especially now. As much death as I've seen, it still creeps back in the dead of the night when all my defenses are down. Laughing would be good for his soul. I wanted him to feel the weight of being involved with the wrong crowd, but at his age, his hormones and emotions could easily send him into a deep depression that wouldn't be good either. Balance was important for all of us, but a good dose of laughter would help him get through the next few days and hopefully the nights when the images came back most vividly.

At the church, Reverend Hamilton had apparently calmed the women down. Mrs. Green was kneeling at the altar in fervent prayer and didn't even notice when we entered. Reverend Hamilton, usually reluctant to interrupt someone in prayer, tapped her on the shoulder and pointed to Chris, who was standing beside me at the back of the church. Upon seeing Chris, Mrs. Green burst into tears. At the sight of his grandmother's distress, Chris rushed to the altar and threw his arms around her. They hugged and wept at the altar. The few ladies who remained shouted praise and thanks to God for Chris' safe return. I caught Reverend Hamilton's eye and gave him a thumbs-up as he mouthed a silent, "Thank you." I nodded and slipped away.

Leaving the vestibule, I went outside. That's where I saw Mama B sitting on the concrete wall that surrounded the church porch.

"I thought you went home."

"Was downstairs waiting for you."

I sat beside her on the porch. "How did you know I'd be here?"

"When Reverend Hamilton told us you were taking care of everything, I knew you'd bring the boy home okay."

I felt a moment of silly pride at her faith in my ability to get results. But Mama B had always had faith in me. "You want a ride home?"

"Yes, indeed. I'm bone tired. My knees aren't what they used to be. I thought you were going to have to find a crane to get me up off that altar." Mama B laughed her wonderful, full, hearty laugh that made her entire body shake.

"You know you shouldn't have been down there on your knees. I believe God would have understood entirely if you had prayed from the pew."

"Honey, I know God can hear me whenever and wherever I pray, but there are times in your life when you just have to get down on your knees and talk to the Lord. I guess it's more for us than for Him. I can't explain it, but it's true just as sure as I'm sitting here. You're too young to understand now, but someday you'll know what I'm talking about. You just keep on living and you'll see."

Mama B hoisted herself up, and I helped her down the church steps to my car.

The short drive through the alley to Mama B's house took less than five minutes. At the house, I was disappointed to see Paris wasn't home from work yet. I considered accepting Mama B's offer of dinner, but given the situation with Chris, I had left the station without shutting down my computer and had a few other files to clear up. So, I reluctantly took my leave.

I still had a murder to solve.

CHAPTER ELEVEN

———

Back at my desk, I located an address in Detroit to go with the telephone number Viola Rutherford gave me. I debated driving up. Detroit was only a three-hour drive from St. Joe. But I decided against it. Instead, I called the metro police station in the Motor City. It didn't take long to pass along my request, and within twenty-four hours, someone from the department was set to question Tonya Rutherford.

Finally, I sat back and started in on the endless paperwork that was the bane of every policeman's existence.

I had just about decided to do something about the emptiness in the pit of my stomach and the crick in my neck when my cell rang. Noticing it was Paris' number, I grinned.

"Hello. How—"

"Someone broke into my house. I went home to get some things and … they've trashed my house."

I was already halfway down the hall and out the door. "Paris, I want you to get out of the house and go wait in the car."

"There's no one here. I—"

"Paris, I just need you to do this. Did you call the police?"

"They're here. RJ, I'm fine. Really," She was taking deep

breaths and calming her nerves and her voice. "The officer made me wait outside while he checked the house. Don't worry. I'm okay. I'm just shook up, that's all. There's a police car outside and a couple of police officers in the house. Trust me, whoever did this is long gone."

"Good. I'll be right there. *Don't* leave. Just wait for me."

"Okay. I will."

There was a police car parked in front of Paris' house, and the neighbors had come out to see what happened. In the midst of all of this, I saw Paris standing outside. She had been crying and I gave her a handkerchief.

Inside the house, I saw what had upset her. The house was trashed. Every drawer was pulled out. Every cushion was ripped. In essence, every potential hiding place had been exposed. Whoever broke into Paris' house was looking for something and didn't care who knew it.

I wasn't surprised to hear Harley's voice behind me, since I'd called him on my way over.

"Do you think they found what they were looking for?" It always amazed me how after working together for such a short time, we were thinking the exact same thing.

"I don't know. But we'll find out soon enough."

"How?"

"If they come back."

"Any idea what they're after?"

"No. But we better figure it out soon."

We boarded up the house as best we could. Paris gathered up her clothes and essentials and we left. I had just gotten her bags in the car and was heading back to Mama B's when she reached up for my hand. "Stop. Pull over."

Pulling the car to the side of the road, I took a closer look at her and waited.

"I don't think I should go back to Mrs. Bethany's."

"Why not?"

"I don't know what this whole thing is about, but I can't put her in danger. I *won't* put her in danger. What if they think I have whatever it is they are looking for? They might come looking at her house."

I saw where her mind was going and I appreciated her concern for Mama B's safety.

"Look, you're right. They might come looking at Mama B's. I don't know. But anyone crazy enough to break into Mama B's will get a lot more than they bargained for."

"Are you sure?"

"I'm sure." I turned the key in the ignition and pulled away from the curb. It must have been a full five minutes before Paris realized we weren't heading toward Mama B's.

"Where're we going?"

"I need to go by my house." If she was surprised, she hid it well. "I have to pick up some things. I'll be staying at Mama B's too."

TONIGHT, MY NEAT habits were a relief. Many women expect men to live in messy apartments with clothes strewn all over the floor and dirty dishes in the sink. The truth is, I'm lazy. If you hang your clothes up when you take them off, then you've only had to touch them once. If you throw them on the floor or the furniture, you'll have to pick them up again. Maybe not today, maybe not tomorrow, but someday you'll have to pick those clothes up and move them. Then you've had to move them twice. It's the same with dishes. As soon as I finish eating, I put the dishes in the dishwasher. Not only have I eliminated the step of moving them from the counter or sink to the dishwasher, but I also don't have to look at them. Maybe my laziness is a sign of a controlling personality, I don't know. But it's helped me keep my home neat, and that's a plus.

I gave her the fifty-cent tour.

"I like it."

"Really? I thought you preferred older, more traditional décor."

"I do, but that doesn't mean I don't like other styles and can't appreciate open spaces." She walked around, noticing every detail. "I normally don't care for modern décor. I find it cold and uninviting. But you've done a nice job of making it warm and comfortable. I really do like it."

I was amazed how much her opinion mattered, but then I decided I'd better give up being amazed and just go with the flow.

While I packed, Paris plopped on the floor and amused herself with my CD and album collection. I have hundreds of CDs, tapes, and albums. Old or new, it doesn't matter. I have one large storage unit that houses my collection.

She had to yell from the living room for me to hear. "I would have expected you to be an iPod man."

I had just finished adding my toiletries to my bag and was standing at the door, watching unobserved while she browsed. She looked at home. Perhaps I breathed too hard, but somehow she sensed my scrutiny and turned toward me.

"I even have an old record player I picked up in a junk store. It plays everything—33s, 45s and 78s. Music touches so many senses. It's not just an auditory thing. I like to hold the albums and read the back covers and breathe in the old smell. I don't know how to explain it."

"I think you've explained it very well. Music is an experience you have to savor. I like that."

"Look, I don't want you to feel weird or anything, but I need to take a shower. It'll only take a few minutes and then we can go."

"No problem. I understand completely. I love Mrs. Bethany too, but she has very little water pressure."

"Yeah, and if someone flushes a toilet, you get scalded."

We both laughed.

"I'll just sit here and listen to music if you show me where the CD player is."

I pointed her in the right direction and then went to take a nice hot shower. I made it a quick one and was hurrying to dry off and get dressed when I heard the familiar sounds of Al Jarreau floating through the house. He's one of my all-time favorite singers. It seemed like a happy omen Paris chose him from the hundreds of CDs and albums I had. I couldn't help smiling to myself that here was something else we had in common when I heard her singing along. She had a really good, strong voice. It was rich and mellow. Usually, when someone sings along with a record, they drown out the artist. But Paris wasn't trying to compete with Al Jarreau. Instead, she was complementing him. She wasn't just singing, she was harmonizing, filling in, accompanying. It was as if they were singing a duet. The song she chose was "Mornin'," another favorite.

I peeked around the door. Paris wasn't just singing but dancing too. I watched in silence as she swirled and turned, dancing with a pillow from the sofa. After the song ended, she hugged the pillow and replaced it on the sofa, then she turned and noticed me watching for the first time. I applauded, and she threw her head back and laughed and then bowed.

"I didn't know you could sing like that. You're amazing."

"Thank you. I thought you knew I sing in the church choir."

"A lot of people who sing in the church choir don't sound like that."

She smiled. "Are you ready?"

"Almost."

I grabbed my bag from the bedroom, and when I returned, Paris was on the floor, replacing all the CDs she'd taken out earlier. When the last one was in place, she reached out to me, and I helped her to her feet. I pulled her close and held her in my arms. Her hair had a faint smell of citrus. She leaned up and we kissed. It was soft and sweet and gentle. After a moment, she held up the CD I didn't realize she was still holding. Without saying a word, I put it into the CD player. The song she'd picked was a cover of one of my favorite James Taylor tunes, "Don't Let Me Be Lonely Tonight," by David Sanborn and Liz Wright, whose smooth voice gave life to the suggestive lyrics. Paris started to sway and dance alone as the music filled the room. Smiling at me, she said, "Don't get any ideas. I just love this song." That lightened the mood, and I laughed and took her in my arms.

We danced. Sad, but I can't remember the last time I danced. It was probably at my sister's wedding. Fortunately, with a slow song like this one, I didn't need to be Fred Astaire, preferring to stand in virtually the same place and sway. But it was nice to dance, to hold someone close and just dance. There was something old fashioned and romantic about slow dancing. The song came to an end, and we stopped.

"I'm a bit rusty," I said.

"Maybe we can get some practice in at Cesselly's. I used to love to dance. I work so many long hours now with the salons, I rarely have the time."

It was nice that our conversation included references to the future. "I would imagine you have a long line of men waiting to take you dancing."

"Officer, I would have thought your investigative techniques would be better than that. If you want to know if I'm dating someone, why not just ask?"

"Well, are you dating anyone?"

"No, I'm not. Are you?"

"No. But I think you knew that already. There is no way you could have known Mama B for more than twenty-four hours, let alone spent several days in her home, without her telling you everything there is to know about me."

"I guess I was wrong. You are a good detective after all. But she only told me things that presented you in the best possible light. She loves you as if you were her own son."

"And I love her like she was my mom," I added with sincerity. "We'd better go."

I called Mama B to let her know what time we'd be coming. I knew she would have heard about the break-in over the police ban radio, so by the time we arrived, she had clean towels laid out in *my* room. When I was young and stayed with her, I slept in the blue room. It was upstairs and faced the backyard. I don't know what it was about that room I loved so much. It had a weird ceiling that was angled and sloped down, allowing for very little head clearance. But there was a window seat, and I would sit there and look outside or read and lose myself in some imaginary adventure. The room hadn't changed much over the years, except to seem even smaller as I grew taller. But there was something comforting about its sameness I appreciated.

I LEFT EARLY the next morning, not wanting to wake Mama B or Paris. As usual, my sleep was short and interrupted by visions. It was always the same vision of a tiny girl with one shoe, but last night the visions were not quite as painful, somehow.

By the time Harley came in, I had sorted through a ton of paperwork, answered all my emails, and was starting to return telephone calls. The first call on my list was to First State Bank President Henrietta Thomas. Mrs. Thomas had left a message asking me to call, and although the bank didn't open for another hour, Mrs. Thomas had assured me she would be in the office by 7:30 a.m. I called and found myself speaking to the lady herself.

"Good morning, Detective Franklin. I was wondering if you had time to stop by my office sometime today." Not waiting for my response, she added, "Will nine thirty work for you?"

"Yes, certainly."

"Good. I will talk to you then. Thank you."

Mrs. Thomas apparently didn't believe in wasting words. I wondered what she had found out, but didn't have time to ponder long because my phone rang. It was Sgt. Harris at the front desk. I was taken aback to hear Mrs. Warren was downstairs asking for me. After informing the sergeant I would be right there, I stood up. Perhaps it was something in my attitude, but Harley asked, "What's going on?"

"Mrs. Tyrone Warren's downstairs."

Harley joined me, and we headed downstairs to discover what had compelled Mrs. Warren to travel two hundred fifty miles to see us just two days after her husband's memorial service.

Mrs. Warren was impeccably dressed in all-white, including a white cane that appeared to have an ivory handle. She was wearing so much jewelry I was concerned about her safety, even in a police station.

"Mrs. Warren, it's a pleasure to see you looking so well. How may we help you?" I decided to get to the point while Harley, ever the gentleman, offered her an arm to lean on as we entered a nearby conference room.

Once seated, we played the generous hosts and offered Mrs. Warren coffee, but she declined.

Now that the time to speak had finally arrived, she seemed reluctant. "You know, I think I would like a cup of coffee if it wouldn't be too much trouble."

"No trouble at all," Harley assured her as he left the room, giving me a wink so subtle I barely noticed. Fortunately, we've worked together enough that I knew he would be taking his time returning with the coffee, first stopping in the room next door to listen.

I thought to repeat myself and ask why she was here, but decided instead to simply sit and wait for her to speak. Silence can be a valuable tool when you are trying to get people to talk. Most people can't stand the silence. Mrs. Warren was no exception. It didn't take long.

"I guess you want to know why I'm here."

"Well, I did think your recent surgery might have you

incapacitated for some time. However, I am glad to see you are able to get around quite nicely."

Her hands twitched. I could see her jaw tighten and a vein on the side of her head start to pulse. I thought she was going to give me a piece of her mind. But in a split second she took a deep breath, sighed, and regained her composure. "Well, it is difficult. I'm in a lot of pain. But I felt compelled to come here."

Taking a handkerchief out of her purse, she put it to her eyes, and then added, "The loss of my husband has hit me so hard I have had trouble sleeping. I can't stop thinking of him and how he died. I just had to come here, to this place where he spent his last days. I felt I needed to see the things he saw, go to the places he went to, and touch the things he touched." Overcome by her emotions, Mrs. Warren stopped and once again put the handkerchief to her eyes.

I'd give the performance quite high marks. She was certainly a first-rate actress. "How can I help you?"

"Well, I wondered if you could share with me a little of my husband's life. Who were his friends? Where did he hang out? Also, I know most of his things were destroyed in the fire, but they can do wonders these days restoring your memories and keepsakes that have been damaged by fires and floods. As his wife, I wondered if I could have his things. They would mean so much to a woman at a time like this."

Now we had arrived at the heart of the matter. Mrs. Warren had come over two hundred miles less than one week after surgery to get her husband's belongings. The idea was touching, but it seemed to me too little too late.

"Well, Mrs. Warren, as you know, your husband was in a fire. What items were not destroyed in the fire were ruined by the water from the hoses as the firemen tried to put out the flames. I've gone through the house and I am sad to say there is virtually nothing left."

"But he must surely have had some other place where he

kept things. I believe he was doing some auditing work while he was here. He must have had an office."

"Unfortunately, we are not at liberty to share any information because this is an ongoing investigation."

She struggled to find some way to get what she was after. Before she could try again, Harley entered with a steaming cup of coffee.

"I wasn't sure if you wanted cream and sugar, so I brought both." Harley dropped a few packets of powdered creamer substitute and sugar on the desk and handed Mrs. Warren coffee that looked strong enough to stand a spoon in.

"Oh … thank you so much." The look on Mrs. Warren's face spoke volumes. She would clearly rather die of thirst than drink anything we might present, but being the trooper she was, she forced herself to take a sip before putting it down on the table.

"Well, I do think I have wasted your time, gentlemen. I had hoped for some … keepsake that might help me through this grieving process. But I see I shall have to satisfy myself with memories."

That last bit was laying it on a little thick, even for her. Harley helped her to her feet and once again provided an arm for Mrs. Warren to lean against. He helped her to the door, but she refused assistance to her car. Back inside, Harley found me at the reception desk watching the security cameras as Mrs. Warren made her way to her car.

"What was that BS? Do you really think she honestly thought we would buy that grieving widow routine?" Harley couldn't hide the disbelief in his voice.

"I guess she did."

"How dumb does she think we are?"

"She must be really desperate to find whatever he left," I said.

"Do you think she broke into Paris' house?" Harley asked.

"No. She may not be a grieving widow, but she did just have surgery and there's no way she could have been responsible for that damage … at least not by herself. But I don't believe she is here by herself. Someone put her up to that charade and I think I know who."

CHAPTER TWELVE

———~~~———

I SAT IN the office of Henrietta Thomas, the president of First State Bank, and faced one of their in-house attorneys, an internal auditor named Dudley Hogan, and an external auditor from Starling and Schuck. The room was large, but with all these people, it felt crowded.

"We've reviewed the information, as you requested. Unfortunately, we have not been able to find anything that will help you with your investigation," Mrs. Thomas said.

"Why the crowd?"

"Frankly, your request was unusual. We wanted to be thorough, and there were a couple of items that made this issue a serious concern."

"I'd like to hear anything you have." I pulled out a notebook and waited for her to elaborate.

Mrs. Thomas nodded to Hogan and waited for the internal auditor to explain.

Hogan didn't fit my preconceived idea of a numbers cruncher. Instead of a blue suit, white shirt, and glasses, he sported an extremely loud Hawaiian shirt, white shorts, and flip-flops. He was in his mid-twenties and was chewing gum as he explained the intricacies of the transactions Thomas Warren had allegedly conducted.

"Detective Franklin, as an internal auditor, my job is to monitor the controls setup in the bank to prevent fraud and ensure security and independence. An external auditor audits the books. I have a background in information security, which is primarily why I was called in for this situation." Hogan chewed his gum faster the deeper he got into the narrative. "So, while we can't find anything specifically illegal in the transactions Mr. Warren conducted, they are suspicious."

The external auditor from Starling and Schuck, a conservative gentleman in his mid-forties with fiery red hair and a face full of freckles, interrupted Hogan. Despite his somewhat youthful appearance, I judged his age to be early to mid-forties. Mallory, as he was introduced to me, was a partner at Starling and Schuck.

"Perhaps I should start. As an external auditor, my job is to validate the financials. One of the unique characteristics here is that Mr. Warren chose to target service organizations with irregular income. Unlike most businesses, churches have incomes that fluctuate greatly, not only from one month to the next but from one week to the next. If the church were in the midst of a fundraiser, the congregation might rally around a specific program and donations increase. This is also an area where cash is often collected, which is harder to trace than checks."

As exciting as Mallory's information was, I found my mind drifting. Having successfully stifled two yawns, I missed the third.

"I don't want to bore you with the details," Mallory said.

"I'm sorry, Mr. Mallory, please forgive me. I had a long night. Please continue."

"Thomas Warrendale was brilliant. He set up a series of accounts and routed funds in and out of banks."

"It's like following an artist," Hogan said. "He used every loophole, every exception, and every trick in the book."

"Are you saying everything Warrendale did was legal?" I asked.

Hogan had the common decency to at least fidget. "Not exactly legal, but not exactly illegal either."

"We traced some of the funds," Mallory said. "We've found a few that are going to offshore banks."

"So?"

Mallory smiled as if humoring a child. "Well, most individuals in St. Joe don't use offshore banks in countries that don't share information with the United States. It's a technique called layering, and it's commonly used by money launderers."

Now I was starting to see where this was heading. "Are you saying Thomas Warrendale was laundering money?"

No one seemed eager to answer the question. Hogan finally responded. "Actually, no."

For one of the first times since his initial introduction, Mr. Reed, the attorney, jumped in. "That's what is so unusual, Detective Franklin. The techniques used are not illegal. But they are unusual, especially when dealing with a local church. Most local churches of this size would not need to have multiple offshore bank accounts."

"Not unless they are trying to hide something," Mallory said.

"These techniques are often used by companies with ties to terrorists and drug cartels," Reed said. "Or by individuals who have been laundering money."

"So, where did the money go?" I said.

Shrugs all around. Finally, Mrs. Thomas said, "Hence, my call to you, Detective Franklin. Obviously, Mr. Warrendale was involved in activities of a suspicious nature. All signs point to some type of deception. I promise to keep you posted as we continue."

AFTER MY VISIT to First State Bank, I swung by one of Paris' salons to see if she was free for lunch. Hair 2 Dye 4 Salon was a flurry of activity.

The salon was located in a transitional neighborhood on River Park Avenue, which featured neither a river nor a park. The side streets were predominately residential, with smaller single-family homes and converted duplexes. In spite of the excessive number of cars that went up and down River Park Avenue, it reminded me of *Cheers*, where everyone knew your name. It was lined with churches and small neighborhood diners, bookstores, and second-hand furniture shops. There was limited parking on the main street, but Paris had a narrow lot behind her shop.

The salon was a small brick storefront with a waiting area that consisted of an old sofa, folding chairs, and tables with outdated hair magazines strewn all over. There was also a television broadcasting one of the many daytime court shows, a pop machine, and vending machines with snacks. I stepped into the inner sanctum, where eight styling stations were arranged. Each station was small but serviceable. Hair dryers lined the walls. All the stylists who worked in the shop were African-American, as were the clients waiting. It was loud, and there was a lot of laughter and talk. I stuck my head in to look around, and one of the stylists came forward and looked me up and down.

Wearing pink flip-flops and smacking her gum, she cocked one hand on her hip and said with the warmth of an iceberg, "Help you?"

I gave her a big smile. "I'm looking for Paris Williams."

"She ain't here today." She smacked her gum and then shuffled back to her customer.

"Do you by any chance know where she is?"

I got a shrug. One of the other stylists, noticing my consternation, put down her curling iron and came over.

"I'm sorry for that. Tamika don't have no manners. My name's Khamela. Can I help you?"

"I'm looking for Paris."

She pulled me aside and whispered, "She at her other salon."

"Can you tell me where it is?"

Reaching into her smock, she pulled out a business card and handed it to me. "It's downtown in the old Fullers Building."

I pocketed the card. "Thank you."

I debated making the trip to the other salon. It wasn't far away, but I was starting to feel self-conscious. I decided to drive by the shop. If I found a parking space, then I would take it as a sign I was meant to go in. But given the time of day and the location, I most likely wouldn't find one and would just keep going.

The old Fullers Building was a converted warehouse downtown on the river. In former days, it was the home of a cheese manufacturer. Fullers Cheese used to be a big favorite in St. Joe and a major employer. In the eighties, the factory closed down the St. Joe location and moved all operations to Wisconsin. The warehouse was converted into a retail space with small specialty shops, a restaurant, and now apparently a hair salon.

Remarkably, a car pulled out of the parking spot immediately in front of the building, and I pulled in. Here was my sign.

Inside the warehouse, I saw a sign that indicated Un Jour à Paris was located down a flight of stairs. I might not have recognized the name if it hadn't been for the small icons of blow dryers, scissors, and curling iron. The entire lower level looked like a Paris street. In direct contrast to Paris' other salon, this one was more upscale—a high-class spa. Plush carpeting, soft music, dim lights, and a pleasant receptionist greeted me enthusiastically.

"*Bonjour, et bienvenue à* Un Jour à Paris. May I help you?"

"I'm looking for Paris Williams."

"Your name, please?"

"Just tell her RJ is here."

"Certainly. Please have a seat, and I'll let her know you're here.

Can I get you a beverage? Coffee? Water? I have candy." She smiled as if enticing me with forbidden fruit. This receptionist was seventy-five if she were a day. She was happy, perky, and sported a bright-red hat. Her enthusiasm was refreshing. The atmosphere was the exact opposite of the other salon.

I took a seat in one of the comfortable guest chairs that lined the waiting area and declined the offer of refreshments. After a few minutes, Paris came out to greet me.

Any doubts about my welcome were quickly dispelled as she smiled, genuinely glad to see me. I found myself smiling too as she gave me a quick kiss. She smelled like orange blossoms.

"What a pleasant surprise. What brings you down? I certainly hope it's not business."

"Actually, I just thought I'd see if you were free for lunch."

I saw the smile vanish as she turned to check with Amy, the perky greeter, who reviewed the appointment book and shook her head.

"Sorry. I have an appointment due here any moment. I wish I could, though. Why don't you come back to my office until she gets here?"

I followed Paris to her office. This salon looked expensive and appeared to cater to all the senses. It was relaxed and Zen-like, with thick, sumptuous drapes, high-tech chairs, soft music, and the light aroma of jasmine and lavender.

Paris' office was a modern, Asian-inspired room with a fountain, a large Palladian-style window, and a high ceiling. On the glass desk was a slim laptop. The office fit the space but contrasted with the old-fashioned, traditional décor I knew filled her home.

"This space is a surprise."

"It's my new venture. I've always wanted to open a high-class, full-service salon. I've only had this shop for six months, but it's doing very well. Of course, the renovations cost a lot more than I originally planned, so I've had to scale back a little."

"Doesn't look like you've scaled back at all. Very elegant and classy."

"People pay for the atmosphere in a place like this, so I had to cut back on services. At the moment, we only offer the basics, hair and nails. But eventually we'll offer spa treatments— Shiatsu massage, facials, the works."

"I'm impressed." And I meant it too. Paris was a good businesswoman and an entrepreneur. Just then her phone rang, and I knew it was her expected client. I started to head to the door as she came around her desk to go out.

"I'm really sorry to be missing out on lunch," she said, "but if you're free later, maybe we can have tea or coffee. I try to take a break around four each day to get refocused."

"Not sure yet, but I'll try."

"Good enough."

I saw Paris' client, an extremely well-preserved older woman, waiting for her in the lobby.

"If you can make it," she said, "I'll be at the St. Joe Chocolate Factory for tea at four. If not, that's fine. I'll eat a chocolate scone for you anyway." She winked at me then turned and escorted her client to the back of the salon. The receptionist gave me a friendly wave on my way out.

I grabbed a quick sandwich and headed back to the precinct to finish up some additional paperwork. The mayor had scheduled a meeting at two, and I wanted to make sure I had all my ducks in a row.

Just before two, Harley, Chief Mike, and I walked over to the mayor's office to meet with the district attorney. It went about as well as expected. He refused to make any commitments, first wanting to ensure they had reviewed all appropriate statutes. Mayor Longbow thanked everyone for their time and ushered us all out.

Back at the precinct, I waded through a ton more paperwork, some related to Thomas Warrendale, some related to other cases. There was no report from Detroit on Tonya Rutherford. If I didn't hear something soon, I was going to have her picked up for questioning.

Though I wondered why she was avoiding answering my questions, I found myself unable to concentrate. Harley asked, "Do you have some place to go? You keep looking at your watch."

I was annoyed with myself. Paris Williams was turning into a big distraction. I thought about her a lot and that wasn't good for a lot of reasons. First, she was part of an ongoing murder investigation, and although that thread was pretty loose, there were still rules about cops getting involved. Second, she was a successful businesswoman and I was … a cop. Apart from the adjunct teaching class I'd just committed to, I didn't have much going for me. A bum leg, nightmares, and insomnia weren't great assets.

"I need to ask Paris Williams some questions … about the case." I saw the grin Harley didn't try to hide and grabbed my keys.

If I was honest with myself, I would have acknowledged I just wanted to see her. But I didn't want to be honest with myself.

I walked into the St. Joe Chocolate Factory at four and saw Paris standing at the counter. Bypassing the people in line, I added a coffee to the order and paid.

The St. Joe Chocolate Factory is a local company that started with a license from SMACU and made three items that were sold through a catalog. A couple of decades later, the St. Joe Chocolate Factory makes over five hundred items and has shops throughout Indiana and Southwest Michigan.

"I'm glad you could make it," Paris said in between bites of her scone and sips of Earl Grey tea.

"Me too. I like this place. It's pretty close to the precinct, but I rarely get to come here. Too busy, I guess."

"I used to be the same way. I worked a lot of hours and drove by this place all the time. I'd say, 'I should take time to go there,' but I never did."

"So, what changed?"

"Me. I went to the doctor and had a physical. She told me

my blood pressure was sky high. My cholesterol was through the roof, and if I didn't slow down, I would be dead before I hit forty. So, I decided to make some changes."

I laughed. "Like coming to the Chocolate Factory every day?"

"You have to start someplace. I needed to slow down and make time for myself. I still work a lot of hours, but I realized I didn't have to do everything myself, and I got some help. I hired a maid service to come in and clean my house once every two weeks. I contracted with someone to do the yard work at home … and someone to do my books."

"Ah, so that's how you got involved with Tyrone Warren?"

"Warren?" Paris looked confused before the light bulb came on. "Oh, yeah, that was his real name, wasn't it? Yeah, I hired him. I started walking in the morning. And I come here every day and treat myself to tea." Leaning in, she whispered, "And if I've been especially good, then tea and a scone."

"Sounds like a plan. How's it working?"

"My cholesterol is down a little. My blood pressure is down a lot. And I have a lot more energy and am enjoying my life more."

"That's good. You should enjoy life. It's pretty short."

"Exactly. I get so busy working and taking care of others, I rarely take care of myself. This is one thing I do just for me. And I'm glad, because otherwise I wouldn't be enjoying a tea break with you." She smiled.

I took a drink of coffee, trying to dial down the enormous grin I knew was plastered on my face.

"How is the investigation going? Or are you not allowed to talk about it?"

"I can't comment on an open investigation."

She nodded.

"I feel like we're missing something, but I can't put my finger on it. Normally, I zero in on someone right away. But this is harder, probably because I know a lot of the people involved."

"It must be hard to suspect people you have known your whole life." Paris sipped her tea.

"Not everyone is a suspect, but you're right. Can you remember anything different or unusual that happened recently?" I asked.

"Like what?"

"It's difficult to believe that Tye Warren—ah, Thomas Warrendale—had been here for almost a year with nothing strange happening. Then all of a sudden, he's murdered. There had to be something that led up to that moment. Something that changed recently and led to his murder. Was there anything different at choir rehearsal?"

Paris thought for a moment, but then shook her head. "Honestly, I can't think of anything different or unusual that happened in the last few weeks. Certainly nothing that would lead to someone getting killed. But maybe if I think about it, I'll remember something."

We sat and talked for about thirty minutes and then Paris looked at her watch and got her things together.

"Well, this has been pleasant. I've enjoyed the company, but I have an appointment in fifteen minutes and have to get back to work."

I walked Paris back to her shop, which was just up the block.

THE REMAINDER OF the afternoon was filled with paperwork. I'd finally gotten a report from Detroit on Tonya Rutherford. Her statement said she'd only seen Thomas Warrendale at church. She also denied she was pregnant by him. Only time would tell. It was possible she was telling the truth, but my money was on Mama B and her gossip network.

"Let's see if we can locate the key players from Warrendale's life. Maybe that'll help eliminate someone."

Harley and I got to work trying to physically locate the people connected to Warrendale. We knew Mrs. Warren was here in the city. We learned Bryce Chandler was out of town on business, although no one at Benson, McCormick, and Chandler would tell us where he was. Harder to find was Mrs. Hartford-Graham. We had Detective Hastings working quietly to see if her location could be pinpointed.

Ascertaining several of the key suspects were no longer in Cleveland wasn't exactly a breakthrough in the investigation. However, it gave us something to focus on. Next, we tried the local hotels. Given the lifestyles of the parties involved, there were only a few I thought likely. St. Joe boasted only two four-star hotels. I couldn't see Mrs. Warren—in her condition—parking her own car or carrying her own bags to her room. She was a valet-parking woman if ever I'd seen one, and there were only two hotels in town that valet-parked. I lucked out and got the right hotel with the first call. Feeling today was my lucky day, I decided to try my luck a little further. Calling back, I learned not only that Mrs. Warren was a guest at the St. Joe Hilton, but Bryce Chandler was also a resident. Imagine that? Two for one.

Mrs. Hartford-Graham wasn't checked into any of the hotels in St. Joe. Two hours later, I learned she also wasn't checked into any hotel within a hundred-mile radius of St. Joe, at least not under her own name. Sometimes in police work what you don't find is just as important as what you do. This wasn't one of those times. There were probably a hundred possibilities for Mrs. Hartford-Graham's whereabouts, including safely back home in Ohio. St. Joe's geographical position—ninety miles from Chicago with its extensive list of grand hotels, stores, theaters, and high-rise condos, thirty miles from the beaches of southwestern Michigan, and a couple of hours from Detroit and Indianapolis, meant she could conceivably be staying within a very short drive of St. Joe. The notion that she might be using a different name also crossed my mind. No, Mrs. Hartford-Graham wasn't going to be easy to track down. Unless Detective Hastings was able to get a visual confirmation she was in Cleveland, I was going to assume she was here. And why not? Everyone else involved in this case had managed to make their way to St. Joe. Why not her? I was becoming a bigger skeptic as each day of this open murder case passed.

The best way to locate her would be to track her credit card use. Most people paid for hotels, flights, and rental cars by credit card. In fact, most of these establishments required one just to make a reservation. I would try to get a subpoena, but that would take a few days. It would give me something to do. However, someone with her resources would easily be able to slide through by using cash.

A middle-class person like Mrs. Warren and an upper-middle-class person like Bryce Chandler most likely flew first class. But the truly rich either owned their own jet or they knew someone who did. Bryce Chandler and Mrs. Warren might stay at the nicest hotels in whatever city they chose. The Mrs. Hartford-Grahams of this world owned the hotel. Of course, if Bryce Chandler or Mrs. Warren were looking for something, they could come to St. Joe and look personally. But Mrs. Hartford Graham was different. Would she come herself, or would she pay someone to come in her place? Someone like her man, Gerald. Or she might have hired someone else to find whatever it was they were all looking for. Regardless of whether Mrs. Hartford-Graham was in St. Joe, the bottom line was, she had to be someplace. I was determined to find her, so I kept working.

"I'm starving. Let's get something to eat." Harley stretched and rubbed his eyes.

I didn't say a word, just grabbed my coat and stood up.

Harley and I had fallen into a routine. Most of the time we didn't need to talk anymore. During times of stress we just put everything on autopilot and sat back and observed. This was one of those times.

Without a word, Harley and I got into my car and I drove to Marty's. Marty's was a local diner that had been in St. Joe for well over fifty years. The food was good, not great. The diner was clean and fast. We could also sit quietly and talk undisturbed. It was never too crowded and stayed open twenty-four hours, which was great for cops. And it was close to the precinct, so there were always a ton of cops. If the number of police cars parked outside was any indication, it was one of the safest places in the city at any given point.

It wasn't until we had both eaten and sat drinking our coffee that we talked about the case.

"Maybe she isn't here."

I knew Harley was referring to Mrs. Hartford-Graham.

"Do you have any other ideas?"

"I'm just saying she could be anywhere in the entire world. And if she doesn't want to be found, there's no freakin' way we're going to find her."

"I know. But, do you have any other ideas? Because if you do, let's hear them," My tone wasn't quite as harsh as the words imply.

"Maybe we could set a trap for them."

"What kind of trap?"

"I don't know. If we knew what they were looking for, we could pretend we had it and then ... never mind."

I knew Harley was as frustrated as I was, but there was something in what he said.

"Maybe we've been looking at this all wrong." I wasn't sure of where I was going with this, but his idea of setting a trap had given me an idea.

"Okay. How should we be looking at it?" Harley asked.

"Maybe we need to focus on the item they're all looking for. If we find it, then we find the killer."

"Sounds good, except for one small problem. We have no idea what it is."

"Maybe we do know but just don't know that we know."

Harley shrugged. "Same thing as not knowing."

"No, it isn't. It's a puzzle. We just have to fit all the pieces together."

Harley and I talked through what we knew and what we thought we knew. We made some assumptions. Policemen don't like assumptions. You know what they say about "assume." In addition to making an ass out of you and me, to do so can also get your case thrown out of court. We had been conditioned to work with facts. Facts hold up in a court of law every time, but we didn't have all the facts.

We started with the assumption that Thomas Warrendale took something. Whatever it was, it was important enough to someone that they were willing to kill for it. We assumed he took it when he left Cleveland and came to St. Joe. We also assumed his wife, Bryce Chandler, and Mrs. Hartford-Graham all knew what *it* was and they all wanted it. If all these assumptions were true, Warrendale had hidden it and they hadn't found it. If they had, they wouldn't be in St. Joe. One fact was Thomas Warrendale stole money from the church and from Paris' Salon and had set up offshore accounts. Why? Force of habit or was he planning to relocate again?

When we finished talking, we weren't a lot closer to a solution, but at least we had some additional leads to follow instead of hunting down an old woman. Harley was going to look into the money angle further. I decided to try and tackle Thomas Warrendale from a different angle—a spiritual one.

IT WAS SATURDAY night, and that meant choir practice at FBC. The Gospel Chorus rehearsed from six to seven, and the Senior Choir rehearsed from seven to eight. I wondered who'd take control of the choir now. I arrived at the church just as the Senior Choir was finishing and found Mrs. Miller-Jones had come out of retirement to help out in this time of need. Mrs. Miller-Jones was a legend at FBC. She had directed the FBC choirs for well over fifty years and had retired a year ago. The church had been looking for a replacement for three months when Thomas Warrendale landed at FBC.

I knew Reverend Hamilton liked to listen to the choirs

rehearse, and also knew I'd find him in his office in the lower level sitting at his desk. Seeing me, he smiled and waved me into his glass box. Unlike the warm, book-lined office of the rectory, this office was an addition meant to give the pastor a place to pray and meet with people without having to track back and forth to the rectory.

"RJ, what a pleasant surprise. Come in and have a seat. You just missed an excellent concert."

I entered and sat in one of the modern chairs.

"Sorry to bother you so late on a Saturday evening. I don't want to disturb your preparation."

"I've already got my outline for tomorrow. I was just enjoying the beautiful singing. It really does my soul good to hear it. What can I do for you?"

"I was just wondering what you can tell me about Thomas Warrendale. Knowing you as I do, I can't believe you hired him as the minister of music without thoroughly checking his background."

Reverend Hamilton sat quietly for a few minutes. "As you know, the conversations between a man and his spiritual advisor are considered sacred. But, given that the man is dead, I believe a little latitude is in order."

"So, you knew who Warrendale was?"

"I did."

I was astounded. Reverend Hamilton saw my reaction and immediately added, "But I didn't know he'd done anything illegal. I knew his real name was Tyrone Warren and not Thomas Warrendale. I knew he came from Cleveland and he wanted to leave his old life. That's not a crime."

"If he had done nothing wrong, why come here and hide?"

"Many people run from their pasts. It doesn't make them criminals. Thomas Warrendale and I talked. He'd been successful and gotten caught in the trappings of success. He said he wanted to start over. He said he'd found God."

Something in Reverend Hamilton's words and tone alerted

me that there was more here than he was letting on. "He *said* he found God," I repeated, "but you didn't believe him?"

Reverend Hamilton paused and then shook his head. "No. I didn't."

"Why?"

He looked at me, puzzled by the question, then shrugged.

"No," I said. "That's not good enough. There must have been something that made you doubt his sincerity. What was it?"

He looked down and I could almost see the wheels turning in his mind. "I can't put my finger on it. It was just a feeling. I didn't have any proof he wasn't telling the truth. I knew he was weak where women were concerned. But, none of the women he approached were married and they were all adults. I didn't know he was married and had left his wife. I certainly wouldn't have allowed him to hold a position of authority if I had."

"But what about the money? You knew something wasn't right there. You're the one who got me involved in the first place."

Reverend Hamilton looked me in the eye for several seconds. "I did not *know*. I had suspicions. I prayed and asked God for guidance and then Warrendale was murdered. I asked you to investigate, but I shouldn't have put you in that position." His eyes pleaded. "I went to the trustees. We've hired someone to look into it. If they confirm money is missing, then we'll look into what steps to take next. I'd prefer to handle this within the family if we can. But if not, then we'll do what needs to be done." Reverend Hamilton sighed.

"Did Warrendale tell you why he came? What happened? What led him to leave Cleveland?"

"No. He didn't. I hoped one day he might confide in me. Unfortunately, he never got the chance." He looked at me, and I saw sadness in his eyes. Here was a shepherd who'd lost a sheep, and apparently the loss was weighing heavily on him. With a shake of his head, he got up and walked out. I used to think Reverend Hamilton had X-Ray vision and could see into souls. I guess he could and he did. As I got into my car to leave, I found myself hoping he had looked into my soul.

I decided to call it a day and headed to Mama B's. If I was lucky, Paris would be home, although I doubted she would be home that quickly. One of the valuable pieces of information I learned during our talk this afternoon was that hairdressers often worked late to accommodate their clients who had full-time jobs and couldn't get their hair or nails done until they got off work at five or six. With two salons, Paris typically didn't get home before ten or eleven after she'd closed the shop and finished up all her paperwork. I wondered if she had time for something or someone more in her life.

I PULLED UP to Mama B's and saw her and Mrs. Green on the front porch watching the game across the alley and waving at cars that honked as they drove down the busy street in front of the rec center.

When I went up the steps, Mrs. Green didn't say a word. Instead, she got up, gave me a big hug, and kissed my cheek as she whispered in my ear, "Thank you! Thank you! Thank you!"

"Mrs. Green, I didn't do much."

"I don't want to hear it. You were there and I praise God you were there. I don't know what …." Mrs. Green had to choke back the tears, and I gave her a handkerchief and helped her back into her seat.

"It's okay. I truly didn't do anything. Chris was merely picked up as a witness."

"You did more than you can ever know. I haven't had one problem with that boy. He is a changed young man. He is respectful. He isn't hanging out with those crazy fools all day and all night anymore. I have my boy back." At this, Mrs. Green rocked as she cried.

"He's a good boy. He was just trying to fit in. I don't think you'll have any more problems with him." I patted her back and tried to comfort her, but these were tears of joy.

"I better not have another second of grief from that boy," Mrs. Green sniffed. "I told him if he got in trouble again, I'd take my husband's old gun and shoot him dead myself."

Mama B rocked and smiled as Mrs. Green unburdened her soul and thanked God, me, and Reverend Hamilton, not necessarily in that order.

"Dorothea, I told you everything would be okay," Mama B added.

"Well, I pray for him every day and every night. God knows I would go through fire for that boy. I just wish I could knock some sense into him sometimes."

After a while, Mama B had Mrs. Green laughing rather than crying, so I figured it was safe to go inside. "What's for dinner?"

"I don't know. I didn't feel like cooking today."

That stopped me in my tracks. "What's wrong? Is your blood pressure up? Did you check your sugar? Are you feeling okay?"

"Stop firing questions at me like I'm some kind of criminal." Mama B tried to sound stern, but I saw a glint in her eye as she kept on rocking. "I'm fine. Sometimes you fuss like an old woman." She and Mrs. Green both laughed at that.

"Dorothea brought me some sweet peas and I'll snap those and let them soak for tomorrow."

"Well, what about the chicken I saw in the fridge? Is any left?"

"Well, yes, but not enough for everyone."

Mama B rocked for a while and smiled. "Maybe I have a date?" Mama B and Mrs. Green both laughed. Eventually Mama B said, "You got police driving by the house every few hours, and one of them is Eugene King, Marla's boy. You remember him?"

I shook my head. Mama B was always trying to jog my memory about people I hadn't seen in more than twenty years.

"Well, Marla used to be on the Missions Board with me. Her boy Eugene is a policeman now. He stopped by earlier and we talked for a minute. He said he would come back when he got off work, so he could tell me how Marla's doing. You know she moved down to Memphis to stay with her sister after she had that stroke a few years ago."

"Mama B, you do not have to feed the entire city." I tried to sound stern but she wasn't paying any attention to me.

"He didn't have time to eat earlier. I just gave him a plate to take back."

Mama B laughed as I leaned against the rail on the front porch, trying to figure out what she had up her sleeve.

"So that chicken in the fridge is spoken for. I guess you and Paris will just have to go out someplace tonight and get something."

So that was it. Mama B was plotting.

"I don't think she'll be back until late. She'll probably grab something fast on her way home."

"Uh-huh, that's what she said when I talked to her earlier. But I wasn't sure what I felt like eating then. So, I told her to check with me first. I told her I might want her to bring me something too. So she said she'd wait." Mama B grinned and rocked.

Mrs. Green laughed and then started to sing, pretending, not very convincingly, she had no idea what was going on:

> Why should I feel discouraged, why should the shadows come
> Why should my heart be lonely, and long for heaven and home?

"Mama B, I don't need a matchmaker."

Mama B just rocked and smiled while Mrs. Green kept on singing.

I gave up and went into the house. As the door closed, Mama B yelled after me, "I bought you a new shirt. It's hanging up on the door in your room. I think it will look really nice on you."

I ignored the laugher I heard from the front porch and went

upstairs to my room. I refused to give her the satisfaction of asking how she got to the store or why she bought me a new shirt. That's what she wanted me to do, but I wouldn't fall for it. I can't remember a time in all my years of knowing her when Mama B didn't have a full-course dinner in the fridge or freezer. She came from that old school where women actually baked and made sure there was a cake or a pie in the pie shelf in the event of company.

It was a very nice shirt. Mama B knew my style. I tried it on, and she was right: it did look good on me. I decided to take a shower. Since we were being sent out on a date, I might as well make the best of it.

I took my time with my shower. The poor water pressure was always an issue when you had to compete with others in the house. In the evening, there would be no other people to compete with, so I was free to shower as long as I wanted.

By the time I was dressed, I heard voices downstairs, which indicated Paris was home. I wondered if Mama B had purchased clothes for her also. I went down to join the crowd.

Paris noticed my new attire and lifted an eyebrow. "You look nice. What's the special occasion?"

"Apparently, I have a dinner date."

Paris looked puzzled and then embarrassed. "I'm sorry, I didn't realize …."

I could see she was confused. "With you."

"Me?" I saw the relief on her face, and I felt a moment of pride.

"Didn't Mama B tell you? She plans to feed our dinner to the patrolman assigned to drive by the house."

"You're serious?" Paris asked.

"Oh yeah, she's serious. So you better go get changed so we can get out of here."

Paris went upstairs to get dressed and I sat on the front porch and watched the basketball game and listened to Mama B and Mrs. Green gossip. If I were lucky, I'd pick up something that would help with my investigation. Sitting there brought back memories from my childhood. I'd spent many a lazy evening and summer afternoon on that front porch.

It didn't take Paris long, and she came downstairs wearing a skirt and blouse. It wasn't a fancy outfit, but it seemed bright and fresh and appropriate.

We said our goodbyes and then got into my car.

"Do you have a taste for anything special?" I asked.

"You pick. I chose Cesselly's."

"What about Roma's?"

"Sweet potato fries and ice cream sounds fantastic. Good choice."

Roma's was a small Italian restaurant on the south side of town. It had great food, and every day there was a new featured ice cream. They were well known for the sweet potato fries, which weren't greasy, and had an incredible dip that I hadn't yet figured out.

We spent the evening talking and getting better acquainted. Paris was one of four children. Her mother had always wanted to travel but never got the opportunity, so she named her children after all the places she longed to see. London, Paris, and Savanna were the girls, and Rome was the youngest and the only boy.

"It could have been worse," Paris said. "She could have wanted to travel to Guam or Belgium." She had a great laugh.

"Is your mother still alive?"

"She passed away about a year ago."

"Did she ever get to see any of those places?"

"When we found out she was dying, we wanted to take her traveling. We pooled our money and planned to take her around the world. But when it got time to go, she didn't want to. She was afraid reality wouldn't live up to her imagination and didn't want to die disillusioned. So, my sister and I went together."

Paris paused and stared into the distance before shaking off the momentary melancholy. "What about you? Do you have brothers and sisters?"

I told her about my sister, Caroline. My mother was a big John F. Kennedy fan, and my sister was named after Caroline Kennedy.

"Does she live here in St. Joe?"

"They live in Houston. She's married with two kids, Morgan aged ten and Madison aged seven going on forty."

"How cute. Do you have pictures?"

"Of course. I'd be a horrible uncle without pictures." I pulled out my phone and showed off pictures of my niece and nephew, which she oohed and aahed over. Then she pulled out pictures of her family, including all eight nieces and nephews.

Before we knew it, we were the last ones in the restaurant. I paid the check, and we left.

It was a pleasant evening, and I enjoyed the drive back to Mama B's. The house was dark; Mama B had to already be in bed. I unlocked the door, and we went inside, careful not to make too much noise since Mama B's bedroom was just off the living room. Her door was closed, but she had left a lamp on to help us see our way in the darkness. Inside, Paris turned to go upstairs, and I grabbed her and kissed her. It was intense and passionate, and her response matched my own. It seemed only a second before my cellphone rang.

"This had better be good," I pulled myself away.

It was Harley. Someone had broken into Paris' other salon, but were scared off by the burglar alarm. The conversation didn't take long. I filled in the gaps that Paris hadn't heard from Harley's side of the conversation.

"Nothing was taken, and best I can tell, there was no damage. The burglar was frightened off by your alarm system."

In her eyes, I saw the storm of anger rising. "They aren't going to stop until they find whatever it is they think I have. I wish I knew what it was because I'd just give it to them."

She was tired and scared. She started to shake and I held her in my arms until the shaking stopped.

After a long moment, she pulled herself together and looked at me expectantly.

"I'll find them. I promise."

Death went out to the preacher's house,

Come and go with me

The preacher cried out, I'm ready to go,

I've got my travellin' shoes

Got my travellin' Shoes, Got my travellin' shoes

Preacher cried out, I'm ready to go,

I've got my travellin' shoes

CHAPTER THIRTEEN

———∼∼∼———

I RARELY MAKE it to church two consecutive Sundays. I'm doing well if I go twice in the same month, so for me to not only make it to church two weeks in a row, but to make it to the early service two weeks in a row, was a miracle of God. A miracle, I might add, that didn't go unnoticed. There were more than a few raised eyebrows as members of the congregation greeted me. I wouldn't have gone to the early service, but Paris was singing, and I wanted to hear her.

I knew she could sing well from the little bit I'd overheard in my living room a few nights ago, but with the Gospel Chorus backing her up, she was amazing.

Each one of the choirs was good in their own way. The Senior Choir sang a lot of spirituals, hymns, and old-time gospel favorites. The Children's Choir sang cute little songs that brought a smile. The Young Adult Choir consisted of the teenage set and sang the hip-hop-inspired and gospel-rap tunes. They were loud, energetic, and flashy. The Gospel Chorus was the twenty-to-forty-year-old bunch, and they typically stuck to contemporary gospel. All the members, as far as I could tell, were excellent singers, and were the most requested for special concerts and singing engagements.

Paris was good, and I'm not saying that simply because I was falling for her. She had a deep, rich voice, but she also had a good range and could sing quite high when she wanted. The song had a blues/jazz feel to it, and Paris was remarkable. I, like most of the congregation, found myself standing and clapping before she finished her last note.

The major differences between the early service and the other services were fewer songs, fewer people, and a shorter duration—only an hour and a half. So the early service kept to a pretty tight schedule. The later service often spilled over to a later time if the Spirit moved. Paris confessed that was one of the reasons she preferred the early service. The hardest part, of course, was getting up. But since my accident and the lack of sleep, I was up early anyway.

Reverend Hamilton preached a message about forgiveness, and I wondered if it was directed at anyone in particular. He cited the text in the Gospel of John where the Pharisees attempt to discredit Jesus. In the story, the Pharisees bring a woman to Jesus who has been caught in the act of adultery. According to Mosaic Law, this act was punishable by stoning. When the Pharisees challenges Jesus to judge the woman, Jesus responds by saying, "He who is without sin among you, let him cast the first stone." The people pressing him are so troubled by their own consciences, they leave. When Jesus finds himself alone with the woman, he asks who her accusers are. She replies, "No man, Lord." Jesus then says, "Neither do I condemn thee: go and sin no more."

It's possible the message wasn't directed toward anyone in particular, but I still felt like those Pharisees and wanted to depart. I intended to stop by the rectory later, after Reverend Hamilton was done. I hoped I hadn't been too forceful or judgmental last night when talking to him. For me, the law was clear. You steal, you go to jail. That was what the Oath of Honor I'd sworn to required. But I realized that Reverend Hamilton dealt in a lot of gray. The money was important, but it wasn't his primary focus. He was concerned about the eternal soul.

After the service, I made my way into the vestibule when what to my wondering eye should appear but a white Mercedes and Mrs. Tyrone Warren. I watched as Mrs. Warren parked in one of the handicapped spaces near the front door and hobbled up the stairs into the church.

Now, I supposed she might still be looking for comfort that would help her recover from the death of her dear husband, but my cynical nature wondered if there wasn't a bit more to it.

I'd planned my Sunday differently. I'd intended to take Mama B and Paris out for brunch at Cesselly's, but those plans would have to wait.

I hurried out the door and found Mama B sitting on the church porch. Just as I arrived back on the steps, Paris came out with her choir robe in hand.

"I'm sorry, but I have something I have to take care of," I said. "Can you please take my car and drive Mama B home?"

Surprised, Paris hesitated about a half second before replying, "Sure. No problem. Would you like us to wait for you for lunch? Or do you want me to come back and get you?"

"There's no need to come back for me. I can walk. I'm not sure how long I'll be, though, so you might want to go on without me."

"That's okay. We'll wait a little while, but if we get hungry, we'll go on."

With that, Paris helped Mama B down the stairs to the car, and I went back into the church to track down Mrs. Warren.

I tried the sanctuary first but didn't see her. Everyone was getting ready for the next service, so I went downstairs, where I saw Mrs. Warren sitting in the office with Reverend Hamilton. Now, this was tricky. They were obviously involved in a conversation. I couldn't very well interrupt. Well, I could, but it might shut down the conversation, which was the only reason I was there. Just then, Reverend Hamilton looked up and noticed me. He smiled and waved for me to enter.

"RJ, it's so good to see you. I believe you know Mrs. Warren?"

"How are you, Mrs. Warren? I'm surprised to see you here."

Mrs. Warren did not look pleased to see me, although she plastered a fake smile on her face and extended her hand.

"Yes, Detective Franklin and I know each other. He's investigating Tye's death. I had the pleasure of speaking with him just the other day."

Reverend Hamilton, who was removing his clerical robe, motioned for me to sit. "Mrs. Warren was just sharing with me how difficult it has been to grieve for her husband without having his things." Reverend Hamilton was masterfully filling me in on their conversation. Mrs. Warren didn't seem pleased. In fact, she seemed downright angry.

"I shared the same thing with Detective Franklin just the other day," she said, "but he was not able to assist me. I was hoping you, Reverend Hamilton, a man of God and Tye's spiritual confidant, would be able to help."

She was laying it on pretty thick. Thankfully Reverend Hamilton was intelligent enough to recognize her flattery for what it was.

"I will certainly help you in any way I can." This drew a smug smile from Mrs. Warren, which was quickly wiped away when Reverend Hamilton added, "I'm a certified grief counselor, and I will gladly spend time sharing words of comfort from the scripture to help you during this incredibly difficult period."

Mrs. Warren's eyes got large. She had not seen that coming.

Reverend Hamilton grabbed his calendar and flipped through it. "We'll need a few hours for the initial consultation and perhaps additional time depending on how things go. How long will you be in town, Mrs. Warren?"

"Well, I don't know exactly. My plans are still very much up in the air. I had thought I might return home tomorrow. I don't think I can commit to counseling sessions."

Mrs. Warren stood and inched her way out of the room. If she weren't still recovering from surgery, she might have run.

"I'm sorry to hear that, Mrs. Warren," Reverend Hamilton said. "I believe I can help you. The Word of God is a great comforter during times of grief. However, I understand if you must leave." As she continued her retreat, he added in a louder voice, "I hope you'll call me if you do feel you need counseling. I'm always here for those in need."

Mrs. Warren had made it out of the office and was almost at the point where she had to shout to make herself heard over the noise of children running around in the church basement. "Thank you, Reverend."

I have never seen anyone make such a hasty exit, and once we were sure Mrs. Warren was out of earshot, we gave in to the hilarity of the situation.

Reverend Hamilton chuckled to himself. "That has to be a record for me. I don't think I've ever cleared a room quite that fast before."

"What do you suppose she wanted?"

"You're the detective. She started asking about any items her husband might have left behind, keepsakes or mementos she could have to help in her grieving process. But that was just a lot of hooey. She's looking for something."

"Any idea what she's trying to find?"

He shook his head. "No, but whatever it is, she must believe he left it here. And she's scared."

"What makes you say that?"

Reverend Hamilton stopped and turned to look me full in the face. "People think ministers are these sheltered creatures who don't know much about life, but I've seen fear many a time. And that woman is scared."

I returned Reverend Hamilton's stare. "Anyone who thinks you 'don't know much' is a fool."

He let out a hearty laugh. Despite our disagreements, Reverend Hamilton knew I respected him.

Now, to solve this murder, all I had to do was figure out what Thomas Warrendale had that everyone wanted badly enough to kill for.

We shook hands, and I left him to prepare for the next service. I was tempted to stay and keep an eye on Mrs. Warren to see how she interacted with the other members of the congregation. FSB was a far cry from the conservative church she was accustomed to in Cleveland. Don't get me wrong. The members of FSB were not rustic, uneducated backwoods folk. But the atmosphere at FSB was certainly a great deal homier than what I think Mrs. Warren would have preferred.

A quick scan of the sanctuary showed no signs of her, and a glance in the parking lot confirmed the white Mercedes was missing. Mrs. Warren was gone. I was relieved I wouldn't have to sit through the service a second time. Twice in one day might have sent me over the edge.

Walking down the alley to Mama B's house took less than ten minutes. When I arrived, both Mama B and Paris had changed into their Sunday afternoon attire and were relaxing on the front porch, drinking lemonade, and watching the morning basketball games at the rec center.

I hurried up the steps to the porch. "You ladies seem relaxed. Just let me change real quick and we're off for brunch."

"Sister Bethany is trying to bail on us," Paris said. "Maybe you can talk some sense into her."

I stopped in my tracks. "What's wrong? You feeling okay?"

"I'm fine," Mama B said. "And you can stop asking me every two seconds how I feel."

"Then why don't you want to go? You ashamed to be seen in public with us?"

"You hush, boy." Mama B rocked. "You don't need an old woman holding you down."

Paris smiled. "You may be right. RJ, do you know any old women?"

Mama B had a big laugh over that. I loved watching her when she was really laughing. Her whole body shook.

I ran inside to get out of my Sunday suit and pull on some casual linen slacks, a lightweight sweater, and loafers. Then, on my way down, I grabbed Mama B's purse and sweater from the dresser in her bedroom and went outside, closing the door behind me. There was only one way to deal with Mama B when she was being stubborn, and that was to bulldoze her.

After handing Mama B her purse, I held out my arm to help her out of her rocker. She rocked a little more, but then gave up and pushed herself out of her chair.

"I was just getting comfortable here. You know you don't want me tagging along."

"I have no idea what she's talking about, do you, Paris?"

"No, sir. Let's go. I'm starving."

Paris climbed into the back of the car, and although Mama B made a feeble attempt at protest, it was easier for Paris to get in the back than Mama B. I got her settled in the passenger seat and we were off.

On Sundays, Cesselly's offered a jazz champagne brunch that was fantastic. There was everything from bacon and hash browns to shrimp and grits and prime rib. Mimosas were included and a jazz pianist played while we enjoyed good food, great music, and excellent conversation. I can say I thoroughly enjoyed the meal, and even Mama B, who can be extremely particular about food when eating out, enjoyed herself. Cesselly's was relatively new but was gaining a lot of notice around the community. Once again, it was full but not packed. There was a steady stream of customers who seemed to know either me, Paris, Mama B, or some combination thereof. I think Mama B enjoyed the atmosphere and the socialization most of all. It wasn't long before the two owners, who were filling in by taking coats, had pulled up chairs and were sharing funny stories from their time as touring jazz musicians. Time flew by, and three hours later, I noticed almost everyone had gone.

We reluctantly got up to leave. The owners not only made Mama B promise to return, but gave her a card for a free meal.

After brunch, we went to the same river-front park where Paris and I had gone last week. Mama B sat on a bench and fed the ducks and geese popcorn I purchased from a street vendor. Paris and I followed the same path as before along the river and across the bridge. It was a beautiful Sunday afternoon.

"I'm so glad we got to come today. I was afraid you were going to stand us up."

"Not likely. Mama B deserved a day out."

We walked in companionable silence for a few minutes before I asked, "How close were you to Warrendale?"

I felt Paris stiffen and then she stopped and turned to face me.

"What are you asking?"

I could tell she was angry, but I needed to know the answer for several reasons, one of which had nothing to do with the investigation. "I'm not accusing you of anything. I'm just trying to find some answers."

She took a few minutes to think and then shrugged. "We weren't close at all. I barely knew him. I knew he was a CPA and he did the books for the church. That's about it."

I was curious as to why anyone would break into both of her salons and her home.

"Did you meet him often? I mean did he come to your house or to the salon?"

"We only met a few times outside of church. He was the choir director and I sing in the choir. But you know how big FBC is. The Gospel Chorus has over fifty members and not all of us sing at every service. I usually sing at the early service. Others only sing at the later services."

We continued to walk as we talked, but the mood had completely changed. I wished I had delayed this conversation, but now that we were in the middle of it, I had no choice but to continue.

Paris went on, "We usually met at my house or one of the salons. He didn't live far from me, so it was more convenient to just meet at home. Plus, that's where most of the records were. I took almost everything I needed home so I could work on the books from there rather than staying late at the salons."

"Did he ever give you any boxes or papers or computer disks ... anything?"

She thought about it for a few minutes before shaking her head. "No. Nothing I can remember. It would help if I knew what you're looking for though."

"If I knew what we're looking for, we would have this case solved. Did he ever talk to you about ... his past?"

She shook her head. "No. I had no idea he was married or anything. I don't think any of the other choir members did either. I know he liked to flirt. Several of the women, especially the really young ones, had crushes on him. But that's natural."

"Really?"

"Sure. It happens all the time. I'd bet not only the choir members but half the women in the congregation fantasized about him."

"Fantasies. Hmm ... really?"

"Why do you seem so surprised? He wasn't ugly or deformed." She looked at me.

"I didn't say he was."

Things were finally lightening up.

After a long moment, she added, "I didn't say *I* fantasized about him."

"You didn't have to say it." I laughed, and after an indignant look, she laughed too.

"He wasn't my type."

I stopped and stared at her. "And what is your type?"

Paris blushed and looked away shyly. "Maybe I'll tell you someday, but not today. Today I am enjoying a pleasant walk with a very nice police officer."

We finished our walk hand in hand.

* * *

THE NEXT MORNING, Harley and I presented ourselves in the lobby of the Hilton Hotel. We showed our badges to the twenty-something clerk behind the desk, who decided perhaps he could override hotel policy and give us Mrs. Warren's room number after all.

Mrs. Warren was staying in the penthouse suite. We waited until the clerk was distracted and made for the elevator.

Harley let out a low whistle as we stepped out of the elevator. The Hilton wasn't a shabby hotel under any circumstances, but the penthouse suites were in a class all their own. The carpet was thicker, and the lighting was nicer. The pictures on the walls were all numbered editions and the atmosphere made you want to whisper.

Mrs. Warren opened the door in a long, white negligee. "What took you so long, I …."

At least she had the decency to blush. After a moment of hesitation and shock, she quickly hobbled off to the bathroom and came back in a robe. "Well, you might as well shut the door and come in."

With that hearty welcome, Harley and I closed the door and entered the suite. Mama B's house would have fit inside this suite at least once, maybe twice. We followed Mrs. Warren as far as the living room/dining room area, where she took a seat on the sofa. *Perturbed* didn't begin to scratch the surface of her demeanor. I decided to launch right in, hoping her anger might make her less guarded.

"Are we interrupting anything?" I asked as innocently as I could.

Mrs. Warren scowled. "Of course not. What could you possibly be interrupting?" Sarcasm was not an attractive cloak for Mrs. Warren.

"I only asked because when you opened the door, you looked as though you were expecting someone."

"I ordered room service. I thought you were the waiter. That's all." She couldn't even look me in the eye.

"In that case, do you mind if we sit down and ask you a few questions?"

She obviously did mind very much. She looked at the gold Rolex on her arm and sighed. "I guess I have a little time. As you can see by the way I'm dressed, I was just about to turn in. I'm very tired."

"Before you ate?" I asked.

"I get tired very easily after my surgery. I got tired of waiting and had just decided to get ready for bed. I don't think that's a crime, not even in St. Joseph, Indiana, is it?"

Harley took this opportunity to jump into the conversation. Summoning all of his Southern charm, he said, "Of course not, ma'am. We just wanted to ask one or two more questions if you're feeling up to it. May I get you something—a pillow or a glass of water?"

Sometimes he can really come on a little strong with the Southern-gentleman thing. But Mrs. Warren, like most women, ate it up. She actually smiled.

"No, but thank you so much. I think I'll be fine *now*." The implication being she wasn't fine while I was talking, but she was now that Harley was taking charge.

I moved away from them to look out the window while Harley sat at her feet and asked her, "Mrs. Warren, we were wondering if your husband mentioned any papers or files he might have had in his possession?"

I waited just a moment for the response when I heard Harley say, "Mrs. Warren, are you okay? You don't look very well." The anxiety made me turn to see Mrs. Warren, who had suddenly lost all color and slumped back onto the sofa.

"Are you okay? Do you need a doctor?" Harley's concern was obvious. Mrs. Warren wasn't faking. She wasn't that good of an actress to pull this scene off.

"Mrs. Warren, do you have any medications? Is there anything we can get for you?" I asked.

She nodded.

I was already on my way to the bathroom. I barely had time to register the fact there was a man's travel case with razor and clippers on the counter before I filled a glass with water and rushed back.

"Here, drink this." I handed her the glass, and she gulped it down while Harley tried to get her consent to call an ambulance.

After finishing most of the water, Mrs. Warren seemed slightly more in control of herself. Her hand was steadier as she gave the glass back to me. She shook her head and whispered, "No. I don't want an ambulance. I don't need a doctor. I'm so sorry. I don't know what came over me. I just suddenly felt light-headed and ill."

At that moment, there was a knock at the door. I didn't think it possible, but Mrs. Warren got paler. Her eyes darted back and forth and she made an attempt to rise, but Harley stopped her.

"No, ma'am. You stay right there. I'll be more than happy to get that. It's probably just your room service."

Harley rushed to the door and opened it to Mr. Bryce Chandler.

He looked even more shocked to see us than Mrs. Warren had been. Surprise, anger, and frustration all registered on his face in less than half a second before he said, "Oh, is anything wrong with Mrs. Warren?"

She had recovered her wits enough to yell, "Bryce. I'm in here!"

Harley stepped aside as Bryce Chandler hurried into the room. Seeing Mrs. Warren on the sofa, he halted.

She held out a hand as he advanced. "Thank you so much for coming by on such short notice." Mrs. Warren was providing the excuse and Bryce Chandler seized on it.

"Well, of course. When I got your call, I hurried here at once. It's the least I can do for such old friends as you and ... and Tye. Are you okay?"

"Yes. I just had a bad spell, and these two policemen were kind enough to look after me, but I really would like to lie down. Can I trouble you to help me?"

"It's no trouble at all." He turned to us. "Gentlemen, Mrs. Warren isn't well. I think it would be best if you left. I can help her back to bed."

I'll just bet you could help her to bed, I thought. We couldn't force her to answer our questions now, and as soon as we left, she'd brief Bryce Chandler.

Harley tried one last time. "Mrs. Warren, are you sure you wouldn't like me to call a doctor for you? You looked deathly ill a moment ago when we were talking about your husband's books."

Harley had gotten a strike in, and we both watched for a reaction. Mrs. Warren was on guard this time, and Bryce Chandler was a much cooler customer. However, his hands tensed. A vein pulsed on the side of his head.

"No. No. That won't be necessary. I just wasn't feeling well and I haven't eaten. I was just a little light-headed. That's all."

"Well, if you're sure." Harley was so good at that charming routine, I almost believed his show of sympathy and compassion.

"Thank you both so much for your concern, but I just want to lie down."

With that, Harley and I made our exit from the luxurious penthouse suite of Mrs. Warren. Neither of us said a word as we walked down the hall and rode in the elevator.

I'd have bet my pension that Mrs. Tye Warren and Mr. Bryce Chandler were both staying in the same room. Apparently, his wife didn't review the credit card statements or maybe he didn't care if she did.

HARLEY AND I went back to the precinct. Obviously, we'd hit a nerve with Chandler and Mrs. Warren. They were both in town and could have broken into Paris' Salon. Mrs. Warren's alibi was tight; she couldn't have killed her husband. But Bryce Chandler was another story. He was starting to look like an excellent suspect.

We spent the rest of the day in the never-ending battle to keep up with paperwork. Solving one case didn't necessarily mean an end to the paperwork and we both had a lot to do. By the time I looked up, it was late. I got another message from First State Bank, but given the hour, I'd have to call them first thing tomorrow.

It was late and my day had started very early. I decided to swing by the salon. I told myself I was checking on the shop. After all, it had been broken into just two days earlier. I knew Paris tended to spend the mornings and most workdays at her new salon, Un Jour à Paris—which I'd learned meant, A Day in Paris. And her evenings and weekends were spent at Hair 2 Dye 4. Apparently, most African-American women like to get their hair done close to the weekend. Mama B said it was so their hair was fresh for church on Sunday. Paris said her younger clients wanted their hair to be fresh for going out to the clubs. Regardless of the reason, the evenings and weekends were extremely busy at Hair 2 Dye 4, while A Day in Paris was busier during the mornings and weekdays. The upper-class salon tended to attract a different clientele.

She was at Hair 2 Dye 4 and had one client in the chair, one under the dryer, and another waiting. Seeing me, she smiled and waved me in. At almost seven at night, things were still bustling. Two other stylists were here too, and one appeared to be sewing something into Mercedes Jackson's head.

"What brings you down?" Paris was styling her client's hair with large, elaborate curlers in a device like an oven.

"That looks extremely dangerous," I said, staring at the huge oven and the curlers she wielded as if on autopilot.

"I suppose they are … in the wrong hands." She smiled. "But I'm a highly trained professional."

I smiled back, recalling the first time we'd met, when I'd said the same line to her.

"What is that thing?" I pointed to the oven looking device.

"It's called a Marcel Stove. It heats the curlers." She patted it with her hand. "They're actually going out of fashion, but some of my clients prefer them."

I stared at the device, but tried to move on. "I'm just making sure everything's okay after the break-in."

"Everything seems fine. Nothing was taken."

"Will you be here long?" I asked. "I mean, if you aren't comfortable being here late, then maybe I can escort you to your car ... for safety," I added.

She grinned. "Thank you. That's very thoughtful, but I've got two more clients after this. It'll be about two more hours before I get out tonight. I'll make sure to walk out with my last client."

"Are you going to see Mama B tonight?"

"I don't know. It's been a long day, and I'm about ready to crash." I supported that statement with a yawn. Amazing how just a couple of weeks ago, I couldn't sleep more than a few hours, and now I was actually feeling tired and looking forward to a good night's sleep—well, at least a few hours. The nightmares hadn't stopped altogether, but they were not as intense.

"You'd better get some sleep."

I took a few steps away and beckoned for Paris.

She put down the curlers and told her client she would return in a minute, then followed me to a corner. Leaning in close to her ear, I whispered, "What is she doing to Mercedes?" I darted my eyes toward Mercedes Jackson, who was sitting in a nearby chair.

Paris smiled and whispered back, "She's sewing in hair. It's called a weave or a sew-in."

The stylist had a long needle shaped like a fishhook. Paris glanced over at Mercedes and noted she was turned in such a way that she would be unlikely to notice the extra attention before continuing in a soft voice, "She used to come in to get her sew-in done every two weeks, but for several months she's slacked off. It's very expensive."

"How much?"

"Two hundred dollars."

"Every two weeks?

Paris nodded.

"That's a lot of money to spend on your hair."

She shrugged. "Most women can't afford to come that often. But if you want it to look really nice and fresh …." She shrugged again. "I'm guessing that between her weave and her nails, she drops about five hundred dollars a month."

"I wonder how she affords it." I was genuinely puzzled.

"I doubt if she pays for it herself," Paris whispered. "Mercedes is the type who would have someone … supporting her."

"Ah … I see what you mean."

Seeing me yawn again, she said with a laugh, "You better get home before you fall over."

I was so tired, I skipped dinner and headed straight to bed. For the first time since the accident, I was too tired to dream. I thought I might even sleep through the entire night.

As soon as my head hit the pillow, I fell into a deep sleep. But a full night's sleep was not to be. At two, my cellphone rang. A body had been found at the church.

CHAPTER FOURTEEN

P OLICE CARS SWARMED in front of the church. The area
was cordoned off, but an officer manning the barricade
recognized me and let me through. I took the stairs two at a
time and rushed inside.

Reverend Hamilton, wearing an old bathrobe, was at the
back of the church giving a statement to a uniformed officer.

"RJ, praise the Lord." Reverend Hamilton sighed with relief.
"I'm glad to see you."

"I'm pretty happy to see you too, Reverend." I took a few
extra breaths to release my tension and steady my nerves.
"What happened? Who died?"

Reverend Hamilton shrugged. "Beats me. I've never seen
him before."

I walked over to the body crumpled in a heap at the front of
the altar. I stood over the man and looked down.

Harley joined me. "Bryce Chandler."

"What happened?" I asked Reverend Hamilton.

"I have no idea. I was at home asleep and heard a gunshot.
It sounded like it came from the church. I looked out the
window and thought I saw a light, so I threw on a robe and

came running. When I got here, I found the side door of the church open and him on the floor."

The coroner was fairly confident the cause of death was a gunshot to the side of the head at close range, but of course the official cause of death would have to wait until the autopsy. Within a few hours, he'd be able to tell us if the gun was the same caliber as the gun used to kill both Warrendale and Bryce Chandler.

"How'd he get in?" Harley asked as we examined the side door. The door had been dusted for prints, and as expected, there were a ton of them. Lots of people used that side door each and every week. The side door was just to the right of the piano at the front of the church. It was the closest door for choir members who parked in the side parking lot to reach the choir stand. It was also the area designated for smokers.

"No signs the door was forced." Harley examined the frame. "Who has a key?"

Reverend Hamilton thought for a minute. "Myself, Minister Chapman, the musicians, Deacons, Warrendale had one, the head of the Usher Board, the head of the Mother's Board—"

"In short, just about everyone."

He nodded. "That pretty well sums it up."

"But why did he come here?" Harley asked. "And why in the middle of the night?"

Only one possibility made sense to me. "He met someone here."

HARLEY AND I decided to take the bull by the horns and tackle Mrs. Warren first. She was still at the Hilton, and the desk clerk remembered us.

Mrs. Warren looked furtively around the room for a moment before she stepped back for us to enter.

"What do you want now?"

"I think you should sit down." I indicated a chair in the living room area of the suite.

She seemed taken aback, but she sat down and invited us to do the same.

"Let's stop playing games. We need the truth. Mrs. Warren, have you been here all night?"

"Yes, of course."

"And Mr. Chandler?" Harley asked.

"He went out last night. He said he needed to meet with someone. Why? What's wrong?"

"Do you know who he went to meet?" I asked.

"He didn't say. I don't think he knew. He just got a call asking for a meeting. They said they had information about Tye." Mrs. Warren was fidgeting as she asked, "What's happened?"

"Mr. Chandler was killed last night." I watched her response carefully.

I expected screams or cries. Instead, Mrs. Warren slumped over and collapsed. Harley called for an ambulance.

I lifted her onto the bed. Then I got a cold compress from the bathroom and applied it to her forehead. It seemed every time we met with Mrs. Warren, she fell ill. Normally, I would be extremely suspicious if it wasn't so obvious that she was truly unwell.

Soon, Mrs. Warren was on her way to Memorial Hospital. Given the events of the last twenty-four hours, the hospital might prove to be the safest place for her. I couldn't be sure the murderer wouldn't be coming for her next.

THE REST OF the day was spent almost entirely in meetings. We met with Chief Mike, who was upset that not only had we failed to solve Thomas Warrendale's murder but now our prime suspect had been murdered. Then we spent an hour hearing how frustrated and disappointed the mayor was. That was followed by another meeting with Chief Mike. By the time I got outside again, it was dark.

Detective Hastings called to tell us Mrs. Bryce Chandler had taken the news of her husband's demise with surprising good humor. She voluntarily shared that she had wanted a divorce for a long time but had signed a prenuptial agreement. Now that Chandler was dead, she could finish out the rest of her days in style. If she hadn't had an iron-clad alibi, and if I weren't so sure Chandler's murder was connected to Warrendale, I might have suspected her.

Harley and I reviewed the coroner's report and the crime scene investigator's evidence again, looking for some clue we had missed. There had to be something. We reviewed all the forensic information and looked at the photos and evidence bags taken from the first death. The photos showed the charred furniture covered in soot and ashes, but something struck me as odd.

Moving into one of the conference rooms, Harley and I took the photos and laid them out so we got a sense of the house. Modern technology being what it is, we also had a video. After we'd watched the video at least four times, Harley was ready to throttle me.

"Are you seeing something in that? Because I can't take much more of this."

"I'm not sure. It seems like … wait. Freeze it!" I shouted.

Harley pressed the pause button on the laptop. "What's that?" I pointed to a shiny object on the floor under a suitcase and a lot of debris.

Harley squinted to identify the one object shining amid a sea of gray before giving up and attempting to zoom in for a better look.

"I can't quite make it out," he mumbled as he continued to manipulate the shot. Finally, after a few more seconds of adjustments, the image became clear. "Looks like a lighter. Did Warren smoke?"

Rummaging through the evidence bags, I found the one containing the lighter. It wasn't as shiny, since the soot and ash had dulled it. Rubbing my finger across the plastic, I was able to clear off enough soot to see the gold of the metal and the faint scratches that indicated the engraving.

I stared at the picture and the evidence-bagged lighter, then got up and grabbed my jacket. "That's not *just* a lighter," I said. "That's a solid-gold, engraved lighter."

We hurried to the home of Tonya Rutherford, and on the way, I filled Harley in on the solid-gold lighter that Mrs. Rutherford had received when she retired from Tucker Car Manufacturing. I also told him about Mama B's suspicions that Tonya had been "messing around" and gotten herself pregnant.

"So, you think Tonya Rutherford killed Warrendale?" Harley said.

"Looks that way. Although I would have bet money she wasn't the type. Really smart kid. Sad to throw away her life like this."

We arrived at the Rutherford home at the same time as the two black and whites I'd called for before we left. The neighborhood was alive with flashing lights and people sitting on their front porches.

Harley sent the other two officers around back. Weapons drawn, Harley and I led the way to the front door.

I pounded on the door and shouted, "Mrs. Rutherford, this is the police."

The house was dark and silent. I pounded again and then kicked in the door. Inside, the room was dark, silent, and empty. We'd missed our prey … this time.

We looked for Tonya and Viola Rutherford for most of the day, checking out neighbors, relatives, and any place that seemed even remotely plausible as a hiding place. After hours with no results, I was worn out and decided to go get some rest.

Back at Mama B's, both Paris and Mama B were on the front porch drinking sweet tea and rocking.

"You look worn out," Paris said. "Let me get you something to eat."

I plopped down on the steps "I just need to sit down and rest."

Bryce Chandler being murdered at the church was already headline news.

"Did you know Tonya Rutherford well?" I asked.

Paris shook her head. "Not really. She seemed like such a nice girl. She's really smart too. I hate to say this, but I really hope you're wrong about her."

"I hope I'm wrong too," I said, although it sure didn't seem likely. "I've known her all her life, and I really hate thinking she could have thrown everything away on a low-life like Thomas Warrendale."

"Young girls are very impressionable," Paris said. "He made a big impression on a lot of women at the church."

"Is there anything you can think of that might help?"

"Like what?"

"Did Warren ever say or do anything that was unusual ... anything different or odd?"

Paris thought for a moment. "Well, he was different."

Mama B snorted. "You can say that again."

"No," Paris said, "I mean he was really good with numbers."

I turned to look at her. "How so?"

"He could glance at a column of numbers and tell you what the total was just like that." She snapped her fingers.

I didn't think being able to add quickly got him killed. "Anything else?"

"He could remember large blocks of numbers, like account numbers, without writing them down. When he first started doing the books for my business, I mentioned something about the accounts, and he just rattled off the account numbers like a grocery list."

That was interesting. I wasn't sure how it fit in, but it might prove significant. I filed it away. "Anything else?"

"This is going to sound weird, but I think he used numbers to help him remember things," she said.

"How do you mean?"

"He always carried this little book with him. He called it his 'hymn book.' "

"That doesn't seem unusual for a choir director."

"I know, but it wasn't a real hymn book. It was just a blank notebook he wrote in."

"Like a composer?"

"No, he didn't write the music, just the titles and numbers. Lots of numbers."

"Did you ever see inside this book?"

"Only once. We were rehearsing and trying to get a particular part. His hymn book was just lying on the seat, and I picked it up. But I couldn't make heads or tails out of it."

"How did Warren respond when you picked it up?"

"He got mad at first, but then he just laughed. He said he had his own methods, and his hymn book was special."

Something wasn't right, but my brain was too tired to do much figuring, so I decided to call it a day and try to get a little more sleep.

Unfortunately, tonight was not going to be my night for rest. At two a.m. my phone rang. It felt like déjà vu.

"RJ, I am sorry to bother you at this hour," Reverend Hamilton said, "but I really need to speak to you. Can you please come by the rectory?" The words themselves didn't convey much, but the soft tone and the timing let me know something serious had occurred.

"Sure, Reverend. Give me a few minutes, and I'll be right there."

I hurried to get dressed. I sure hoped there wasn't another dead body at the church.

Reverend Hamilton opened the door, and without a word, led me to his office. That's where I found Tonya Rutherford and her mother Viola already seated. The office was small, but

Reverend Hamilton had brought another chair into the room for me.

Reverend Hamilton motioned for me to sit down then took his seat behind his desk. Tonya was crying, and Miss Viola looked like she'd been through World War III.

Reverend Hamilton gave a nod toward Tonya.

She gulped and started to talk. "I thought Minister Warrendale was the most wonderful man I'd ever known. He was so exciting and so talented and … and I fell in love."

"Tonya," I said, "I need to tell you that anything you say can and will be used against you in a court of law. You have the right to speak to an attorney and to have an attorney present. Do you understand these rights?"

She nodded. I took out my notebook.

"He was the first man I … I had never *been* with a man before." She stumbled over the words and looked sideways when Miss Viola, sitting in the corner, caught her breath and began to sob. "He made me feel so special. I mean, here was this man who was so talented, and he wanted to be with me." She choked, but after a moment, she sniffed and continued, "At first, I was so happy. Proud and happy. But then I started hearing the rumors. I started hearing there were other women. I didn't believe it. I thought they were all just jealous. Everyone wanted to be with him. I thought they were just making it up to make him look bad because he wasn't interested in any of them." Pausing, she took some tissues from the box on Reverend Hamilton's desk. "But then one day, I saw him. I went to his house, and there was a woman there. I crept into the back of the house and listened to them talking. She was his wife. He was married."

This gave me a clue about the timeframe. It had to have been the Sunday Mrs. Warren discovered his whereabouts.

"He was married," she said again. "I couldn't believe it. He told me he was going to take care of me. I thought he meant he was going to marry me. But he didn't. He meant he'd give me money to get an abortion or go away someplace and have the baby."

More sobs from Miss Viola. Reverend Hamilton's face wore a pained expression.

"I didn't want to see him after that," Tonya said. "I was so ashamed. I had to tell my mom about the baby. I was starting to show."

Miss Viola looked haggard. But she was a tough woman and wasn't about to give in without a fight. With clenched fists and jaw, she spat out, "And that's when I decided to kill him. I went to his house and had it out with him …. I killed him. I hit him."

Reverend Hamilton shook his head, while Tonya went over to her mother, held on to her grief-stricken body and soothed her. At that moment, their roles were reversed, and Tonya rocked and consoled Miss Viola as any mother would an upset child. Finally, in a soft, soothing voice, Tonya said, "No, Mama. You can't take the blame for me. I won't let you."

Looking at me, Tonya Rutherford said, "It was me. I did it. I went to his house, and we got into a fight. He had a suitcase and was leaving. I got mad. I hit him with a statue. I didn't mean to do it. I swear to God I didn't mean to. But I killed him."

CHAPTER FIFTEEN

REVEREND HAMILTON ACCOMPANIED Tonya Rutherford and me down to the police station, where she told her story again. Later, Reverend Hamilton and I sat alone at my desk.

"What will become of her? That poor child doesn't belong in jail any more than I do."

"I doubt she'll even be arrested for the arson. She didn't kill Thomas Warrendale."

He looked shocked. "But she confessed."

"She confessed to hitting him over the head and setting the fire later, but that's not what killed him. He was shot."

The light finally turned on and Reverend Hamilton said, "So that's why you kept asking her about a gun when you questioned her."

I nodded. "She shouldn't have tried to cover it up with the fire."

"That was Viola's idea," Reverend Hamilton said.

"I know. When Tonya told her mother what she'd done, her mother thought they could hide it by setting fire to the house. She should have come to the police. But I think she'll be okay.

She just turned eighteen a few days ago. So technically she was a minor when Warren impregnated her. That will carry some weight. She'll be questioned and released."

"It would kill her mother if she goes to jail."

"She has no priors. She's pregnant. I'll call Judge Browning. He's retired from the bench but he can recommend a good attorney."

"But the cost?"

"Don't worry about the cost. Judge Browning owes me a favor." I smiled to myself, thinking teaching that class would be a small price to pay if it meant helping Tonya.

Reverend Hamilton breathed a sigh of relief. "That would be wonderful. Do you really think it's possible?"

"I do. Plus, I'll be happy to speak on her behalf if it comes to that. A wise man once said, 'anything's possible if you can believe.' "

Reverend Hamilton smiled, "Mark, nine, twenty-three. A truly wise man indeed." He sighed and I saw the weight he had been carrying ease a fraction. Slowly he rose. "Thank you, RJ, I believe God placed you here in this position for just such a time as this."

"Perhaps." I stifled a yawn.

I WENT HOME. I knew I wouldn't be able to sleep, so I didn't even try. A hot shower and two more cups of coffee did nothing to stimulate my brain cells. Back at the precinct, Chief Mike was inclined to close things out and wanted to charge Tonya Rutherford with murder. Fortunately, I disagreed.

From behind the desk in his small office, Chief Mike made his case. "You have your murderer. The mayor will be happy, and that young girl will most likely get off with probation. This case is done."

"That's fine, except she didn't kill Thomas Warrendale. And she definitely didn't kill Bryce Chandler."

"How can you be so sure?"

"Harley, do you have the coroner's report?"

Harley went to his desk and hurried back with the report. Quickly scanning through it, I found what I was looking for.

"According to the coroner's report, Warrendale was shot. The ME found a hole in the skull consistent with a forty-five-caliber handgun. There's no way Tonya Rutherford shot him."

Chief Mike paced. "So she lied. She shot him. Maybe she doesn't have a license for the gun and didn't want to admit she had it."

"But why hide it? She already confessed. She thought she'd killed him. There's no reason to hide it if she'd shot him instead of hitting him over the head. Besides, she didn't kill Bryce Chandler."

Harley just looked between Chief Mike and me as though watching a tennis match.

"How do you know?" Chief Mike asked.

"Her alibi checks out. I verified it before I went home last night ... ah, this morning. She was on a Greyhound bus traveling from Detroit to St. Joe. The bus driver remembered her."

"He must have had hundreds of passengers."

"Apparently, she sat behind the bus driver and cried most of the trip. She reminded him of one of his daughters. She was traveling alone, so he kept an eye on her. He even remembered what she was wearing."

I laid the report on the desk and waited.

"Maybe the two murders aren't connected?" Chief Mike looked up, but even he didn't believe that. He flopped down in his chair. "Never mind."

Harley looked at me, puzzled. "What's really bothering you?"

"Too many questions. We still don't know who shot Thomas Warrendale. We don't know who shot Bryce Chandler or why."

"We also still don't know what they're looking for," Harley said. "Why break into Paris' salon or her house?"

Chief Mike had already sent word to the mayor that we had

solved the murder, and he was not excited about having to backtrack.

"You two better get busy. Find this murderer and find him quickly," he said through gritted teeth. He picked up the phone and placed a call to the mayor's office. Harley and I got out as quickly as possible.

I did run into a little bit of luck in tracking down Mrs. Hartford-Graham. The casino owner's credit card had been used at a restaurant just outside of Chicago two days ago. That was promising. So Mrs. Hartford-Graham was within two hours of St. Joe. Still, no matter how I tried to stretch my imagination, I just couldn't envision the elderly Mrs. Hartford-Graham breaking into the church rectory. It didn't take a great deal of imagination to visualize her bodyguard, the Hulk, breaking in. In that case, Mrs. Hartford-Graham would have ensured that she was far away and had an iron-clad alibi. No, my gut told me Mrs. Hartford-Graham was much too smart to arrange the killing and then stay close by.

At lunch, Harley and I tried to organize our thoughts.

Harley reviewed his notes. "We know Thomas Warrendale took something. That's why he ran."

"We're assuming what he took was the reason he left Cleveland and hid in St. Joe."

"And whatever he took was so important someone was willing to kill for it."

"We know that whatever it was, they haven't found it yet," I said.

"It would have to be relatively small. It couldn't be anything too big or he wouldn't be able to hide it so well."

"We know Thomas Warrendale was a brilliant accountant," I said. "He was somehow stealing money from First Baptist Church and Paris' salon." I couldn't help feeling I was missing something.

Harley noticed my puzzled look. "What?"

"It's just something Paris said. She said Warrendale was talented with numbers. For that matter, everyone else we've talked to kept mentioning how brilliant he was with numbers and accounts. She mentioned something about a hymn book too."

"So what?" Harley asked.

"Well, the money stolen from the church was pretty obvious. I don't know anything about accounting, but the records I saw before I handed them over to the forensic accountant were pretty sloppy. I mean, Reverend Hamilton figured it out. That doesn't sound like a financial genius."

"So, you think someone else was involved?"

"Yeah, I think so."

"Okay, so who and why, and is it connected with the murders?"

"Let's look at the connections. Warrendale worked for Bryce Chandler. He did the books for the Easy Street Casino, which is owned by Mrs. Hartford-Graham. Warrendale did the books for Paris' salon, and she's had two break-ins. He did the books for First Baptist Church, and money was stolen." I paused. "What's the common denominator?"

"Thomas Warrendale."

"The stuff we got from Hastings showed someone was laundering money and embezzling. I think that was Warrendale and probably Bryce Chandler. For some reason, Warrendale decided to run."

"Maybe Mrs. Hartford-Graham figured it out," Harley said.

"Could be. She probably went to Chandler. Warrendale got scared and ran, but not before he took some papers, books, files, or something." I didn't have any solid facts to back up my theory, but it felt right.

"Chandler?"

"He and Mrs. Warrendale have been looking for something. I think that's why they came to St. Joe, and that's why he was murdered."

"So, we've got to find *it* before the killer does."

Later that afternoon, we went back to the mayor's office
to provide an update.

"This case has gone on way too long," he said. "I want this
thing resolved. What's the problem?"

Chief Mike looked from Harley to me. "We think we know
why he was killed and have a couple of likely suspects, but we
can't prove anything yet."

"Maybe you should pull someone in for questioning. Even
if you have to release them, it would be better than doing
nothing. At least the media would *think* we have a clue what
we're doing."

I was frustrated. "Mayor, we *do* have a clue what we're doing.
We're doing our job, but we can't just pull people in and give
away our hand. I think that would be more detrimental than
helpful." I wasn't even trying to keep the frustration out of
my voice. Harley looked nervous, and Chief Mike looked as
though he would love to crawl under a rock. But I hadn't had
much sleep, and my patience had waned.

Mayor Longbow stopped pacing, flung himself into a seat,
and said, "Look, I want this cleared up. You have forty-eight
hours."

Back at the precinct, Chief Mike said, "If we don't find the
solution fast, we're going to look like incompetent fools. Tell
me you have a plan."

"My plan is to find whatever Warrendale took before the
people looking for it find it and before anyone else is killed. I
believe that if we do, it'll lead us to his killer."

"Great." Chief Mike paced. "So how do you do that?"

We talked through some ideas, then I got a call from the
hospital that Mrs. Warren was doing better. So Harley and
I headed off. I had a feeling Mrs. Warren was the key to

unlocking this entire case. Now my job was to convince her to talk.

I DISLIKED HOSPITALS more than I disliked the morgue. Memorial Hospital was a huge, meandering complex with miles and miles of halls, painted with different-color stripes. The stripes served as a legend designed to lead each visitor through a maze, which, if followed correctly, would culminate at the room of a loved one. But it was the sterile atmosphere and smell of disinfectant and death I objected to most. This was where my mother battled cancer. Month after month I watched as she slowly deteriorated. Eventually, they sent her home with the telephone number for Hospice.

After what seemed like miles of walking, Harley and I arrived at the private room where Mrs. Warren stayed. She looked even frailer in the hospital than she had the first time I saw her after she'd had her appendix removed. The death of her lover on top of that of her husband had obviously taken a terrible toll.

I approached the bed. "Mrs. Warren, are you feeling up to answering a few questions?" I asked in the hushed voice people used in hospitals.

For a moment, I wasn't sure she'd answer. She looked at Harley and me as though she couldn't quite place who we were. After a few seconds, her eyes widened in recognition. She clamped her lips shut and shook her head.

"Mrs. Warren, it's very important," Harley said quietly with soft eyes as he placed his hand gently on her arm.

The blood drained from her face and a pale, ashen woman stared back. After another pause, she turned away and clutched the sheets more tightly to her throat. She was terrified, and we would have to tread carefully. The room was small, with only one chair. I motioned for Harley to take the chair, but he said, "I'll just go grab another chair. Be right back."

He was back in less than thirty seconds with another chair,

which he placed next to the bed. He sat down and took out his notebook. I sat in the other chair and tried to shake off the gloom that flooded the small room.

"Mrs. Warren, can you tell us who Mr. Chandler was going to meet?" I waited for her response.

Her eyes darted around like those of a frightened rabbit. After a long pause, she shook her head.

The hands that clutched the sheet were shaking. Normally, I would have come down hard on her to force her to cooperate—a firm hand can do wonders at opening locked lips—but she was terrified. Given her current medical state, I was reluctant to push too hard. I glanced at Harley. With one nod, he put down his notebook and took Mrs. Warren's hand. Keeping his movements slow and gentle, he stroked her hand, and in a soft, kind voice, he soothed her troubled mind.

"I need to tell you that anything you say can and will be used against you in a court of law. You have the right to speak to an attorney. If you cannot afford an attorney, one will be provided for you. Do you understand?" I asked.

Mrs. Warren looked ashen and terrified.

I tried again. "Mrs. Warren, do you understand?"

"I understand," she whispered. Her eyes and words seemed to search for reassurance. "You can protect me?"

"Yes. We can protect you if you tell us the truth," I responded.

Mrs. Warren closed her eyes. For a moment, I was afraid she'd fallen asleep, but she sighed and opened her eyes.

"I'll tell you what I know, but I need your word." Mrs. Warren looked from Harley to me. "I need a deal. I want protection and," she struggled to find the right words, "I want immunity."

I didn't have the authority to grant immunity. The district attorney was the only one who could do that, and I wasn't sure if even he could do it without talking to the DA from Cleveland. I explained that to her while Harley went into the hall and called Chief Mike to fill him in and get further direction.

"Mrs. Warren, if you tell us what you know, I promise to do everything in my power to help you."

Mrs. Warren looked more tired and frightened. With a heavy sigh, she nodded.

Just as Harley returned and gave me a slight nod, Mrs. Warren laid her head back on the pillow.

"Mrs. Warren, can you tell us who Mr. Chandler was going to meet?"

"I have no idea. I got a call in the middle of the night."

"Can you tell us anything about the caller?" Harley asked. "Was it a man or woman?"

"It was a man. I didn't recognize his voice," she said softly.

That ruled out Reverend Hamilton, since she had talked to him previously. I'd never seriously considered Reverend Hamilton a suspect, but it felt good to rule him out.

I hoped we could zero in on the caller based on the conversation itself. "What exactly did he say?"

She paused before responding. "He said he knew why I was there and that he could get what I wanted, but it would cost fifty thousand dollars."

"Do you carry that kind of money around with you?" I asked.

She shook her head. "No. I told him I didn't have that kind of money on me. He said, 'Then we have nothing to talk about.' He said goodbye and I think was about to hang up, but I yelled for him to stop. I told him I would get the money."

I doubted if the killer would have actually hung up, but then Mrs. Chandler probably didn't deal with as many criminals as I did. "What did he say then?"

"Well, he sort of laughed and said, 'That's better.' He told me to bring the money to the church at three. He said to come to the side door and to come alone."

"What happened next?" I watched her face, but couldn't detect any sign she was speaking anything other than the truth as she knew it.

"Nothing. He hung up."

"So how did Mr. Chandler come to be there that night?" Harley asked.

Looking as though she might cry, Mrs. Warren said, "Bryce was there. He was with me at the hotel. I told him what the man said and he said he would go and meet him. I wanted to go with him, but he told me to wait at the hotel. He said it would be better if I let him handle it."

Mrs. Warren started to cry. "I should have gone with him."

"If you had, you would both be dead now." I hoped my bluntness would snap her out of her melancholy. "What, specifically, was it you were paying for, Mrs. Warren?"

She pondered the question and I could almost see the wheels turning in her head. For about two seconds, I thought she would lie. Then she lowered her shoulders and sighed. "It was a book, a code book."

The hymn book. It had to be. At last, we knew what we were looking for. "What was in the code book?"

"I'm not sure exactly—"

"Mrs. Warren, your husband and your lover have both been killed. I think it's time you leveled with us and told us the truth."

The blood rose into Mrs. Warren's previously pale face and her nostrils flared. "Before I was so rudely interrupted, I was about to say I'm not exactly sure what's in the book. I haven't seen it, but I believe it's a coded list of accounts."

Harley looked up from his notes. "Accounts? What kind of accounts?"

"Accounts that contain the money Tye stole from his clients," Mrs. Warren said with only the slightest look of shame. "Tye transferred the money into banks all over the world. He was brilliant when it came to finances. Bryce said Tye had stashed away close to thirty million dollars."

Another half-hour of questions didn't yield any new information to help us learn who had killed Warrendale or Bryce Chandler. Mrs. Warren's strength and energy petered out, and we left after securing her promise to call if she remembered anything that would help us solve the murders. I arranged for a guard to watch her.

Lack of sleep had really started to catch up with me, and I decided to head back to Mama B's and get some rest. At the house, I tossed and turned for several hours before finally dropping off.

Unfortunately, my morning started much the same as the past two mornings—with a phone call in the wee hours.

CHAPTER SIXTEEN

———∼∼∼———

Someone had tried to break into the rectory. With that shock, I was wide awake. The scene in front of the rectory was similar to what I had witnessed just a few days earlier outside Paris' house. There were six police cars, with lights flashing.

The officers outside recognized me so I didn't have to show my shield before rushing into the rectory to find Reverend Hamilton. He sat at the kitchen table in a flannel bathrobe and slippers. As I entered, he nodded at me and then stood up to get another mug from the cabinet. Without a word, he filled the mug with coffee and pushed the sugar and cream in my direction before sitting back down at the table.

I thanked him and took several sips before getting down to business.

"What happened?"

"I was sound asleep when I heard a noise downstairs. Then I heard the floorboards creaking and a bang. I knew someone was in here. I got up and turned on the lights and started down the stairs."

"What? You could have been killed. You should have picked

up the phone and called the police. The last thing we need is a dead hero." Concern made me speak more sharply than I'd intended. I took a deep breath. "You should never confront a burglar. Most burglars just want to get in, grab small stuff, and get out. Many of them don't even carry weapons."

"I have no desire to be a hero, dead or otherwise. I turned the light on and came downstairs for two reasons. First, I thought it was some kid trying to grab loose change or a television. I thought if he saw the light he would get scared and run."

He was probably right about that, but I was still angry. "And the other reason?"

"I have one of those confounded cordless phones my nephew bought me for Christmas and I'd left it downstairs. I had to go down there to get the phone in order to call the police."

I left him sitting in the kitchen with his coffee while I went to talk to the officer first on the scene. Apparently, nothing of value was stolen. The lock at the front door was pried open. The intruder must have tripped over the boxes Reverend Hamilton had stacked up outside his office.

Back in the kitchen, I sat down and tried again.

"Do you have anything of value someone would want to steal?"

"The most valuable things here are my books, and very few thieves would recognize the value of a sixteenth-century copy of the Bible in Latin or a book of sermons that once belonged to Martin Luther King Jr. He signed it when I had the pleasure of meeting him at his church in Atlanta years before he was killed."

"Anything missing?"

He shook his head and then looked at me in that piercing way he had. "RJ, we both know this is connected to that poor man's murder."

"We have no evidence …." I barely got the words out before he snorted.

"I'm not a policeman. I don't need evidence. I *know*."

Reverend Hamilton tapped his chest as he talked, indicating that this knowledge came from inside.

"Did Warrendale give you anything to keep for him? Papers, books, anything?"

He thought for a few minutes, shook his head, but then stopped. "Well, he didn't exactly give me anything but—"

"What? What is it? Anything. Whatever he gave you. It might be helpful."

"I'm thinking. Hang on."

Reverend Hamilton thought and then shook his head again.

"I can't think of him giving me anything. I mean, we talked about the church books and he gave me the books and the records, but those weren't his—he was merely returning them to me."

"When was the last time you talked to him?"

"Saturday night."

I wasn't expecting that one. "*What*? You didn't mention that?"

"RJ, there was nothing to tell. We have choir rehearsal on Saturday night. I was—"

"Wait. I thought choir rehearsal was Friday night," I said, thinking back on Moe Chapman's statement and what I'd learned from Paris.

"Yes, well, the children, the young adult choirs, and the eight o'clock choirs rehearse on Friday night, but the other choirs rehearse on Saturdays," Reverend Hamilton elaborated. "I was there, like always. Afterwards, he came down to my office and asked what I thought. I told him it sounded wonderful. We talked for a few minutes. He gave me the books for the church." He paused and thought back, looking as though he was reliving the scene. "He looked tired. But I chalked it up to the rehearsals. I offered him some coffee and we walked back to the house. There was nothing unusual in that. We often sat in my office and had coffee."

There was something nagging at the back of my mind. I just couldn't put my finger on it.

Harley walked in during this discussion and stood there quietly. He looked worse than I felt and I wanted to laugh. He must have gotten dressed in the dark. He wore mismatched shoes, his T-shirt was inside out, and a patch of hair at the back of his head was sticking straight up.

Reverend Hamilton noticed him and stood up to get another mug. As he poured the coffee, I realized what was bothering me.

"When Warrendale came here that evening, why did he return the church's books? Did you ask for them?"

"He said he was going to be on vacation and wanted to leave the books with me for safekeeping while he was gone."

Harley drank a full cup of coffee before asking, "Did he say where he was going or when he was planning to return?"

"He said he was feeling tired and wanted to go someplace … he mentioned something about the sea or blue oceans. I assumed he was going to the beach. He didn't volunteer the information and I didn't want to pry."

"Had he mentioned anything about a vacation before? Wouldn't he have told some of the choir members? I mean, is that normal?" If Warrendale saw his wife at church on Sunday, then he must have decided to leave before the week was out.

"It wouldn't be unusual if he were going to be back for the next week's service."

The pot of coffee we were drinking had run out, and Reverend Hamilton made more. The kitchen of the rectory was very small, as it was in many old houses. Unlike the modern kitchens of today, which are open to the living areas, the kitchen was closed off from the rest of the house. And the refrigerator was around a corner in the back of the kitchen. Reverend Hamilton kept his coffee in the freezer and had to leave the kitchen to get it, which got me thinking.

"Where did you have this coffee? In the kitchen?"

"No. We talked in my office."

"So, when you left to make coffee, did he follow you into the kitchen?"

Reverend Hamilton stopped at that. "No. He sat in the office and waited." Light dawned on all of us at the same time.

I headed for the office with Harley and Reverend Hamilton close behind. But at the sight of the office, we stopped. There were hundreds if not thousands of books lining the walls and piled on the floor.

Harley said, "You think he left something in here?"

"If he was going to make another run for it, he might have," I said. "Maybe seeing his wife in the congregation made him see that he'd have to move on. If his wife had found him, it was only a matter of time before whoever he was running from did too."

Harley continued, "So you think he took whatever it was they wanted and hid it in here somewhere."

All three of us looked daunted by the task ahead.

"It would help if we knew what we were looking for," Harley said.

"Paris mentioned the notebook he carried around. He called it his 'hymn book.' Paris actually looked at it. Perhaps she can describe it to us? That might not be the book we're looking for, but it's worth a try."

I tried calling Paris, and left a message for her to call back.

"Well, we know he had some kind of book, probably a small notebook ...." I waved at the books that filled the shelves, the floor, and every flat surface of the office. "Reverend Hamilton, after Warrendale left, did you notice anything unusual? Any books or papers out of place, moved, missing?"

He shook his head but scanned the room anyway. "I know what you're thinking, but he didn't have anything else with him but those books. He didn't bring anything I saw and I didn't notice anything was disturbed."

Paris called back to say the book was probably black and about half the size of an actual hymnal.

We spent the next three hours looking through the books and papers in the office. By the time the sun came up, we'd gone through three pots of coffee and more than half the books in the office with no luck. When Mrs. Mattie Young arrived, she was so shocked by the mess, she was almost speechless. I say *almost* speechless.

"What in the name of God Almighty do you think you're doing?" Mrs. Young stood with one hand on her hip and was so furious I think even Reverend Hamilton was surprised.

Reverend Hamilton climbed over a pile. "Mattie, I know it looks bad, but—"

"Bad? You think it looks *bad*? I spent days straightening that office and cleaning and rearranging. Those books were in alphabetical order. Do you know how long it took to get that mess as organized as it was? And you bringing home new books every time you step out the door."

"Mrs. Young, I can explain," I began, but the look in her eyes froze my lips and I stopped. We had made a mess of the room and that was a fact.

"Don't you even start with me, RJ Franklin. I don't think I can speak to you right now without profaning God."

Harley smiled, but the smile vanished as soon as she turned her stone-faced stare to him. "And you can drop those books right now and get out of this room, or as God is my witness, I'll take you over my knee and tan your hide."

Harley dropped the books and got out of the room without another word. Reverend Hamilton and I put down the books we had in our hands and left the room as well.

The patrol cars had long since left, and only one black and white sat outside on duty, watching the front door.

Reverend Hamilton shepherded us to the front porch. We heard books and doors slam as Mrs. Young attempted to pick up the pieces of her once neat and orderly rectory.

"She's pretty upset right now, but she'll calm down soon. Just leave her to me. I know how to handle her." Reverend Hamilton might have been more convincing if he wasn't whispering. "Don't worry about a thing. I'll get through the rest of the stuff in there and let you know if I find anything."

But I had a thought. "Reverend Hamilton, did Warrendale go into any other rooms?"

He rubbed his head as he thought back. "We sat in the office talking, and I asked him if he wanted a cup of coffee. He said yes and I told him I'd be back in a minute. I went into the kitchen and started the coffeemaker."

"Did you talk about anything while you were making the coffee?" I asked, hoping to spark a memory in his mind.

He paused before shaking his head. "We talked about the choir and how well they sounded. Then he ...." Reverend Hamilton took in a sharp breath.

"What?" we asked simultaneously.

"He went to the bathroom," Reverend Hamilton said as he took off back into the house. Harley and I followed.

There was a small powder room on the first floor, just off the study. It wasn't big enough for three, so Reverend Hamilton stood outside while I looked around. There wasn't much to look at. The room had a toilet, a pedestal sink, and a mirror. I looked at the only hiding place available, the toilet. Reaching into my pocket, I found a pair of latex gloves. I looked in back of the tank and then lifted the lid. In a Ziploc bag taped to the inside, I found a book about the size of a small diary. I pulled out the bag and opened it. Inside was a series of numbers.

Harley whistled softly. "Bingo."

HARLEY AND I looked through the code book, but none of it made any sense. We would turn it over to our geek guys to decode when we went in to the precinct, but it was still pretty early in the day. I was tempted to head to my townhouse for a shower, but Mama B's house was closer, so Harley followed me. As I drove the short distance through the alley, I couldn't get over the feeling that some piece of the puzzle was still just out of reach.

Back at the house, Harley and I reassured Paris and Mama B that Reverend Hamilton was fine. I left Harley to fill them in while I hurried upstairs. After a shower and a shave, I dressed in fresh clothing and headed back downstairs. I could smell the ham and biscuits when I was halfway there.

In the kitchen, Paris was setting the table while Mama B finished scrambling eggs. Harley ate ham, eggs, grits, and biscuits, and washed it all down with coffee.

"I timed that just right," I said as I slid into the dining room chair. Mama B put a plate in front of me.

Harley and I were the only ones eating fried ham, biscuits, and eggs. Mama B ate oatmeal while Paris had a small bowl of fruit and yogurt she must have purchased herself. I knew Mama B wouldn't buy it.

"Why are you guys eating so healthy?" I said. "You trying to fatten us up or something?"

Paris spooned her yogurt. "If I ate that type of stuff every morning, I'd be big as a house. I already need to lose about ten pounds."

"I think your pounds are just fine where they are," I said and dropped my head to finish shoveling in the food. "Besides," I added in between bites, "you need to keep your strength up to hoist those huge curling iron things around."

That lightened the mood. Harley and Mama B chuckled.

"That reminds me. I have a message for you."

I could tell by the way her lips were twitching that something was amiss. "What's the message?"

"Mercedes Jackson saw you leaving the shop the other night, and after a few comments about your anatomy, your appearance, and what she would like to do to you, she had the nerve to ask me to make sure you had her phone number."

I rolled my eyes.

Mama B snorted and Paris burst out laughing. Even Harley was laughing, which I found annoying, since he hadn't even met Mercedes.

"What did you tell her?"

Paris smiled and adopted a look of wide-eyed innocence. "I told her I would pass along her message." Reaching into her pocket, she pulled out pieces of paper that had been torn to the size of confetti and placed them on the table near my plate. "Here you go."

For about two seconds, the room was quiet while we looked at the pile of ripped-up paper. Then we burst into laughter. After another moment, I collected myself enough to ask, "I'm still investigating a murder, so what if I need to ask Mercedes some additional questions?"

Paris smiled and shrugged. "You're a detective. I'm sure you can figure out how to put the pieces together." After a second she added, "Of course, Mercedes would need to find a new hair salon and I'll miss the income. She's one of my best-paying customers."

The back and forth seemed natural and comfortable. I was about to take another jab, but decided instead to put this topic to rest. "Mercedes will not need to change hair salons. Your income is secure."

Mama B's eyes sparkled, and she barely hid a smile, but she soon turned serious. "I didn't think Mercedes was still going to your shop anyway. I haven't seen her there for months."

"She used to be as regular as clockwork. She had a standing appointment every two weeks for years. But then, about six months ago, she stopped coming. I thought she'd found another stylist."

Something had been triggered in the back of my mind, but before I could figure it out, Harley asked, "What happened six months ago?"

Paris shrugged. "I'm not sure. That's when Moe Chapman started preaching. I just assumed he wasn't making as much money as a minister as he had as the financial secretary and wasn't able to support Mercedes' expensive habits anymore."

"Yeah, her weave was looking pretty raggedy for a while there," Mama B said.

"But that doesn't make sense. I mean he should have made *more* as the associate minister. The financial secretary job is a non-paid position," I said.

"I have no idea why she stopped coming to the salon. At first I thought she found someone new, but Mrs. Bethany's right. She looked pretty scruffy for several months."

I glanced over at Harley, who was also looking puzzled. We were obviously out of our element when it came to women's hair routines, so Harley asked, "Is that uncommon, for someone to stop coming for a while?"

Paris thought for a moment. "Lots of women have standing appointments. That's not uncommon."

Mama B added, "I have a standing appointment with Paris every two weeks."

"But most of the people who come on a regular basis don't have a weave. Mama B wears her own hair. I would say every one of my standing appointments is for people who wear their own hair. Weaves, or sew-ins, can be very expensive, especially the kind Mercedes has done."

"What makes her sew-in expensive?" I was trying to wrap my head around this.

"She only uses real hair, not synthetic, for one thing. And she has the hair sewn in and glued. It lasts longer that way and looks nicer. Women with a sew-in usually don't come every two weeks. Mercedes came in religiously, every two weeks. So, missing six months for *her* was uncommon. Plus, she gets her nails done, and that's expensive too."

I looked at Harley. "So, when Moe Chapman was financial secretary for the church, his girlfriend Mercedes dropped over five hundred per month at the hair salon, but once Warrendale took over the books, she stopped."

Paris nodded.

"Well, isn't that interesting," Harley said.

Mama B broke in, "Used to be a time folks had respect for the church. They would never dream of stealing from God or from a man of God either, but not anymore. Now, folks will kill you and steal the gold right out yo' mouth." She paused. "I'm still surprised that boy lived as long as he did. If looks could kill, he should have died a week earlier." This was perhaps the third time Mama B had shared this sentiment since Warrendale had been killed.

"What do you mean?" Paris asked.

After a moment's hesitation, Mama B said, "I think that boy was messin' around too much. You can't roll around with dogs without getting fleas." She finished with a nod, as though that explained everything.

I was confused, but I wasn't about to stop her now. So, I waited patiently for her to explain.

When it seemed no explanation was forthcoming, Harley prompted her, "Who do you think he was … ah … lying down with?"

Mama B waited a moment. "Well, that woman RJ said was his wife looked mad enough to bite the heads off nails. She looked like she wanted to kill him right there in the church. Then, there was Tonya Rutherford. She was madder than a wet hen. And Moe Chapman tried to hide it, but I could tell he wanted that little fancy pants dead."

Something Mama B said earlier was floating around in my head, so I asked, "You said Moe was jealous of Warrendale but Mercedes claimed that was just gossip."

"I don't gossip." Mama B leaned across the table. "I was there at the church and I know what I heard."

"What did you hear?" Harley and I said simultaneously.

I added, "If you know something that can help solve this murder, you should have told me a week ago."

"Don't you raise your voice to me, Robert James Franklin Junior," Mama B said. She only used my full name when she was really angry. I took a deep breath and tried to calm down.

"I'm sorry. Please tell me what you heard," I said in a clipped voice that was as polite as I could muster.

Mama B sat fuming for a moment. Finally, she said, "Well, it was my turn to help Mother Applewhite set up for communion."

I knew the Mother's Board was responsible for putting out the crackers and grape juice for communion the night before the first Sunday.

"Okay, so you and Mother Applewhite were at the church …" Harley prompted, as he took out his notebook and held his pen poised to take down her words.

"Choir rehearsal had just finished."

I mulled this over. "So, Mercedes was at the church on Saturday night." I shot a quick look at Harley, who nodded at me. He would check her statement, but I was pretty sure she'd claimed to be at home waiting for Moe to take her out.

"I had to go in the office and get soap for the washing."

The washing was the ritual where the ministers washed their hands in front of the congregation prior to administering communion to the congregation.

"What happened next?" Harley asked.

Mama B squirmed a bit in her seat. Finally, she said, "Well, I heard Warrendale, I mean Warren, laughing. He was saying Mercedes wasn't his type, but he would keep her entertained while Moe was gone." Mama B shuddered, not from cold, but as though shaking off a mood. She continued, "It wasn't exactly the words he said but the way he said them."

"How did he say them?"

I watched as Mama B looked up at the ceiling, as if trying to come up with the right description. Finally she gave up. Shaking her head, she said, "It was as though he was laughing at the poor man. Now, I'll grant you, I don't care much for Moe Chapman with all his teeth—always smiling at you and sayin' *praise the Lord* every other word—but he is a home boy."

In Mama B's world, a hometown boy was better than someone from another state like Thomas Warrendale. I was focused on something else Mama B had said. "What did he mean by when 'Moe was gone'? Was Moe Chapman supposed to be going somewhere?"

"I don't know," Mama B said. "I might have missed that part when I was getting the water."

I stood up from the table. "Looks like I need to have a talk with a couple of people."

MOE CHAPMAN WASN'T at home, at the church, or at Mercedes Jackson's house. So Harley and I started with Mercedes, who lived in a small house not far from the university. The house used to belong to her parents, now both deceased. When I knocked on the door, she smiled big until she opened it wide enough to notice I wasn't alone.

"RJ, what a pleasant surprise," Mercedes said. Her big smile looked even more fake than her nails and hair.

I had no time for games. "We need to talk to you."

"Well, of course, come on in." Mercedes held open the door and stepped aside just enough for Harley and me to enter. We had to turn sideways to avoid brushing against her.

The house was decorated with cheap, gaudy plastic furniture. There was a large red-pleather sofa and black lacquer pieces too big for the room. Pictures of African tribal women covered the walls, surrounded by statues of the same subject. Mercedes slinked to the sofa and patted the cushion next to her. Harley took the only chair, another red-pleather piece, and I chose to stand.

"We have some additional questions for you," I said as Harley pulled out his notebook.

"Sure, RJ. You can ask me anything at all," Mercedes said.

"I want to start by telling you that anything you say can and will be used against you in a court of law. You have the right to an attorney. If you can't afford one, an attorney will be provided for you. Do you understand these rights?" I tried to make my tone as cold and stern as possible.

Mercedes' jaw dropped open. "Well yes. I understand .... I mean I understand what you said. But I don't understand *why* you're saying it. I haven't done anything wrong."

"Obstructing justice and interfering in a police investigation are serious offenses," Harley said.

"I haven't done any of those things. I never lied to a police officer." Mercedes was all wide-eyed innocence.

"Tell me what happened at the church the Saturday night Tye Warren was murdered," I said flatly.

Fear flashed in her eyes for a fleeting moment, but then she pulled herself together. "Nothing happened."

"The truth, Mercedes. You're in big trouble, and unless you're completely honest now, I will arrest you," I said.

She thought for a second and then leaned back on the sofa. "Moe used to be really good to me. He'd buy me things and take me to fancy restaurants. But then, when he started preaching, he changed."

"Changed how?" I asked, although I could guess what was coming next.

"He *said* everything was the same, but he wasn't taking me out anymore. He wasn't buying me gifts. I couldn't even get my nails done." Mercedes paused for a few seconds. "So, I thought maybe he'd cooled off. I thought he needed a kick-start."

"What kind of kick-start?" Harley seemed puzzled.

Mercedes tried to look coy but her smile came across as more of a smirk. "Well, no man wants a woman unless some other man is interested in her."

It took a minute for that to sink in, but Harley got her drift soon enough.

"So, what did you do?" I asked.

"I let him think there was something going on between me and Thomas Warrendale."

"Tye Warren," Harley corrected.

"What?" Mercedes looked confused.

"His real name was Tye Warren," Harley said.

"Oh yeah, whatever. Well, I flirted with Mr. Warrendale whenever I knew Moe was around. Thomas, I mean *Tye*, was a big flirt himself. He knew the score. That's all there was."

"So what happened after choir rehearsal?" I watched her closely to see if she'd try to lie her way out.

"Well, I knew Moe would be there. He usually came to the church to listen to the music and pick me up. So, after rehearsal, I flirted, and when I heard Moe's voice in the vestibule, I let Tye kiss me." Mercedes was unable to avoid a smile at the recollection.

"And what did Moe do?" I was pretty sure I could imagine the answer.

"He was angry. Specifically, I think, because Thomas … ah … Tye just laughed. I think that hurt more than anything."

"Did Moe do or say anything?" I wanted to see how this version would align with Mama B's account.

"Not while I was there. I just grabbed my purse and left. I think they had a few words, but then those old ladies were fixing the table for communion."

"Why didn't you tell me this before?"

"There wasn't anything to tell. Everything worked out great. Moe was mad a little but he got over it." Mercedes smiled. "And ever since then, he's been extra attentive and generous. I don't even have to hint about things I want; he just buys me gifts and spends time and money left and right. So, see? Everything worked out great."

Mercedes was so self-centered she had no idea she'd most likely been the catalyst for a man's death.

We escorted Mercedes to the station to make a statement and then rushed to find Moe Chapman. He still hadn't shown up at any of his usual places. We obtained a warrant and searched his house. I had an unmarked car stationed outside his house and the church. Mercedes claimed not to know where he was, and I believed her this time. She called his cell but got no answer. I gave the number to Harley to track using the GPS in his phone. But I needn't have bothered.

CHAPTER SEVENTEEN

———————

I GOT A text from Paris to come to Mama B's. When I tried to call her back, she didn't pick up. I told myself maybe she was busy, but something in the pit of my stomach wasn't buying it.

I knew something was wrong when I pulled in front of Mama B's house. The first thing I saw was three people sitting on the porch: Mama B, Paris, and Moe Chapman. Moe sat in between Paris and Mama B, and he had his hand inside his jacket in a way that told me he had a gun pointed at Mama B's ribs.

I made a move toward my gun, but Moe shoved the gun into Mama B's side and she flinched. I slowly raised my hands to show there was no need for panic. Moe smiled his big alligator smile as I climbed the few steps to the porch.

"That's close enough," Moe said. His voice sounded calm, but the gun he had in Mama B's ribs didn't look very steady, and sweat dripped down his forehead. "I don't want to hurt nobody, RJ."

Mama B rocked with her eyes closed.

"That's good, Moe, because I don't want anyone to get hurt. So why don't you let the women go, and you and I can go inside and talk about this."

He laughed. "Oh, I don't think that would be good."

I looked out of the corner of my eye. There was a black and white parked nearby, empty.

Noticing the glance, Moe said, "Don't worry. He's okay."

I looked at Mama B. She still had her eyes closed. Her skin seemed pale, and her lips were moving. It took a split second for me to realize she was praying. I was almost afraid to look at Paris. But I did. She looked frightened but uninjured.

"You okay?"

She nodded and tried a half-hearted smile.

My stomach flipped. The blood pumped so loudly in my ears, I could barely hear. I needed to remain calm. I had to try to figure out how to get between Moe Chapman and Mama B. I took some deep breaths to help steady my nerves.

Moe said, "He's tied up in the back bedroom." I realized he was referring to the policeman who drove the black and white.

"It's Eugene King," Mama B said. "He came to return my plate and use the bathroom." She still had her eyes closed.

"I just need that book," Moe said. "I heard from Reverend Hamilton you found it. I just need the book, and then I'll get outta here."

"Take my car. I'll give you the keys." I started to reach in my pocket, but Moe got nervous and shoved the gun into Mama B's side.

She gasped.

I moved my hands back to where Moe could see them.

"Don't try to be a hero, RJ. I don't want to shoot Sister Ella. But I will." Moe sounded weary. "I've already killed twice, so I don't think one or two or even three more will make much difference now."

"Why did you kill Tye Warren?" I needed to buy some time to think up a plan to get us all out alive.

Moe sighed. "He figured out I had been taking money from the church when I started preaching and he took over the books. But he didn't turn me in. No. He made me pay him.

I had to pay him double what I had taken. That money was already gone. I tried to explain that to him but he just laughed. I had to get a part-time job and sell everything I could to try and come up with the money. Then he went after my girl." Moe shook his head and tried to wipe the sweat off his forehead.

"Mercedes is high maintenance, but a woman like that is an investment. When we walked into a room, heads turned."

Something made me look at Mama B. She was still, but she was smiling. Moe happened to look too. What made her smile? She was being held at gunpoint, but she seemed to be at peace. Then she started to hum. She had to be in shock. I needed to work quickly.

Paris looked at Mama B and shrugged.

The noise from the recreation center was louder than usual. Young men were descending on the center and a major game was about to go down. But I was focused on a different game—a game of life and death.

"So, Warren was blackmailing you," I said to keep Moe talking.

"Yeah, but I heard her," Moe cocked his head toward Paris, "arguing with him, and I knew I had some leverage. So, I went to his house Saturday after I took Mercedes home. He was there. His head was bleeding, and he was in a really bad mood. He wouldn't even listen. He just kept threatening me. He said he'd turn me in to the police. He laughed and said he'd keep Mercedes busy until I got out. That's when I snapped. I shot him before I even realized what I was doing."

I heard a noise and thought I saw something move around the side of the house. Moe must have heard it too. He started to move but changed his mind. He must have decided it was more important to keep his eyes on me.

I tried to think of something else to keep him focused on me. "And Bryce Chandler?"

"Warrendale had that book. I saw him writing in it. He called it his 'hymn book.' I looked for it when I searched his house, but I never found it. Reverend Hamilton said you found the book at the parsonage. I should have started there. But I thought maybe *she* had it." Moe motioned toward Paris. "She kept talking about books when she was yelling at him at the church. I thought there might be notes in there about what I'd done with the money."

The sweat poured off Moe, and he struggled to keep his eyes on everyone at the same time. "That lady came to the church looking for his belongings. I thought I could get some money so Mercedes and I could get away. I called her. But she didn't come. Some guy came." Moe shook his head at the memory. "He didn't have the money, and then he started threatening me too. But I'd had enough threats. So, I shot him." He looked around like a trapped rat. "Now it's time to go. Get up."

Moe started to stand but halted when Mama B started to sing.

> I will trust in the Lord
> I will trust in the Lord
> I will trust in the Lord until I die

Paris looked at her for a moment and then started to sing quietly too.

"Okay, that's enough, Sister Ella," Moe said, "Let's go in the house."

But Mama B didn't seem to be listening.

I knew we stood a better chance of survival outside, and if Moe Chapman got his hands on that code book, he'd have no reason to leave us alive. I was going to have to make a lunge for Chapman and hope Mama B or Paris wouldn't get hurt. Forcing that thought from my mind, I took a deep breath and said a quick prayer. I spoke to God for the first time in months.

Paris and Mama B continued to sing. Moe pulled the gun out of his jacket. He pointed it at them. It was now or never. That's when I heard a noise around the side of the house, but I refused to look. I kept my eyes focused on Moe Chapman. On the gun. I watched his hand. It was now or never. I started to leap toward Moe. From the corner of my eye, I saw two men leap over the back of the porch rail. Moe turned. I made my move. I pushed Mama B aside and hurled myself at Moe. The force of my body weight knocked him backward. He tried to steady himself. Over the rail came the two men. I recognized one as Tiny, the gang banger Mama B often fed. He was holding a switchblade to Moe's throat while another man held a gun pointed at the back of his head. I reached behind my back, pulled out my gun, and placed it on Moe's forehead.

Tiny said, "Make one move and I'll slit your throat, mother—"

"*Tiny*," Mama B yelled, "watch your mouth."

"Yes, ma'am," Tiny said, although he didn't move his blade.

Needless to say, Moe remained perfectly still.

I relieved him of his weapon, but kept mine pointed at his head.

Paris helped Mama B back into her chair.

"You okay?" I asked.

Mama B nodded and said, "Tiny, I told you about using language like that."

"I'm sorry, ma'am," Tiny apologized.

"Yo Yo, Five O. You want us to take care of this?" the other thug said, meaning Moe Chapman, and for the first time I saw genuine fear in Moe's eyes.

I hesitated a split second. "No, I got this."

Tiny and his friend nodded and put their weapons away.

I was too thankful for their help to ask questions about their weapons—maybe another time, but not today. I rolled Moe onto his stomach. With my knee in his back, I cuffed him.

"I got some lemonade and a pound cake in the kitchen. Ya'll go on in and help yourselves," Mama B told her two rescuers. She looked peaky and her voice was understandably shaky.

"You okay?" With Moe immobilized, I took a good long look at her to make sure she hadn't been injured in the commotion.

"Yes, praise the Lord. I'm okay, but my legs are a bit wobbly. I'm just going to sit here for a while," Mama B said.

I had pulled out my cellphone to call the station when I heard a voice from inside.

"Yo, Five O, you want us to untie your friend?"

I had forgotten about Eugene King the patrolman tied up in the back. "Yeah. Untie him."

Once Moe Chapman was cuffed, he hung his head and cried like a baby. I had an overwhelming desire to kick him, but refrained. Mama B wouldn't have approved.

Paris stood up and said, "Hold me."

And that's what I did.

To SAY MOE Chapman sang like a bird would be a serious understatement. Once Reverend Hamilton arrived, he cried, confessed, cried, and then cried some more.

Harley, Chief Mike, and I briefed the mayor. He had his nerds working on cracking Warrendale's Hymn Book. I suggested they use a Baptist hymnal to help with the cipher. The numbers in Warrendale's hymn book represented the letters from various hymns. Once they had that key, they made progress. I hoped one day Paris and the church would get some of their money back, but it could take years to sort through everything, especially with off-shore banks. I also doubted we would find anything in the hymn book that would convict Mrs. Hartford-Graham of anything unless it was tax evasion. Maybe with the evidence from Carl Hastings Senior, the account information from Warrendale, and testimony from Mrs. Warren ... but even if we did get the evidence, it was unlikely she'd ever stand trial. Lawyers would drag this out until she was dead and buried. Perhaps Mrs. Hartford-Graham would one day face justice for money laundering—if not in this lifetime, maybe in the next.

At least the people of St. Joe could rest easier knowing the murder of Thomas Warrendale had been solved. And the people of Cleveland could rest easier knowing Bryce Chandler wouldn't be laundering or embezzling money anymore. All in all, it was a good day.

After the briefing, we spent several hours filling out paperwork. Paperwork was still my least favorite part of being a cop. However, this case hit pretty close to home for me and involved a lot of people I knew and cared about. So, I took extra care to make sure it was perfect.

It was dark when I got back to Mama B's. She was in her chair. I knew Paris would be there along with Reverend Hamilton. Mama B refused to go to the hospital to get checked out. I was worried the strain had affected her blood pressure. But Paris promised to keep an eye on her. I noticed Tiny and a few of his friends were sitting on the hood of the car in the rec center parking lot. Mama B was definitely well looked after.

The color was back in Mama B's skin and the sparkle was almost back in her eyes. By tomorrow, she'd have a full house of busybodies all wanting to hear the story.

"Is everything wrapped up?" Reverend Hamilton asked.

I flopped down on the sofa. "Pretty much. He confessed to the killings, so it should be a quick job. We've got him on suicide watch."

Reverend Hamilton shook his head and then added, "I hope he will accept the forgiveness of God. He has always looked at God as a vengeful being to be feared rather than an understanding parent full of love and forgiveness. If he can change his outlook, he can still serve God."

"Are you kidding me? He killed two men, assaulted a police officer, and held three people hostage. What kind of work can he do?"

"The Bible is clear, RJ. 'If we confess our sins, He is faithful and just to forgive our sins and to cleanse us from all unrighteousness.' " Reverend Hamilton was quoting I John 1: 9. I didn't know a lot of scriptures by heart but I remembered that one. That had been one of my mom's favorite verses.

"Amen, Reverend," Mama B said.

"God doesn't view one sin as greater than another. If we can confess and turn from our wicked ways, He will forgive." Reverend Hamilton spoke patiently, and he seemed to be looking through me. At that moment, I knew he wasn't talking about Moe Chapman anymore. The person who needed forgiveness was me. I needed to forgive God and I needed to forgive myself for not saving that little girl in the accident.

"Forgiveness is a gift," Reverend Hamilton said. "In order to receive this gift, you have to be willing to accept it in return. Only then will you be open to all the other gifts and benefits God has for us … like love."

I might have been mistaken but I would have sworn Reverend Hamilton looked at Paris.

She blushed.

I knew forgiving myself would take time and I would never forget the tragedy of that accident, but I was ready to travel the path to forgiveness and peace.

Mama B hummed and rocked in her chair. I settled back on the sofa and couldn't help smiling. I'd caught a killer. The streets were safer. As Robert Browning wrote in "Pippa's Song," "God's in His heaven, all's right with the world."

Death went out to the sinner's house,

Come and go with me

Sinner cried out, I'm not ready to go,

Ain't got no travellin' shoes.

Got no travellin' shoes, got no travellin' shoes

Sinner cried out, I'm not ready to go

I ain't got no travellin' shoes

Death went out to the gambler's house,

Come and go with me

The gambler cried out, I'm not ready to go,

Ain't got no travellin' shoes.

Got no travellin' shoes, got no travellin' shoes

Sinner cried out, I'm not ready to go

I ain't got no travellin' shoes

Death went out to the preacher's house,

Come and go with me

The preacher cried out, I'm ready to go,

I've got my travellin' shoes

Got my travellin' shoes, got my travellin' shoes

Preacher cried out, I'm ready to go

I've got my travellin' shoes

RJ'S FAVORITE MEALS

BJ Magley's Pork Chops

~~~

Serves 4

4½ to 4¾-inch-thick center-cut pork chops
Lawry's® Seasoned Salt
Pepper
2 cups all-purpose flour
½ cups vegetable oil
½ cups milk
1 egg

1.   Sprinkle Lawry's® Seasoned Salt and pepper on both sides of the pork chops.
2.   Beat the egg and milk in a shallow bowl.
3.   Heat the vegetable oil in a cast-iron skillet on medium heat for approximately 10 minutes.
4.   Drip the pork chops in the egg and milk batter.
5.   Dredge in flour on both sides.
6.   Fry on medium high until gently brown.

BJ's Quick and Easy Peach Cobbler

2 29-oz cans of sliced peaches in heavy syrup
1½ cups sugar
¾ cups butter plus 2 tablespoons
¼ cups lemon juice
1 teaspoon cinnamon
2 boxes of Pillsbury™ Refrigerated Pie Crust

1. Preheat oven to 350 degrees F.
2. Pour peaches into shallow 10x13-inch glass pan and then pour lemon juice over the peaches. Add sugar and mix well.
3. Sprinkle cinnamon over the top of the mixture.
4. Slice ¾ cups of butter into approximately 10 slices and place them in dots over the top of the mixture.
5. Unfold the pie crust and place over the top of the peach mixture. Using a fork, poke holes across the top of the crust.
6. Melt remaining butter and pour over the top of the crust.
7. Bake until golden brown, approximately 45 minutes.

Sweet Potato Pie

———∼∼∼———

Makes 2 pies

2 9-inch pie shells
2 cups cooked sweet potatoes
8 tablespoons butter
1 ¾ cups sugar
1 teaspoon ground nutmeg
1 ½ teaspoon vanilla extract
2 eggs
1 cup (8 oz) evaporated milk

1.   Preheat oven to 350 degrees F.
2.   Place sweet potatoes in a five-quart sauce pan and cover the potatoes with water.
3.   Boil over medium heat until the sweet potatoes are soft when poked with a fork (approximately 30 minutes).
4.   Drain potatoes and remove skin and beat with an electric mixer until smooth.
5.   Cream butter and sugar together and add to sweet potato mixture and beat well.
6.   Add nutmeg, vanilla, eggs, and evaporated milk.

7. Mix ingredients thoroughly and pour into unbaked pie shells. Bake until the pies are set in the center (approximately 35 to 40 minutes).

Elvira Burns' Fried Corn

———∽∾∾———

Serves 4-5

12 ears of sweet corn
½ cup of water
¼ tsp pepper
2 tbsp all-purpose flour
3-4 tbsp. bacon drippings or olive oil
½ tsp salt
2 tbsp sugar (optional)

1   Using a sharp knife, scrape the cob downward into a large bowl.
2.   Heat a heavy skillet and add the bacon or olive oil.
3.   When hot, add corn and cook for 15 to 20 minutes, stirring constantly to prevent sticking.
4.   Add water to flour mixture and stir, and then stir into corn to thicken.
5.   Add salt and pepper to taste. If desired, add sugar to sweeten.
6.   Reduce heat and cover tightly, cooking for 20 to 30 more minutes until done.

Photo by Sophia Muckerson

V.M. Burns was born and raised in the Midwestern United States. She holds a bachelor's degree from Northwestern University (Evanston, IL) and master's degrees from the University of Notre Dame (Notre Dame, IN) and Seton Hill University (Greensburg, PA). She is currently thawing out in Eastern Tennessee.

V.M. Burns is a member of Mystery Writers of America, International Thriller Writers, and Sisters in Crime. She is the author of the Mystery Bookshop Mystery series and the Dog Club Mystery series.

For more information about V.M. Burns, check out her website at vmburns.com or follow her on Facebook, http://www.facebook.com/vmburnsbooks.